Praise for The Jack Liffey Mysteries

The Concrete River

"Noir master ... Shannon tackles a tough social issue with intelligence and a clear moral compass. His spare, noir style and articulate dialog strike just the right balance between thriller and social consciousness. His growing audience will love this. Recommended."

—Library Journal

"Witty, alert, energetic, talented way above the ordinary."

—New York Times Book Review

"The hands-down winner in the long-running 'Where is the Next Raymond Chandler Coming From?' sweepstakes ... Jack Liffey is the most interesting new private detective ... since Walter Mosley's Easy Rawlins."

—Dick Adler, *Chicago Tribune*

"Shannon has written an intelligent, surprising book, found the heart of his working-class characters, and delivered a first-rate thriller in the bargain."

—George Pelecanos

"Philip Marlowe would have been proud of his contemporary heir."

—Michael Connelly

"Liffey is a most unlikely action hero whose feats of intuition, verbosity, and personal empathy make an interesting contrast to the exploits of his hard-boiled peers."

—Tom Nolan, *Wall Street Journal*

"Shannon matches the master, Raymond Chandler, in several key areas, notably location, characterization and dialogue."

—Dick Lochte, *Los Angeles Times*

"The real rewards of this novel are the wounded and searching souls caught up in the madness ... and his appealingly thoughtful hero."

—John Koch, *Boston Globe*

"Southern California has always been fertile ground for crime writers and one of the very best of them has to be John Shannon."

—Denver Post

"Shannon has mastered the most essential element of the genre, giving us a guy we want to stand shoulder to shoulder with while we try to make sense out of a senseless universe."

—Booklist [Starred]

"The landscape of Los Angeles ... has been deconstructed by writers from Chandler to Didion, but never quite as artfully as does John Shannon."

—James Crumley

The Cracked Earth

"Jack Liffey is an extraordinary creation ... Shannon is the philosopher king of the mystery forum. And long may he reign."

—Charlotte Vale Allen

The Poison Sky

"A stunner of a book"

—*Poisoned Pen*

The Orange Curtain

"Readers who like gritty noir ... will love Shannon's Jack Liffey mysteries. Shannon delivers a tour-de-force climax ... beautifully, driven by each character's needs."

—*Publishers Weekly* [Starred]

"[Liffey] retains his Marlowe-like decency and steadfastness and even his sense of humor. Those new to this superb but relatively unknown series will want to search out the three earlier Liffey novels."

—*Booklist* [Starred]

"Dead-on characterizations, an ear for dialogue, picturesque description of Orange County's Vietnamese community, and wry touches."

—*Kirkus Reviews*

"Shannon pulls off one of those career breakthroughs that make the writing life so interesting ... Shannon's other characters glow with originality and energy."

—Dick Adler, *Chicago Tribune*

"*The Orange Curtain* is both brilliant and readable (not always the same thing)."

—Robert B. Parker, author of the Spenser mysteries

"A smart, well-crafted mystery with convincingly fallible characters and an assured sense of the look and feel of Southern California."

—Thomas Perry, author of *Death Benefits*

"For too long, Shannon has been an unsung hero of the modern crime novel ... he has written an intelligent, surprising book ... and delivered a first-rate thriller in the bargain."

—George Pelecanos

"Shannon has, in Gudger, drawn a portrait of a sad, even forgivable, young man with no social skills, and a deep and terrible thirst for knowledge and friendship ... Here is an author to watch; he is an extraordinary writer, with insight, wisdom, and great feeling for his characters."

—Charlotte Vale Allen

"Jack Liffey ... [is] a complex guy who leads a messy personal life but has a warm way with strangers ... [Shannon] creates interesting characters with rich inner lives and the wit to express their craziest thoughts with some eloquence."

—Marilyn Stasio, *New York Times*

"Shannon's self-confidence is justified ... he matches the master [Chandler] in several key areas, notably location, characterization and dialogue ... [Shannon] has done a remarkable update on the Chandler knight-errant."

—Dick Lochte, *Los Angeles Times*

"Cleverly constructed, freshly written."

—Tom Nolan, *Wall Street Journal*

Streets on Fire

"Liffey doesn't have much left except his marrow-deep decency, doggedness, compassion, and courage. But that will be plenty for Liffey's current fans and the new ones *Streets on Fire* will surely attract. Here's hoping the trajectory of this series continues upward for years to come."

—Thomas Gaughan, *Booklist* [Starred]

"Shannon's latest is still full of memorable, fully rounded characters and richly detailed scenes of L.A. life at its most strange and bizarre. Strongly recommended."

—Wilda Williams, *Library Journal*

"One of the things you've got to admire about Californian John Shannon is his commitment to principles ... he's a good writer getting better with each book."

—*January Magazine*'s Crime Fiction Report

"Shannon's lean prose makes good use of local history without letting it slow down his hero's progress ... this should be enough to satisfy anyone seeking a strong sense of place in a novel."

—Dick Lochte, *Los Angeles Times*

"Los Angeles [is] shown in the blunt and brilliant crime novels of John Shannon ..."

—Dick Adler, *Chicago Tribune*

"*Streets on Fire* ... brings the problems of racism alive. Jack's toughness and compassion, along with his literate style, make this a strong entry in the private eye genre."

—*Milwaukee Journal*

"Shannon writes muscular, evocative novels that also have something important to say. I can't recommend this series highly enough."

—Poisoned Pen

City of Strangers

"Shannon's series is still on an upward trajectory ... If only all mystery novels were this good."

— Keir Graff, Booklist [Starred]

"Superb sixth book ... reading a Jack Liffey novel is no day at the beach. But then again, neither is life in Southern California."

—Publishers Weekly [Starred]

"Most consistently satisfying hard-boiled writers ... Liffey is a terrific character—smart, funny, sad, and a keen observer of social strata and the world at large."

—Booklist, 10 Best Crime Novels of the Year (2003)

"[A] hard-edged, politically savvy series."

—Marilyn Stasio, New York Times Book Review

"Liffey is accident-prone, depressed, mixed up, and fun to hear."

—Eugen Weber, Los Angeles Times

"This is a rare detective novel that's not just entertaining (with Shannon, that's become a given), but also timely ... that, of course, is really what makes this book so powerful, moving and, yes, important."

—Kevin Burton Smith, January Magazine

Terminal Island

"Shannon has mastered the most essential element of the genre, giving us a guy we want to stand shoulder to shoulder with while we try to make sense out of a senseless universe."

—Keir Graff, Booklist [Starred]

"Liffey is intelligent, sensitive, courageous, even on occasion funny."

—Kirkus Reviews

"A fabulous hard-boiled series that deserves more attention."

—Library Journal

"Beautifully developed theme of intergenerational family relationships ... surprises and feels just right."

—Publishers Weekly

"The most heartfelt book yet about the socially conscious, emotionally fragile, increasingly physically vulnerable Liffey ... an interesting contrast to the exploits of his hard-boiled peers."

—Tom Nolan, *Wall Street Journal*

"Interesting, funny, believable and often touching."

—Tom and Enid Schantz, *Denver Post*

"Sympathetic intelligence and relentless honesty."

—Kevin Burton Smith, *January Magazine*

Dangerous Games

"[Shannon] is at the peak of his impressive powers here."

—Dick Adler, *Chicago Tribune*

"Shannon is masterful at creating these and other horrifying, often giddy, scenes of mayhem."

—John Koch, *Boston Globe*

"It is another first-rate effort from an author who always deals sensitively and informatively with Southern California's multicultural society."

—Tom and Enid Schantz, *Denver Post*

"Shannon is the real deal, a knowledgeable writer in full control of his material ... one of this year's most satisfying crime novels."

—Dick Lochte, *Los Angeles Times*

Koreatown

"This underrated series remains consistently provocative."

—*Publishers Weekly*

"There's plenty of action to drive the plot ... Shannon writes with compassion, as well as intelligence."

—*Denver Post*

"Fans of thinking-man's detective fiction will find much to ponder."

—Keir Graff, *Booklist*

"Right now there's nobody—and I mean, nobody—in crime fiction or the broader realm of literature who writes about Los Angeles (and us) as powerfully and with such keen vision, wit and passion as Shannon does. Right now, L.A. belongs to John Shannon."

—Kevin Burton Smith, *January Magazine*

The Devils of Bakersfield

"Another winner from a writer whose own moral compass is holding steady."

—Keir Graff, *Booklist* [Starred]

"These books are modern classics of Los Angeles crime fiction."

—Patrick Millikin, *Poisoned Pen*

Palos Verdes Blue

"The payoff ... is a wild, bumpy, and satisfying ride."

—Shelly Lowenkopf, *BookTalk*

"With a hero as brainy, compassionate, and conflicted as this, the only real mystery is why these books aren't bestsellers."

—Keir Graff, *Booklist* [Starred]

On the Nickel

"[*On the Nickel*] will be a solid addition to a series that consistently provokes and surprises."

—Art Taylor, *Washington Post*

"Liffey's relationship with his daughter is a thing of beauty."

—Dick Adler, *Chicago Tribune*

"Another winner in an outstanding series."

—*Booklist*

"The characters are realistically drawn ... [with] a compelling narrative ... As long as John Shannon writes Jack Liffey novels, I'll gladly keep reading them."

—Patrick Millikin, *Poisoned Pen*

A Little Too Much

"[An] ongoing, ever-bittersweet story of a man, too smart for abstract idealism, who can't help but try to fix the next seemingly unfixable problem in front of him."

—Bill Ott, *Booklist* [Starred]

BOYSTOWN

❧ A JACK LIFFEY MYSTERY ❧

JOHN SHANNON

AN UNNAMED PRESS/RARE BIRD BOOKS JOINT PRODUCTION

Copyright © 2025 by John Shannon

All rights reserved, including the right to reproduce this book or portions thereof in any form whatsoever. Permissions inquiries may be directed to info@unnamedpress.com.

Published in North America by the Unnamed Press.

Unnamed Press and Rare Bird Books support copyright. Copyright fuels creativity, encourages diverse voices, promotes free speech, and creates a vibrant culture. Thank you for buying an authorized edition of this book and for complying with copyright laws by not reproducing, scanning, or distributing any part of it in any form without permission. You are supporting writers and allowing Unnamed Press and Rare Bird Books to continue to publish books for readers to enjoy and appreciate.

unnamedpress.com | rarebirdbooks.com

Cover Design by Ivan Kurylenko and Dusti Diener
Photo Illustrations by Dusti Diener

Hardcover ISBN-13: 9781964008004

Manufactured in the United States of America.
Distributed by Publishers Group West

First Hardcover Edition

2 4 6 8 10 9 7 5 3 1

Library of Congress Cataloging-in-Publication Data available upon request

For Boris Dralyuk, good friend and teacher
Slava Ukraini

The Jack Liffey Mysteries

The Concrete River
The Cracked Earth
The Poison Sky
The Orange Curtain
Streets on Fire
Terminal Island
City of Strangers
Dangerous Games
Koreatown (formerly *The Dark Streets*)
The Devils of Bakersfield
Palos Verdes Blue
On the Nickel
A Little Too Much
The Chinese Beverly Hills
Boystown

We are all cripples, every one of us, more or less.

—Dostoyevsky

INTRODUCTION

From 1996 to 2014, John Shannon produced fourteen highly acclaimed crime novels—all set in the environs of Los Angeles and featuring Jack Liffey, an ex-aerospace worker turned private investigator. Where Michael Connelly's Harry Bosch's mission in life is to find justice for the dead of Los Angeles, John Shannon's Jack Liffey's calling is to find the missing—hopefully before they wind up dead. His searches take him into many LA neighborhoods inhabited by multi-cultural ethnicities and various societal groups. This is Los Angeles down and dirty... and as real as real can be.

Shannon shines a light on people and places that have rarely, if ever, seen that kind of light. When you read the entire series, it's like taking a tour of the city's darkest and most troubled places. Shannon says, "I've tried to capture Los Angeles as it is now instead of the white-on-white world from noir novels of the '40s and '50s. When you write about the totality of this city, when you get down to the grit, you're blown away by the possibilities."

Each of his crime novels deals with difficult societal issues as well as entertaining us with twisty-turny, procedural-type missing persons investigations. A sampling of such issues include corrupt real estate deals, police violence, white supremacy, religious fundamentalism, terrorism, pornography, Satanism, gang wars and homelessness.

Shannon's likeable protagonist is highly-flawed and unpredictable. But Jack Liffey is also a brave and decent man who lost his job in the aerospace industry, floundered for a while, and then found his true calling—finding lost children and every once in a while a lost adult. Booklist called Liffey "a terrific character—smart, funny, sad and a keen observer of social strata and the world at large."

The whims and vagaries of the publishing world have not done John Shannon any favors, but it's hard to keep an excellent writer down. So I was delighted to hear that there would be more John Shannon—Jack Liffey novels in the near future.

You're holding the first of these in your hands right now. Each can be read as a standalone novel if you haven't read the previous ones. If that is the case, after reading *Boystown*, you'll want to go back and read them all, and I hope that you enjoy them as much as I have.

Welcome back, John!

George Easter

ONE

Coercive Nonviolence

"LUNCHTIME!"

Jack Liffey snapped awake at noon, instantly chagrinned as he saw Gloria at the bedroom door. He'd been napping fairly deep down the dark well since his stroke following heart surgery, but he didn't want to give in to some fixed concept of what it meant to be doomed by time. "No time for sergeants!" he called, sitting up in one shot. Too much nap is bad. "Four legs bad, two legs good."

Gloria came across the room and pressed his head against her thigh. "Careful. You don't want to pop open that zipper down your chest. I know your tongue is out of control."

He was glad she was off her crutch and only hobbling a little. Her injury had predated his problems by a lot, and it was his turn to go goofy. After a career as a tech writer in aerospace dried up during the big Peace Dividend, he had fallen into being a finder of missing children for years, but this new wrinkle probably was going to put that on hold.

Some part of him could take in what he said aloud and wasn't entirely pleased by it. But he knew open heart surgery and a stroke had to leave footprints in your psyche. Get it together. At three o'clock, he knew Miss Dentifrice would be there with her big white smile to encourage his physical therapy.

"Come down, Jack. Your enchilada is ready. And your daughter's here."

"The *whole* enchilada!" he blurted.

On the stairs he could at least help, lending his shoulder as she favored a leg.

"Daddy! You look grand!" Maeve ran to hug him like a limpet.

"Grand is a canyon," he suggested.

He felt Maeve turn her neck subtly in his grip to look at Gloria, and he knew Gloria would be shaking her head infinitesimally: he's still the same.

Damn, I guess I am. He slowed his thought process down to near stasis because he knew that tended to still the rush of pointless words. "How are ... your studies?"

"Just super, dad-o-mine. You should see the oil sketches I'm doing of hands. Hands are hard to get right. Those amazing hands by Dürer and Kollwitz."

"The champion ... of avoidance."

Gloria had told him that Maeve was almost certainly playing hooky from all her non-art classes at UCLA in order to have more time for painting. "How's History 1A?" he asked.

"I'm adapting to college fine, dad. How are you doing with your new bubblebrain? That's why I came over."

"Brain is a ... steel trap." He tapped his forehead, as if she might not know where the brain was.

"Eat, you two," Gloria said, plopping down the overflowing chile-redolent plates. "Skirmish later."

* * * * *

PETRO Ivanchuk Pogorelets netted a meandering butterfly above the rising Sierra trail. For no good reason. He knew it was a *Vanessa cardui*—the painted lady—the most widely disseminated butterfly in the world. A specimen from the Eastern Sierra in California had little scientific value, but for the last hour of his excursion bright ladies had been fluttering northeast in a vast ground-hugging migration, a sight most

COERCIVE NONVIOLENCE

hikers probably wouldn't even have noticed. He wanted to see if any of the orange-and-black specimens might be in the process of evolving into a new sub-species—a suitably Nabokovian pursuit.

His countryman, the great exile of *Lolita* fame, had developed a new system of butterfly taxonomy by dissecting their teensy genitalia under a microscope. Petro Ivanchuk had no such scientific ambitions, just a need to relax into his outing. As a Ukrainian Jew, an exile in a country that often presented only a hypothetical tolerance of foreigners, he'd discovered that he had a nasty temper for slights and insults.

Lepidoptery calmed him down from his daily regimen. It had taken an infuriating decade of kowtowing to fools to gain him a lowly instructorship at a third-rate community college. He was an adjunct instructor in beginning philosophy, though he held four PhDs and had once reigned over the great University of Kiev.

Petro Pogorelets wore a bandolier of killing jars across his chest that contained strips of paper towel soaked in ethyl acetate. He waved his capture net backwards and the baloony netting sent the painted lady on her way. So much for science. He loved butterflies, but he'd be damned if he'd spend hours peering at a butterfly's dick under a microscope.

For several minutes Petro Ivanchuk had been overhearing wisps of human chatter from a trail on the opposing ridge. Glancing across the canyon, he noticed four men wearing what would have been considered too-bright hunting clothes back home. They were carrying rifles, though he knew it was well out of deer season. Was it really such a country of anarchy?

When you were an outsider, too much was always opaque—you lacked the frame of reference. Every common detail that was obvious to a local nine year old held multiple ambiguities for you. Maybe the riflemen were professionals sent to kill a mountain lion, or game wardens culling the mule deer herds higher up in the Eastern Sierras.

* * * * *

BOYSTOWN

TALBOT Denny would just about rather have been anywhere else on earth but here—say, a Klan rally in Bogalusa wearing his gay pride T-shirt. To save his serenity he'd decided not to come out to any of these semi-pals from his summer job, rough-and-tumble machinists and electricians. The little workshop, owned by a mostly absent Russian engineer, was near his brother's home and would keep him in white wine and Trader Joe's entrees until he could go back to Columbia and finish up his post-doc. There weren't a lot of temp jobs to be had in European Intellectual History.

Of course, no stab at staying in the closet ever went unpunished, and he found himself slogging up a rough trail in the Eastern Sierras wearing a ludicrous orange jacket following these three yobs from his workplace. He was even carrying a Marlin thirty-ought-six deer rifle that Charlie Beck had loaned him for the occasion. Deer season didn't open until the fall, but they'd told him it didn't matter, nobody cared. To remain buddies, he'd mentioned lightheartedly a few hunts he'd been on in his past, though he hated weapons and had never before touched a rifle. Still, he detected something inside him that fancied the cool Red Ryder look of the lever-action carbine.

Belkin, the stringy gofur at work, held a cigar in the corner of his mouth as he shouldered an assault rifle that he held contemptuously by the barrel like a golf club over his shoulder. He had a hatred of all rules. One day at work Denny had had a glimpse of a lot of crudely drawn tattoos on him, including a couple of swastikas. Rough stuff from Soviet prisons.

Why the hell did I agree to come? Denny thought. He could have told them his brother was at death's door. His kidney had just been removed. Anything.

"Bug off, bug." Zeke Tomlin waved a hand back and forth in front of his eyes. "That's the Mississippi Salute," he guffawed.

"Like we give a shit," Belkin said.

"When's the last time any a' you capped a deer?" Charlie Beck asked from up ahead. He was the master machinist at Gusev and claimed to have been a Recon Marine so he was "taking point."

COERCIVE NONVIOLENCE

"Or shot any fucking enemy," Belkin said.

"You sure is a cheerful bastard, Russky."

"Suck my *huy*, Mississippi."

All at once Zeke stopped and pointed across the ravine. "Look at that big fairy. The motherfucker's gotta be spookin' every deer in miles."

A heavyset man in a khaki safari suit was trotting up the opposite trail waving what looked like a butterfly net. Did people actually hunt butterflies? They all watched open-mouthed as the man swung his billowy net and seemed to catch what he was after.

They had bunched up on the trail and Charlie Beck stretched out his arm to aim a pistol-like finger at the big man across the canyon. "Plink," he said.

Zeke grinned and raised his .375 Ruger rifle.

No one said a word, it was so unexpected. Zeke fired, and maybe a hundred yards away the big man tumbled forward behind brush at the edge of the trail.

"Plink," Zeke said.

* * * * *

"THESE are great, Gloria. You make them?" A few years ago Maeve had had to cook Mexican for a gangbanging lover she'd been in thrall to. Life was full of twists and turns.

"We buy enchiladas and tamales by the dozen from Mamacita's and freeze them. I don't mind cooking but—I don't know..." Gloria seemed to tail off into a funk.

"You look a little peaked," Maeve said.

Gloria didn't answer, which was not like her. She was usually right up on top. Jeez, I've got two completely lame conversationalists here, Maeve thought and immediately felt guilty. They'd both had their troubles. Some vicious beatings for Gloria and open heart surgery for her dad. She couldn't bear to see the fresh scar-track down his chest.

"I gotta say this. You guys should know I'm part of Black Lives Matter."

"Wonderful," Jack Liffey said dubiously.

"Girl, don't lay down in front of no police cars." Gloria was a cop, after all.

"Don't worry, we're training in Gandhian nonviolence."

"With a loincloth?" Jack Liffey said.

"Don't be frivolous, dad. We learned that there's two kinds. One is truth-oriented passive nonviolence—what Gandhi called *satyagraha*. But the more effective one is power-oriented coercive nonviolence, *duragraha*."

"I don't like the sound of that one," Gloria said.

"It just means peaceful resistance that people can't ignore, like a sit-in in a public hospital that's being taken over by a hedge fund. The first kind is a withdrawal of cooperation, but the second interferes with normal life." Time to get around to it, Maeve thought. "Dad, this is kind of why I came today."

"Here I thought ... you loved us."

"Don't be a Jewish-mother father. Listen. I have something to say."

Gloria was frowning, concerned, and Maeve stalled for a moment.

"Go, girl. Don't drop no bomb and then go hide."

"My roommate's nineteen-year-old brother is missing. He was at a bunch of protests against places that discriminated against gays like that Bob's Beanery that had the famous sign *Faggots Stay Out*. She said he came to her birthday party all beat up a few weeks ago. He lived in West Hollywood and his friends told her yesterday that he didn't come home one night. I thought you could give Bunny and me advice how to start looking for him."

"This is a relative of Bunny's?" Jack Liffey asked.

She nodded. She decided it was best right now to pass over Bunny being her lover. "Her little brother. He was in BLM, too, but when I met him I thought he was maybe a little too het-up about things. I don't want you to go nuts on this, dad." A fleeting glance at Gloria. "Just advice. This is my first big case."

Both of them lasered holes right through her with their eyes.

"I gotta help out a good friend, folks. It's what Liffeys do."

COERCIVE NONVIOLENCE 7

"Do-be-do," Jack Liffey said, then winced. "I'd rather have a truant daughter ... than a detective daughter."

Gloria's voice was suddenly as smooth as a phone salesman—Maeve knew it as her official de-escalate voice. "Hon, don't go overboard yet. We're with you. West Hollywood is sheriff territory, but I got friends there. If you go back to school, I'll look into it right away. I promise."

* * * * *

PETRO Ivanchuk had bit his lip falling hard on the trail, but he stayed down, assuming that the *shmendricks* across the canyon were still dangerous. It felt like he'd been shot in the thigh and he wanted to have a look, but it would be infinitely worse to get up and be shot again.

Sookin syn, he cursed softly. Son-of-a-bitch. He knew he'd crushed the male orangetip by falling on his net. An *anthocharis sara* was almost impossible to catch because it rarely settled except to mate.

When his heart began to calm, he slid to the berm at the edge of the North Fork Trail. There they were on the trail opposite, stabbing fingers and shoving one another in heated argument. A couple kilometers back, the trails had diverged at a rocky ford in the creek and he was guessing one of these crazy men would eventually go back and head up his side to make sure he was in no condition to report them.

The smell of ethyl acetate was invading his adrenaline rush and he knew his fall had broken more than one killing jar. A lot of lepidopterists here were net-and-release purists but he found the concept intolerably sentimental. Pussies, so many Americans, if they weren't bullies. There were no in-betweens.

He rolled onto his back, tore the sweep net off its frame and tied it tight around his thigh as a tourniquet. Young Pioneer training, reluctant participant of which he'd been in that goody two-shoes outfit. "Gaidar is Marching First," a song he'd more-or-less liked, a little of what stayed with him from a Soviet childhood.

The bullet hole in his trousers was very small and the wound might not be as bad as he'd thought. The gunshot hadn't hit bone. Why on earth had they shot at him? What had he done? What a country.

8 *BOYSTOWN*

In a last peek over the berm, he saw the hunters heading downhill and disappearing around a bend. If he wanted to live through this, there was only one way out now—unless he wanted to trudge upward to the Taboose Pass at 12,000 feet and then stumble down forty miles to Fresno. Not likely.

He rose on the shot leg and grunted, his brain screaming at him. *Pain, da.*

Okay, leg, down we go until you hear them coming and then we hide. Then we cross the damn creek and climb the canyon to the other trail to wait. Utterly impossible, but he knew he could do it. In the waning days of the gulags, in the 1980s, he'd survived two years at the far north camp of Norilsk. Simple fury against injustice could keep a man standing and defiant forever.

* * * * *

"THE motherfucker was out of bounds," Zeke Tomlin said. "You all know it. Right?"

"A clear case of self-defense," Charlie Beck said, but his tone had darkened well past any ambiguity.

"Fuck you!" Zeke turned and gave him a shove.

"Cool it," Beck said into the man's face. "Squad discipline now." Beck's features were small and blunt, as if he could take a lot of punishment and keep on functioning.

"Who the fuck appointed you general? You the one said 'plink' in the first place, Charles. Not a judge in this country gonna blame me for playing with a dancing fairy with a butterfly net."

"I'm glad you think so."

"This is my turf. I been killing deer here past forever. We don't need faggots running them off."

"You're a freak, Zeke," Belkin said all of a sudden. "Zeke the freak. The perfect American fuckup."

"I ain't talkin' to you, yardbird," Zeke said. "This is between me and Charlie."

COERCIVE NONVIOLENCE 9

Talbot Denny wondered if Zeke Tomlin had gone temporarily insane. How could you potshot another human being out of the blue like that? And how could he disassociate himself from these crazy testosterone-overloads before even worse came to pass?

"It happened," Talbot Denny announced. "Let's just go home and forget it."

"Huh-uh," Squad Captain Beck said with unassailable confidence. "We got to help our poor Zeke—our great Sierra white hunter. Get with the program here, Talbot. We may not like it, but we got to make sure the butterfly man isn't going to squeal."

* * * * *

JACK Liffey stood waiting over the open toilet, aiming his penis and sending repeated inner signals to his sphincter muscles to let go. The damned prostate. *A gland the size of a walnut*, every single medical article began. But did the *Encyclopedia of Edible Nuts* say that the walnut was a nut the size of a human prostate?

Age is not your best friend, he thought. They say the best tunes are played on the oldest fiddles. Hah! His damn fiddle hurt.

His brain still worked fine, he was sure of it, but it was into its own revolt, sparking and flaring unexpectedly when he spoke aloud. It was like being forced to communicate through Monty Python's Hungarian phrasebook that translated "Can you direct me to the train station?" as "Please fondle my bum."

* * * * *

"HONEY, how you doing with the L thing these days?"

"Just fine, Gloria," Maeve said.

"Don't take it wrong. I just don't want you to put some permanent tat on your person—like '*Women are from Venus, men don't exist.*'"

Maeve laughed. "You know I'm already marked." Her dad was lingering in the bathroom or they wouldn't be having this conversation. In one of their woman-to-woman exchanges, she'd shown Gloria the gang tattoo she'd been forced to endure on her left breast. An Olde

English G for the Greenwoods, the *klika* from right on the block that she'd almost been dragged into.

"I'm doing this thing about the missing boy for Bunny. You've got to meet her, Glor. Her heart is solid gold and I love her a lot. And how about you and dad these days?"

Gloria smiled sardonically. "Interrogation, huh?"

They might have gone on dueling a bit more, but the doorbell rang.

"Can you get it, hon?" Gloria said. "I'm still gimpy."

"We'll talk about this again."

"We ain't backers-down, neither of us."

Maeve let it rest and walked to the door, where she found a tall-ish man about fifty with big lips and a belligerent chin a lot like Lee Marvin. She'd run into him a few times at the hospital, looking in on her dad. He was an arson inspector her dad knew. In an instant she remembered his name—Walt Roski.

"Hi, I'm a friend of Jack's. Could I see him?"

"I'm his daughter, remember?"

"Maeve! Sorry, I was preoccupied back at County. Jack and I worked together on the Sheephead Fire."

"I remember. Do you want some coffee?"

"I wouldn't say no."

Jack Liffey was settling at the kitchen table when she brought the man in, and in the warm greetings she could tell they were genuinely pleased to see each other.

"Good to see you up and around, man. At County, I thought I was going to have to send housekeeping in to water you."

"Water—I never even drink it because fish fuck in it. Sorry, Walt. That's W.C. Fields. My brain can't seem to control ... these eruptions ... from my speech center."

Roski waved the apology off and Gloria hobbled over with a mug of coffee for him and squeezed his shoulder affectionately. Maeve's approval rating soared.

"This man is the genius who found the girl that your dad was look-ing for after that fire," Gloria said.

COERCIVE NONVIOLENCE 11

"The genius who found three incinerated bones that we called the girl," he corrected. "That's my job, all right. A penny short and a day late."

"Late, late, for a very important date. You did find ... her killer."

Roski and her dad exchanged a dark look that Maeve couldn't read.

"That was a bad week or two," Roski said. "Let's let it go."

"But at least it made me . . a good friend," Jack Liffey said.

"Me, too."

"Enough of the lovefest," Gloria said. "I don't want him going gay on me." A faint lemonish expression indicated she immediately realized that was the wrong thing to say. "No offense," Gloria said quickly.

"What you really need is a philosophy of life that isn't about rescuing the world from itself," Roski said.

"Got it. Tell Walt about your missing kid," Jack Liffey said to Maeve. "He's another resource."

She went over her tale again.

"Sure, I can help. West Hollywood is county Fire Battalion one. I served there for seven years so I know everybody."

"Wow, thanks," Maeve said. "I want to help, too."

Roski smiled. "You and your dad are both Type Ones. In my experience there's two kinds of people. The anxious ones—like you two—who find life far too short and want to save everybody before it's too late. And the depressives who think life is plenty long enough already."

"The xanax people and the prozacs," Jack Liffey said. "Nothing is ever innocent to you, Walt."

"Which type are you?" Gloria snarled, apparently hurt by the observation.

"Same as you, dear. Too tired."

* * * * *

PETRO Ivanchuk Pogorelets thought he heard bumbling chatter from the hunters coming uphill on his side. He swung his wounded leg quickly over the edge and dug it into the crumbly hillside, suppressing a cry of pain. If he wasn't going to be able to take the pain, he might as well find out right away. Bearable, just. He used the shaft of the butterfly net as a hiking pole to stabilize his reckless descent, pushing himself along. He took hops downward onto his bad leg, partly out of perversity and partly so he could catch himself with the good one if he had to. Once in a while he did cry out a little, but he was sure he had a while before the assholes would see him down here.

A big hawk must have heard one of his cries—thinking it announced forthcoming carrion—and it began circling overhead, not a good sign if the hunters had anything above average intelligence. Okay, Petro Ivanchuk, you proved you can handle the downhill. That's a snow-fed stream you have to cross right there and then a whole lot of up.

TWO

Closer to God

PETRO Ivanchuk lay utterly exhausted after the endless climb, his head and chest flat on the south trail, his butt-end and legs dangling for the world to see, unable to do a damn thing about it. The seep-bleeding seemed to have stopped after his wound hit the thigh-deep icewater in Big Pine Creek. Climbing the south slope, he'd been able to grasp a few subalpine shrubs like chamise and manzanita. The ascent had stretched his limits for what mind-over-body could accomplish. Thank you, Mr. Nietzsche, you fucking *pridoruk*. Idiot. Nobody is a superman.

A breeze came up the opposite trail and it carried the arguing hunters' voices. He knew he had to get his legs out of view very soon. Yes, very soon. He heard a clatter-crash well below. Broken glass?

* * * * *

"YOU killed a man, trashhead," Belkin snapped. "Stop denying it. What a baby!"

"We don't know he's dead, Russky. Give me a turn at that vodka."

The flat pint bottle had emerged from Belkin's vest a few minutes back. Belkin frowned at the bottle that had two fingers remaining. He hurled it hard out over the canyon. "Zeke—*woof*, go fetch."

"Fuck you!"

14   *BOYSTOWN*

"Kiss my asshole!"

Charlie Beck turned back. "Stand down, gentlemen! I mean it. If any of you think I shouldn't be squad leader and you got superior skills, please signify by stepping up." He gave it a beat. "Okay, stay tuned. Let's find the butterfly man. *Then* we deal with him, as is. After that we turn this bus around. Are we with the program?"

Talbot Denny and Zeke Tomlin nodded. Belkin offered his big nihilist who-the-fuck-cares smirk. "Nice nosedive the guy made on the trail, I gotta say. Nine-point-oh. Difficulty, maybe one."

"Knock it off," Beck said. "You screwed up your life years ago in Roosha."

Belkin gave a wolfish grin. "I gave it my poor try, boss. Like everything I do. Mornings I gets a really big hard turd coming down my ass, all scrape and burn, you know. I just got to smile and let it dump away."

"You get a lot of those painful shits?" Beck said angrily.

"I don't know. Maybe I just made it up."

Talbot Denny studied Belkin. The man was wiry and corded with sinew, not very tall, maybe fifty years old, with wavy black hair and a loose confident manner that said he would do his best to cause you pain if you crossed him. That dangerous air meant you couldn't take your eyes off him—like watching a cobra hovering over an infant. Talbot could only guess: a psyche mutilated by whatever horrors Soviet prisons had once inflicted, a sociopath almost certainly who carried that dark confidence that always seemed to attract children and animals. What the hell was it?

"I'm pleased we were able to clear that up," Beck said. "You. New guy. I want you on point now."

Charlie Beck indicated Talbot Denny. There was so little chance of getting ambushed by Viet Cong on the eastern slope of the Sierras that Denny shrugged and moved well ahead of his quarrelling workmates. A relief, really. Hey, dudes, he fantasized saying, you *do* know I'm a fag, right?

* * * * *

CLOSER TO GOD 15

G LORIA had made another pot of coffee and brought it to them. She seemed fascinated watching the men spar in a friendly way. "Nuh," Jack Liffey said.

"You're a rescuer, man. It's your destiny." "Nuh." He finished his enchiladas, slowing down at basic activities like eating to head off any ambush his mind had waiting for him.

"I thought I'd end up a philosopher sitting under a big bodhi tree," Roski said. "I didn't think I'd be poking at bones and ashes to track down guys whose fathers whipped them so much they had to set fires to get noticed."

Maeve watched her dad nod, almost as fascinated as Gloria by the tap-dance between the men.

"I ended up sitting in a trailer in Asia ... watching radar as airplanes dumped bad shit on Asians. What I really wanted ... to teach Mark Twain to bright kids."

"I was struggling with Heidegger," Roski said. "But, hell, the guy never repudiated Hitler." He sipped the superhot coffee. "My poor ex-was terrified of us talking openly about anything our neighbors couldn't fathom. She was sure they'd hate us. She took down my Cezanne print because it was too blurry. Some days I feel like a girl's diary—begging your pardon, ladies—I just feel all alone. I try to go to lunch but my buddies at work argue about if Target is better than Wal-Mart. I guess it's a new form of epistemology. Denny's or Applebee's. McDonald's or Burger King." He sighed. "Maybe something's made me not such a nice person."

"You've got to find another woman," Jack Liffey said. "The soul withers up."

He almost smiled. "You folks ever find somebody to fix me up, I might go for it. Right now I'll call West Hollywood sheriffs for you. What was the name?"

They all looked at Maeve. She was startled out of an inward reverie. "Benjy Walker. Benjamin."

Roski picked up the cordless house phone and dialed, listened, then sighed. "Interrupt his half-caf nonfat latte. I know where you live, Kristen."

Gloria offered an approving look toward Roski's back. "In a world of bad, it's good to have even this guy," she said softly, then hobbled up behind Jack Liffey and hugged him.

Roski was listening hard on the phone and then he carried the handpiece out of the kitchen.

They were all silent for a moment, as if trying to listen.

"Dad, can you tell us what it's like inside your head now?" Maeve asked. "We do our best."

"I can try. I guess I'm standing in a big cave. Bats fly all around me. Walls are full of cubby holes. In the holes are words I need, quotes, puns. Stuff like that." His hands grabbed in midair to catch a phantom. "I grab at one. But I get the wrong one sometimes." He appealed to them submissively with his eyes, an expression Maeve had never seen before, and it chilled her to the marrow.

"Don't be so worried," Maeve said. "Your brain always did flit around. I know the Liffey mind. It's restless. We go off on tangents. Remember how it used to drive mom crazy? She was so straight-ahead normal. You'd take a sudden left turn and laugh and she'd freeze up as if you'd slapped her. But *I* got it."

"Got-got-got it. I was never kind enough to Kathy. She was good people."

"Yeah, dad. We know that, and we don't need any last benedictions. You're not dying."

Gloria put a hand on Maeve's shoulder and her other hand remained on Jack. It was the first time Maeve could remember all three of them being in physical contact. She wanted to cry, but too much important was going on.

"News, folks," Roski peered in through the kitchen archway. "Oh dear, I'm interrupting a touching family moment. I'll go to work now and call later with the news."

"Freeze, motherfucker," Gloria called, making a finger-gun.

CLOSER TO GOD 17

"Maybe not so touching," Roski said.

"You can't win with her, Walt," Jack Liffey said, "But you can lose graciously."

"Report," Gloria demanded.

He sighed. "I can tell you where Benjy lives, which you may already know." Glancing at Maeve. "He's gay and he has a roommate who hasn't seen him since he went trolling leather bars a few nights ago. My fire pals made a few choice comments that I won't repeat. On my better days, I might have tsk-tsked."

"Op-eds later," Gloria snapped. "You learned this from a fire station?"

"We don't all live in separate boxes. Let's say it comes from the West Hollywood sheriff station. They're alerting for the missing boy."

"Any more wisdom?" Gloria asked.

"Keep Jack occupied. I'll have a peek at things."

They were all silent for a while.

"I'm impressed by you guys," Maeve said finally. "When the going gets tough, the tough turn pro." She and her father smiled briefly at one another, both knowing the quote was Hunter Thompson.

"Family code," Gloria said disdainfully. "Maeve, dear, he's given you his info. Thank him and go home. Don't be another Jack Liffey."

"I'm on it." She saluted.

Maeve's wolfish grin hinted she just might have her Dick Tracy clue kit at the ready.

* * * * *

THE hunters were chest-butting and hand-shoving, very near real blows. Petro Ivanchuk, lying fully on the trail now, couldn't make out a thing they were bawling at each other across the canyon. But the panic was obvious, and the overstuffed egos.

They'd obviously found where he'd fallen, and not one of them had the native sense to track his jump over the edge and his hobble-step descent. Some hunters. Blockheads. The kind of guys who made you want to train the deer to shoot back. Petro Ivanchuk would like to turn them all over to the old KGB for a little close interrogation. He was not a forgiving sort. He had a glimmer that he would get back at them somehow.

With immense effort, he crawled a hundred meters down the south trail toward a large bush where the path turned inward and out of sight. He could soon walk upright. Okay, Mr. Fucking Nietzsche, the power of the will again.

He checked his tourniquet. He knew standing on the wounded leg demanded a superhuman effort. The wind shifted to the north and snippets of talk carried to him.

"... Wish to Christ I had my AR ..."

"... You didn't even see ..."

"... Don't touch me ..."

"... Sissy motherfucker ..."

"... I know he got skin left on ..."

He stood and tried to trot, suppressing the anguish. Plenty of time for self-pity later. He had to curse the pain away. A bit of French—*conneries!*—some Yiddish—*putz!*—his poor Polish—*dupek!*—and stretching his informal American—you fuckwads!

Before long the trail wound outward again, taking him to a viewpoint where he dropped flat and dead still, staring across the canyon. There was nothing to see. Only the hawk, still circling.

He wondered if they'd gone on up toward Taboose Pass. Or found his blood track down the hillside and were hurrying back down to intercept him. He needed his leg looked after very soon.

He went on down the trail at a swing-leg pace that seemed to minimize the pain. Approaching the trailhead parking lot, he heard noises and stepped into some trees. What looked like a Young Pioneer group of sixteen-year-olds came into sight in high spirits—Boy Scouts, of course. He kept well out of sight.

"Don't goose me!"

"You spazz!"

A dozen of them passed up the trail, shooed on by their commissar, and then silence settled. He made his way cautiously to the parking

CLOSER TO GOD 19

lot, leaning on trees when he could. A dozen cars were waiting patiently, including his own. He could drive off now, but he didn't. He took his time and wrote down the license number of each vehicle, on a grid that he drew on the back of a butterfly catch sheet.

Four port-a-potties stood beside the trailhead, and he picked the one that gave him the best view of the parking lot. In his breast pocket he also carried sticky labels for the kill-bottles.

Risk of Dengue Fever! Stay out! he wrote on a label and pressed it onto the potty door as he slipped inside.

* * * * *

M AEVE parked across Dicks Street at the address Bunny had given her for Benjy, a road so narrow that the parking was only on the far side. *Dicks Street.* Don't even *go* there, she thought. She was in the dense heart of the male gay universe, the gayest district of the gayest city in America, with half its population male gays, including an open and out mayor and most of the city council. The area had been known by its nickname for decades, even before it had incorporated as the city of West Hollywood in the 1980s.

Maeve had helped her dad out with investigations before—mostly without his knowledge or permission—but she'd rarely done so completely on her own. She knew she was no Nancy Drew, and it was no longer a world where you could count on girlish spunk to give you a get-out-of-jail-free card. If it ever had been.

The house was breathtaking, which she didn't mean in a kindly sense. Her dad would have loved it once he stopped laughing. In the 1970s gays had moved into the Norma Triangle *en masse* with their sensibility fired up to spiff the area up. The tiny bungalow had been rebuilt with a copper mansard roof, a yellow stucco exterior, a double front door almost twenty feet tall and above it, unbelievably, a weird oval frame set into the mansard with the bust of a French royal. Or whoever it was with a curlicue eighteenth century wig. An olde-time streetlight stood sentry beside the door, and just to ice the cake, a row of topiary bushes stood guard at the sidewalk, squared up to resemble—what?—

old gasoline pumps with lollipops on top. She wondered what it would feel like to come home to an eruption of kitsch every night, but she hadn't come here to pass artistic judgment.

A button beside the door played the beginning of Bach's Second Brandenburg Concerto on chimes.

"Hello?"

The guy who opened up looked relatively normal, she thought. Khakis and a blue work shirt, maybe twenty-five. Very chiseled handsome.

"I'm Bunny Walker's friend from UCLA," she said. "Maeve."

"Wow, okay. Wow. Come in, Maeve. I'm Earl. I keep expecting it to be Ben at the door with a big sheepish look on his face ... and a black eye."

"Black eye?" Maeve asked quickly, catching a whiff of something clue-like already. She stepped into an ordinary universe, a college dorm room in fact. Bookcases of pine boards and concrete blocks, Kmart inflatable chairs, a Salvation Army sofa, but a fancy expensive stereo and TV.

He sighed. "Would you like some coffee? Beer?"

"It's a bit early for beer. Coffee."

"Come on. I think I've got some made."

There was an arched alcove into the kitchen, where Earl wandered. "He has this Lamborghini coffee maker. God knows where he got it. It has a big gear shift on the side and I'm afraid if I slam it into the wrong gear the machine will accelerate right out the back door."

"Can I help?"

"I'm joking. The thing fills a pot just like Mr. Coffee." He peers down into an opaque steel pot. I'll warm it in the microwave if you don't mind."

"What did we all do before microwaves? Um, you definitely said black eye?"

"I don't know if Bunny told you. Ben can be a red hanky guy."

"Pardon?"

"Okay. There's a hanky code for cruising bars. You signal what things you like with different color handkerchiefs dangling out of

CLOSER TO GOD 21

your back pocket. It's not stuff you write home about. Yellow is for ... well ... to do with watersports, peeing. Green means you want money. Well, that's in the left pocket. In the right means you're willing to pay. Rusty brown is cowboy. You don't want to know all this." He suddenly seemed weary.

"I want to know red."

He winced. "Okay. It's fisting. I love Ben but I'm pretty ordinary and I don't have the let's-go-crazy gene. He likes a bit of S and M and I won't do it so he'll go off to leather bars from time to time and he'll come home with bruises and worse. He'd hate me using the word fetishes. It's breaking my heart, you know. I keep saying to myself, this time when he gets home I'll ask him to pack up. I try. He's never been gone more than overnight. Maybe this time, I will. Have you ever loved somebody who hurts you like that?"

"Oh, sure. Over and over. Don't get me going. I'll start to cry."

The microwave chimed and he poured them mugs.

"I'm a lesbian, Earl," she told him. "No worries about me dissing your sexuality. I just need to know what I can find out about Ben. I'm an art student and a friend of his sister. What do you do?"

"I'm an architect—and by the way, don't blame me for this clown house. We're renters, or I am. Most days I get a giggle out of it, but I know it's a gayboy's delight. It has every possible violation of good taste. It should have a preservation order to remind us of the seventies."

"You call them gayboy's delights?"

"I'm not sensitive. At least here in the homeland. And with another LGBTQ+." He smiled but only around the mouth and it felt like some sort of antique chivalry. The coffee was pretty good, if old.

"I'm not here to mess with you. My dad is a detective whose only work is finding missing young people, and I've helped him a few times before so I know a little of what I'm doing. Not much, but a little. And I love his sister. Can you help me out?"

"Anything for Benjy."

"Does he have a study here?"

"We have separate rooms. For snoring and for our occasional snits. You want to see his room, of course."

"Please."

He sighed. "The arrangement is for privacy, too. In our computer-snoopy world. Generally, entry is by permission, but I'll make an exception."

"I'll try not to sully the room," she said.

He smiled. "Please. I couldn't go on living."

* * * * *

"HELP me upstairs, Jack. I'm starting to fade." Thank heavens Gloria had become adept with the cane. He'd have been done in shouldering all her weight up the stairs every day.

"We are getting closer to god," he said, as they hobbled upward. As a high school student he'd ridden the red cars to downtown LA on weekends to work as a copy boy for the old *Herald-Examiner*. On the top floor, like all Hearst buildings, they'd maintained an office suite for the legendary Citizen Hearst, should he ever show up. And on the staircase leading up somebody had painted, **You are getting closer to god.**

"Sure, Jack."

"How come you didn't object ... to Maeve's project?"

"Would she stop if I did? She's a grown woman now, in case you been missing those big breasts. We'll catch her when she falls."

He couldn't see it working out so rosy. "Oh, lord help us," he said helplessly.

* * * * *

PETRO Ivanchuk kept one finger crooked around the port-a-potty door, leaving a small gap, but none of the idiot hunters even drifted toward the toilets. One of them even pissed on a Mercedes rather than bother. It was the fierce-looking skinny one whose supremely cocky body movements reminded Petro for some reason of a gangster back home.

CLOSER TO GOD

The stocky one said: "Drop it, Zeke. 'Plink' isn't a fucking order, you know?"

"It did the deed."

"The deed is all yours. You're lucky we didn't throw you over the edge right then for wrecking the trip. Consider it our gift."

They went to a big black Suburban and piled their packs into the back. The rifles went into a plastic Thule container on top. Petro Ivanchuk checked his sketch to make sure he had the license number of the Suburban and he did.

"Let's don't argue," a young one said. "It gives me the bads."

"Another country heard from."

Petro Ivanchuk could hear that at least one of them was deeply frightened. He had no fear himself, none. Something had snapped over inside him with the panic and the ordeal, and though it wasn't even noon yet, all his thoughts were night thoughts, thoughts of revenge.

THREE

They Say They Can Milk Chickens

P ETRO Ivanchuk tottered up to the back kitchen door and knocked for a long time. Eventually Dr. Leonid Trachtenberg arrived, a man with the sharp features and muscular physique of a Slavic peasant.

"My friend—what on earth are you doing ...? *Oh, my.*"

Blood had soaked down his trouser leg even with his net tourniquet still around the top of his left thigh. He'd loosened it every half hour on the three-hour woozy drive back to West Hollywood. The power of the will was indeed astounding.

"You should be in the ER."

"Never. Only *you*, Leonid. My life depends now on discretion."

"Well, then. Come in." He helped Petro Ivanchuk up the two concrete steps, apparently changing his mind at the last minute about the carpeted part of the house and diverting his burden to a utility room with a linoleum floor. "Lie there for now. What sort of wound is it?"

"Hunting accident. Bullet." He sagged to the floor and stretched out beside the washer and dryer, and the doctor gave him a ball of old laundry as pillow.

"How long ago?"

"Maybe six hours."

"You stubborn man. Sepsis—have you ever heard of it? Never mind. Let me go get a big hammer and a chainsaw."

The instant the doctor left the laundry room, Petro Ivanchuk gave himself over to fatigue and plummeted into a deep dark place.

* * * * *

B ELKIN stripped to his boxers as soon as he got home and began his *gimnastika* with fifty press-ups. His regimen took very little space, no more than the standard prison cell at Vinnytsia. Which was fortunate because the has-its-own-entrance room that he'd rented in the back of an old frame house just off Hollywood Boulevard was none too spacious.

This was the underbelly of old Hollywood—hookers, wannabe punk rockers and runaways looking for whatever it was they hadn't been able to find in Kansas. Belkin was on to aerobic, running high-knee hard in place when he heard the scratch at the door. He threw on his jeans and opened to Cat. The girl growled at him in her feral way, then snapped out, "Asshole"—one of her dozen or so words. "Food!"

The hunting trip had made him forget to put out anything for her. She glared at him, arms crossed defiantly. Being a responsible man was a solemn burden, he thought, but lots of things in life were burdens.

"I didn't get to McDonald's today." For her customary Filet-O-Fish sandwich. "How 'bout a bag of Oreos?"

She made the humming growl that could either be rage or assent. "You gotta get a better yes-or-no for me. Here." He fetched the cookie bag and she snatched it greedily.

She sat down on the stoop and bowed her tangled dreadlocks to the task of eating. Belkin squatted down inside the door and ran his hand gently through her red hair as best he could. She would never cross the threshhold and wouldn't bathe at his offer, but didn't really seem to smell. She could have been 16 or 40. Cat wasn't her name, but clearly she was a stray, and it was what he'd chosen to call her. She seemed to accept it.

Cat had adopted him six months earlier after he'd heard noises and discovered her sleeping in the crawl space directly under his room,

THEY SAY THEY CAN MILK CHICKENS 27

snoring like a tree-chipper. She wore his castoffs now to replace the rags she'd begun with. He could only guess what abuse she'd suffered, and he knew quite a bit about abuse.

Their relationship consisted almost entirely of him leaving food on the back steps and occasionally fondling her hair for a hum that was quite like a purr. Once in a great while Cat would say, "Wow." It was the most heartbreakingly tender human relationship that Belkin had ever known. He'd have killed the rest of the human race without hesitation in order to protect this unknowable girl.

* * * * *

A N arson investigator has quite a bit of license, Roski thought. Anything I choose to look into could be related to a suspicious garage fire in Lennox, or the torching of a bankrupt factory in Vernon. Even visiting the apartment of a woman in hip Silverlake who had recruited Bunny Walker and her brother into Black Lives Matter and knew Benjy. Maeve's heavyset girlfriend had said, "For Maeve, I'll tell you. Don't say who told you the address."

"Scout's honor."

"I like Benjy," Karen Bustros told him. "He's one of those bright guys who hides inside, maybe because he's scared, and to prove he's not scared he'll jump off cliffs. Recklessness and confidence can be attractive. He was gay but I like gay guys. They're entertaining and they don't suddenly make a grab for your tits after saying how much they like talking to you. Yes, I've been called a fag-hag. There's peace in lack of sexual threat."

The young woman had two black eyes, raccoon-eyes as the child-abuse people called it, and probably a broken nose under the bandages. She was olive skinned, maybe Middle Eastern. Bustros lay on a sofa under a big painting of Lenin on black velvet that had a big plastic weepy tear on its cheek, a strange creation that he tried not to look at. It was not her place but she'd agreed to meet there. Still, a fierce-looking black guy stood in an inner doorway watching. The man had opposed Roski entering until he'd shown his arson badge.

"Ain't nobody been burned up here, Arson," the man had said.

"It's part of a larger fire investigation," Roski insisted. "Everything is suspicious, my friend, even you."

"Tonio, can I have two of the pills?" the girl pleaded.

"That's a plan." He wandered off and came back with two oval pills on his palm and a glass of water. Probably vicodin, Roski could see. Not unusual in the circumstances.

She gulped them down. "Give us a few minutes," she said.

"I got to go back to work," he said nervously. "You be okay now?"

"I'm fine, Tonio. Love you."

"Sure." He kissed her gently on the forehead. and disappeared again into the innards. The big frame house overlooking the reservoir had the impersonal shabby look of a clubhouse or shared habitation.

"I'll explain all this," she said to Roski, indicating her face. "In a way I did it to myself. Sit down, Mr. Roski. You're welcome here as long as you don't go hassling anybody."

"And if I do?"

"Just don't. You have to understand, we get nothing but trouble from LE and other officers of the state, like you. When we need help we only get scorn. If we're black you shoot us. This Benjy business started when I was at a café with him. I won't go to his leather bar hangout so we just had a couple drinks and a flatbread pizza on the boulevard. Everything I'm going to tell you I told to two sheriffs who didn't give a shit. They wrote it down and probably dumped it the minute they left."

"Did you see their name tags?"

"Is it okay to snitch on cops?"

"You'd better follow your own code. It could help."

"Deputies Smith and Jones. Now I'll tell you and you can not give your own shit, okay. I was leaving the place Andy's and going back to my car around the corner when I saw it just starting. I don't know how to put it. Benjy liked rough guys and he was obviously coming on to some uncooked skinny hunk of meat. The guy started flipping out and then whaling on him, like really crazy, like straight guys who feel

THEY SAY THEY CAN MILK CHICKENS

their manhood is threatened or something. I ran back. I mean, look at me, do I look like somebody who could stop a fight, but, you know, sometimes guys back off when they see a girl. Not this guy. He's out of control, like he'd ODed on angel dust, you know? He goes, 'Fuck you, cunt,' and before I can say a word, my lights are out. I wake up and Benjy's gone, the guy's gone, bunch of rubbernecks are looking down and apologizing like good citizens.

"I know, you want me to describe him. I told the cops. I'll tell you. Thin and swaggery and foreign-looking. I'd know him again, that's all."

"Thanks, Miss Bustros. That's a pretty good description of things, under the circumstances. Thank you. Are you willing to try something else for me and Benjy?"

She bit her lip and nodded.

"Okay, I want you to close your eyes and relax." She did. "Think back to the first impression you had of this man as you got close. What caught your eye? Something about his looks, his manner, maybe his clothing."

"Uh ... yeah. He had on work clothes, you know, working class clothes. I don't know what that means really, not a janitor uniform, but definitely not preppy or dressy. Probably jeans and some kind of work shirt. I don't think there was a name patch. WeHo is full of reverse snobbery so it might not mean anything. Anybody might dress like that."

"Keep your eyes closed now. There's one detail about him you saw right away. As you got close."

"No, I don't think so. By then I was worrying about Benjy who looked hurt."

"Okay, we'll come back to that. What makes you think it was a work shirt he wore?"

"He had long sleeves with the cuffs rolled twice to the middle of the forearm. Stiff cloth. Maybe khaki or tan. The rugged man look, you know?"

"With the sleeves rolled up did you see anything on his arms? A scar, a watch?"

"Sonofabitch!" she said with surprise. "You're right. It must have been my rage, whatever. What a total *creep* he must be. He had Nazi tattoos on the backside of his wrists—not even trying to hide them. Not swastikas. You know, those zig-zag lightning bolts for the SS. On both his arms. What sort of dipshit trash does that?"

"How did you recognize the tattoos?"

"I'm not stupid, mister. I read books. I've got some ink, too, but it's nice. That stuff's just moronic."

"Some people like to wave a fist at the world."

"Or wave the middle finger."

"Or even wave Lenin," he suggested and nodded upward.

She cranked her neck around to look up at the painting of the weeping Lenin and smiled. "Dumb I guess. At least he was trying to make a better world. Nobody's doing that now, are they? The rich have bought the whole planet and put us to sleep."

"I don't know about that."

"You better look closer. I'm happy to help Benjy, and if you find any photos of assholes with SS on their arms, I'll look at them. This guy is burned on my retina forever." Her eyes closed.

"Can I get you more vicodin?"

She just smiled and drifted off into her own la-la land.

* * * * *

MAEVE sat at the high desk in her studio, trying and failing to get back to work on a sketch. She was thinking about her search of Benjamin's bedroom, how inept she'd been at the task. Her dad would certainly have done better.

But something about the Norma Triangle of West Hollywood had been deeply comforting inside. It was a dense area of well-manicured little bungalows, an enclave of in-your-face urban gay culture pinned between Sunset and Santa Monica Boulevards, and you could walk a few blocks north to one of the last great bookstores in LA or south to the trendiest restaurants and clubs. Or, of course, you could step out your front door and disappear off the face of the earth.

THEY SAY THEY CAN MILK CHICKENS 31

Earl had hovered most of her search time so she hadn't been able to do her job very thoroughly. The bedroom had held a mussed platform bed with bodybuilding magazines stacked beside it, a severe IKEA desk with an old Apple G5 tower under it. A very large orange painting over the bed with a big Nike swoosh in blue. Instead of Just Do It, it said Did It Already.

"Could I check the desk drawers?"

"I'd rather you didn't."

"How about the closet?"

"Tell you the truth, Maeve, I'm uncomfortable. How about if I look and tell you if there's anything odd?"

"It's not the usual protocol, but I'm not here to make you uncomfortable."

He'd stirred a finger in each desk drawer and the bedside drawer, naming a few ordinary things, and then stared into the closet for a few moments. His eyes had gone a bit swampy. "Nothing, really. Guy stuff. In a world of bad shit, nothing at all to worry about."

"Do one more thing for me," she'd said.

"Umm."

"Look under the bed."

"Okay," he said dubiously. He'd dropped to one knee and lifted a fall of bedclothes to peer underneath. "*What* the—"

"Dangerous?"

"In a way." He had reached under and plucked out a four-inch square of gauze and adhesive tape covered with dried blood. "We're both HIV positive," he'd said matter-of-factly.

Maeve had stiffened a little, despite herself, as if that bad voodoo could reach out across the bedroom. She knew better. "Did you know he had a wound?"

"I didn't know he made it home."

"Would you do me one last favor, Earl? Check your bathroom and see if there are any packets of gauze and tape. Maybe he was bandaged somewhere else."

He'd glanced at her, wondering why she wanted to know this, but then looked through the bathroom for her. The answer was no gauze, no tape. She'd thought of asking him to put the bandage in a baggy and give it to her, but why? "Please save it," she'd suggested. "It might be evidence."

Afterward she'd started up her balky 2003 Toyota Echo that had almost 150,000 miles on it, feeling in over her head. Dad, what do you think? She was flying alone now, without her dad and without any goddesses. The weight was dreadful.

* * * * *

TALBOT Denny slipped in the back very quietly at the cottage, as if by not making any noise he wouldn't be drawing the world's baleful eye onto himself. The shooting in the mountains had left him on edge. But his brother Alvis was cooking up a storm in the kitchen and saw him immediately.

Al was putting him up while he unwound from his PhD ordeal. There had been two major rewrites and a grueling defense of the dissertation, "Exile: the Essence of Modernism." He'd been warned by colleagues: endless ordeals await the sucker who goes for the really big themes rather than one of the tiny delimited outposts.

"Tal, you look like death warmed over," Alvis said.

"Cook away, bro. I'm exhausted." They hadn't seen each other since the hunt.

"You didn't get to murder any sweet furry creatures in the mountains?"

"I spared Bugs because of his Brooklyn chutzpah. What's all this?" Dozens of bowls of colorful food crowded the table.

"Tapas. Carolyn's coming this evening and the Brownings and Jacobsons. You're more than welcome to join us. I mean it. C likes you a lot."

Alvis had always been straight, or cis, or hetero, any word for it would do. He was a year-and-a-half younger than Talbot, and neither of them had ever felt compelled by any agenda to try to change or modify

THEY SAY THEY CAN MILK CHICKENS   33

the other. Talbot had known who he was since he was about twelve and his family had known since he was fifteen. It was just the way it was, and he blessed his parents' generous Kansas City souls for making it all tolerable. The Paris of the Midwest indeed.

"I probably won't make it tonight. Thanks. I need to hibernate."

"Back early from the trip, weren't you?"

What to tell Alvin? He'd been worrying it a lot.

"It sucked, Alv. I was nuts to try to fit in with all the Charles Atlases. Lord knows why I even wanted this strange job for six months. I guess my brain hurt." In his head, he kept seeing the big man with the butterfly net tumble forward. He begged the fates to make sure Mr. Butterfly was still alive, a possibility that had freaked the others no end. Charlie and Zeke we're still at each other's throats, and Belkin—who could say what a psychopath feels? Belkin had goaded the quarreling at work afterward.

Alvis smiled. "My brain always hurts. Maybe that's why I'm into music. Music comes from your gut."

"Hydrochloric acid comes from your gut, Alv. Don't ask, but a man got hurt last weekend and my zombie friends freaked out. That's all I can tell you right now. Is that good enough? Honestly?"

"You know it is, Tal, if you say it is. Go hide tonight if you need to. But have a prosciutto, mushroom and goat first. That one there. There's going to be some noise, I'm sorry."

"Thanks, my flesh and blood. I've got earplugs. I'm just riding along now."

"Meaning?"

"This seems to be my summer of utter submission to fate. None of this salmon fighting upstream. I'm riding downstream and I want nothing but a world without choices. Decisions will come later."

"You go, guy. Lots of times in KC I didn't understand a damn word you said, but I always trusted you. You know that."

* * * * *

"'M afraid, Jack," Gloria said, tense as a stone. "I admit it. I'm afraid of never feeling any better. And never being able to walk without this damn hitch and drag. Afraid of Captain Henderson telling me I'm out of the department for good, or exiling me to a desk job in records. I'm afraid of losing my self-respect."

"Let it out," Jack Liffey said.

Gloria's face fell all at once and she wept for a while, sitting on the edge of the bed and clinging to him.

"I'll see you through it."

"The world's got my number, Jack. I'm afraid of becoming that lost little Indian girl again, who had to act out by balling and stealing cars. Glomming onto anything for comfort. I'm afraid of you deciding you've had enough of me, and of the awful silence afterward. You know, I can see some cop finding me in this house in high stink because I been dead alone for three weeks. I've seen it."

"I know you have. I know. Do-si-do and around you go." He winced at his involuntary outburst. "Sorry."

Maybe she hadn't even heard the eruption. She was rubbing her eyes.

"Try a beauty nap, hon," he suggested.

"No jokes."

Cranky nap, then, he thought.

She grasped his knee. It was enough to melt him. Any tenderness, just a show of weakness, meant a lot. "We don't say 'love' much do we, Jack?"

"Not a lot." She'd never said it at all, in fact, on some closely held principle that seemed important to her.

"Funny." But she seemed to have retreated deep inside all at once. "I know I don't say it, but you should be glad. It might make you feel caught."

"I'm really pleased you and Maeve became friends." It seemed an unchallenging way to stay in touch. "That makes me happy."

"Okay. Yeah. Persuade me to lie down now and let everything go for a while."

THEY SAY THEY CAN MILK CHICKENS

"Yes," he said.

"I'm not so nice, Jack. I could have told you that long ago." She lay back and closed her eyes.

Why the hell didn't you then? he thought and almost laughed aloud.

As if she'd heard his laugh, she said, "It just never came up when you were first chasing my pussy."

On the way very quietly down the stairs, he thought, Okay, Gloria, you can care about what you're afraid of. But do you care about what I'm afraid of? The thought seemed harsher than he really felt, but mortality hung over him. His split-open half-healed chest ached quite a lot, and his leg gave a shriek from time to time where they'd sliced inside to steal the veins to graft onto his heart. His out-of-control speech lobe worried him, too. And he had to pee too often. It'd be so damn great to be fifty again, he thought.

He found the phone in the entry where Roski had left it and dialed Maeve's cell. As he listened to the burring, he had second thoughts. Would she think he didn't trust her? He cut off the call and went in to tidy the kitchen.

In five minutes, she called him. "Hi, dad. You wanted—?"

"Hi. Damn these phones. You can't even hang up on somebody any more."

"Star-six-nine, dad. Fifty cents to track down a breather."

"Am I a breather?"

"An incoming call. You wanted something?"

Why had he called her? For comfort? To hear her so-alive voice? Just to touch a world that had her in it? He couldn't really say any of that.

"Can I help?" he said. "With your missing boy."

"You mean it? Are you up to it?" He could hear the brightening in her voice, so it was sincere. This wonderful young woman's emotions never lied if you listened close.

"I'll do what I can."

"Dad, that's super. I was only a few hours on the job and I knew I was in over my head. I went to the missing guy's home and met his roommate. I found out he's HIV positive, and there was a bloody bandage under the bed. Don't worry, I didn't touch it. Bunny said he'd been in a fight. His housemate, his lover, was really uneasy about me looking at his things. You probably know how to push harder. Anyway, I can't find my copy of *Detecting for Idiots*. I need to know step two."

Tough to get to step two when you didn't finish step one, Jack Liffey thought. He didn't mean it cruelly, but the methodical and insistent turning over of flat rocks and checking out what started wriggling beneath had been the core of his life for years now, and he'd learned early on that you couldn't ease yourself past the slightest detail, no matter how unpleasant. There was no room for discretion or letting things slide, even for diplomacy. Okay, a little wiggle room these days, he thought. His attitudes had softened with age.

He used to feel his only real possession was the square foot of earth he stood on, and he had to defend it to the death, but lately he'd been thinking that any square foot at all was pretty good as long as you weren't in pain. Growing old was not for sissies. Was that Bette Davis?

"Step two, do-be-do. That's the toughest step of all, hon. Can we meet up?"

"Wow, hands-on help. Can you stand Coffee Bean and Tea Leaf?"

"I can stand Jack-in-the-Box if I have to."

"I can't. Santa Monica Boulevard in West Hollywood just across from the Blue Whale. Forty-five minutes?"

The Blue Whale was the Pacific Design Center, an unmissable Cesar Pelli-designed modernist building in West Hollywood that now housed hundreds of interior designers. The blue building had been joined recently by the equally haughty Green Building and Red Building, a whole campus of the primary colors of an architect's ego, but he liked them.

"I'll be there. Hon—" There was a question, but it was coming out sideways and his brain locked up.

"Yes?"

"Did you get enough love and encouragement? When you were little?"

THEY SAY THEY CAN MILK CHICKENS　　　　　　　　37

"Dad, you're such a weird fucker, you know that? Come to Coffee Bean and I'll buy."

"Hah. Whose money?"

"The money I make selling my body to the football team."

* * * * *

THE first night after the hunt, they'd all flaked out and fled to their homes to sleep, and they'd stayed home the second day, too, Sunday, but now they'd got together to pick up the pieces. Except they'd excluded the squirrelly new guy Talbot. Charlie Beck, to avoid them having any toxic contact with his wife and kids, took them out to his man-cave, a garage that he rented on the alley next door. Over the years he'd converted it with Abitibi faux wood paneling, deer antlers, gun racks and a big blurry out-of-date projection TV. He had a fridge and an inexhaustible stack of Coors cases.

"If the butterfly man is still alive, he's going to report getting shot," Charlie said. "When he does, my pal in law enforcement will tell us who he is."

"What you plotting for him?" Belkin said, addressing Beck but staring at Zeke.

"Why you looking at me that way?" Zeke bridled.

"I ain't aware of looking at nobody no way."

"This is a civilized country, psycho," Zeke said. "Be cool."

"I'm sure you shot that toe-dancer in self defense."

"It was just a impulse, Russky. Totally understandable in the circumstance."

Belkin grinned. "My school pal in Kiev told me Stalin used to say they ain't no greater pleasure in life than laying your plan for revenge, getting it on the way and then going to sleep on it." He chuckled for a while. "You got to admit that Stalin had a finger on the motherfucking roots of the human mind."

"Gentlemen, we came tonight to be realists," Charlie cut in. "Have a beer and let's reason together. If things get extreme, we go to extremes, of course. But first, let's assume Mr. Butterfly is still alive and very pissed off at us, but clueless. Maybe he reported some guys who look like us to the cops. So what?"

"Yeah, they's tons of crackers with ugly faces like you," Belkin said.

"Button it. We stopped for supplies at the Bi-Rite in Lone Pine. Did anybody take notice of us, any of us, in there to remember? Any of you run up into some big-rack housewife to feel her up? Nobody's going to remember my black Suburban, not since I ditched my **Liberalism Is a Mental Disorder** sticker."

"People drive through there all the time," Zeke said. "Hunters, fishers, skiers up at Mammoth, gamblers going to Reno. Nobody give a shit about outsider cars."

"Until you start shooting them," Belkin said. "I agree shooting folk is a good idea mostly. It keeps the population down. You worried that wussie Talbot is gonna fink?"

"No," Charlie said. "He's a stand-up guy. I like him."

"I feel some bad hate here," Zeke said.

"Jerkoff, how much bad do you want? You mighta killed a guy on our heads," Charlie said.

"Doofuses are expendable."

"You mean him or us?"

"My pals," Belkin put in with a mean twist in his voice. "This little talk is all fun and games, but what if Mr. Butterfly wasn't hurt bad and he sat in the trees and got your license number?"

The fridge started buzzing as they played eye-dogs.

"Then we go to Plan B, of course," Charlie Beck said finally. "Call on the gods of war."

* * * * *

I T had been minor surgery for Dr. Trachtenberg, two days ago. A through-and-through wound, torn flesh and thigh muscle but no bone contact. He'd made sure no lead fragments were left behind, doused the wound with the broadest spectrum antibiotic he had available—Vancomycin—and dressed the entry and exit wounds. Both wounds would have to drain for weeks and be allowed to heal by

THEY SAY THEY CAN MILK CHICKENS

secondary intention without being sewn up. Petro Ivanchuk had said he wanted the scars.

The doctor had thought for a while and then called a friend-patient he knew only as Sergei to come over and discuss the issue. Dr. Trachtenberg was sure that the Land of the Free did not allow deer hunting until September, so this was not an accident.

In an hour Sergei had arrived with a mild tap at the back door, and Dr. Trachtenberg explained what he knew.

"Petro Ivanchuk says it was an accident. He says he didn't see where the shot came from. That's so like him. Intent on his butterflies. But really intent on his own issues."

"A complex man," Sergei said evenly, standing imposingly in the kitchen. "I've met him. He's unlike you and I." The big man seemed to smile, but his eyes didn't smile a bit, they bored into various things at random in the room. He wore a horizontally striped blue T-shirt under his long-sleeve khaki shirt, *spetznaz*. Sergei had reputedly been a member of Alfa Group—Soviet special forces. He was aging now, but in the Soviet Union's own Afghan war in the 1970s, it was known that twenty-four Alfas had taken down the entire Afghan government in one night. In America, at random intervals, Dr. Trachtenberg had treated Sergei for a variety of strange injuries, mostly gunshots or stabbings, but knew never to inquire.

"I like Petro Ivanchuk a lot, Sergei. I like his family and I'm godfather to his grown-up girl. I feel he's in trouble."

"Why would somebody shoot a philosopher? Enemies from the old country? I owe you a lot, Doc."

"Help me here and we're even."

"There's never even, my friend—and never uneven. Life is give help and get help back. I wish to help now. It's my privilege."

"I knew you were a good man."

"Don't like the word. Women often tell me I don't care enough, but they also say they can milk chickens, don't they? This is my sort of problem. I have my friends here and we will all be on this."

The doctor had watched Petro for a day and a half after the surgery, lying in his spare room, warning Petro's wife that he would bring him home later. She had once been the doctor's lover and she still trusted him.

* * * * *

D R. Trachtenberg parked in front of the rambling arts-and-crafts house which always seemed a little overwhelmed in its Plummer Park neighborhood amongst the newer bulky apartment buildings. A great many older Ukrainian Jews had emigrated here after the collapse of the Soviet Union, largely because the area had been a historic Ukrainian and Russian community as far back as the 1920s. It was cheap and adjacent to LA's existing Jewish community along Fairfax Boulevard. Dr. Trachtenberg smiled to himself whenever he passed through the shabbier eastern end of West Hollywood. The elderly Ukrainian Jews here—who spent their days slapping down cards in their *preferans* games in the park while their women shambled home with wire carts of cabbages and beets and jars of pickled eggplant from the Odessa Market and Kiev Mart. Nobody had told these aging and socially conservative people that they were moving into an odd little American city governed by hip young homosexuals.

Each community had ended up clutching its own end of town, and their worlds tended to coast past each other with puzzled frowns, like matter and anti-matter that dare not touch. Plus, as a kind of quiet irony, the best Russian and Ukrainian restaurants were imbedded on the trendy west side, and the gay porn cinema was islanded in the east.

Dr. Trachtenberg and his family had arrived early and settled without ill will in the Norma Triangle on the west side, right next to Beverly Hills, but he knew his countrymen. Who but a doctor like Chekhov could appreciate his people and their trials so profoundly? Few of the immigrants were religious Jews but they all honored the grim old world core of every Jewish holiday, which could be translated as: *They tried to kill us. We're still alive. Let's eat.* As Dr. Trachtenberg's grandmother had always said, For us it will either rain or it will snow.

THEY SAY THEY CAN MILK CHICKENS

He slid in the back screen door without knocking, looking for Alina Abramovna so the woman could help him carry her half-asleep husband into the house. She wouldn't object to his unannounced entry. In the early days of the migration she had slept with him many times, half as barter for medical service for her and her husband, but they had both enjoyed it.

It was the great lesson of Soviet times: if it's in the stew pot, cook it. His sexual tastes had trended younger these days, but he was not a cad, and he had stayed a good friend.

"Alina Abramovna, it's your naked goose!"

FOUR

I Am Both Wound and Knife

EVERYONE in the small electrical workshop seemed to be battling the effects of a rocky weekend. Either downing massive paper cups of coffee, going slow on their machine tools, or dogging it over by the vending machine.

The open building had once been a muffler shop on the southern edge of West Hollywood, which had left them a legacy of six swing-up garage doors facing an asphalt apron. Gusev Emergency Power employed a dozen technicians to hand fabricate its blue special-order power panels full of inch-thick electrical cables and massive solenoids that could trip in a few microseconds to block a current surge of up to 100,000 amps. Once in a while they got an order for a Big Red that would trip at 400,000.

Charlie Beck focused on his Johannson digital drill press as he bored holes through thick sheets of Bakelite that would hold laser diodes the size of his fist. Three days after their ill-fated excursion, plus late nights of Coors self-medication, and he was still recovering.

To his left the fucking new guy Talbot Denny—who was obviously a slumming college kid—was nudging a drafting machine to mark and center-punch the metal shelves of the cabinets, not a critical chore. On the other side of him Zeke Tomlin was using a pneumatic guillotine to shear electrical cable to lengths. It was all man's work and Beck loved it. For years before the aerospace bust in LA he'd worked himself slowly up from machinist to machinist II and III and then tool-and-die maker, which required real application and expertise. These days, with all his certificates and a few bucks he could just about get a cup of coffee.

"Parts!" Beck called.

The oddball Belkin, Mr. Fetch-and-carry, pushed his head-high cart along the workstations as he taunted each worker in turn, insults carefully tuned to what would annoy each of them.

"Here I am, bossman."

"I'm no bossman, dipshit. Two Eaton 600s."

"I heard you used to jump out of airplanes, big man. A fighting soldier from the sky. You gotta tell us all about being brave back then." Belkin tossed two large cardboard boxes onto the workbench.

"I bet you had a great time as a troopie in Chechnya," he shot back. "Killing little boys for throwing rocks at you."

Belkin was impossible to insult. "*Nyet*, bossman—just raping little girls."

Beck plucked up the nearest carton on the workbench, a cardboard box roughly the size of a football, and wondered all at once if he could still plant a twenty-yard spiral on the psycho's head as he pushed his cart on down the line. But he figured he'd be hurling the five-thousand dollar circuit breaker into an indestructible concrete dome and only hurt the device.

* * * * *

FINDING parking in West Hollywood was like hunting for a contact lens in a sand box. There were meters that took the cash-keys that only West Hollywood sold, and most of the neighborhoods were full of confusing residents-only signs where the fourth or fifth sign down the pole might offer you an hour between 3 A.M. and 5 A.M. The redeeming factoid was that when he'd acquired his old pickup truck long ago, it already had commercial plates so he hunted up a yellow delivery curb and slapped his magnetic Acme Plumbing sign on the driver's door. He'd had it made up with a logo of the Roadrunner speeding to the rescue with a pipe wrench held out in front of him.

I AM BOTH WOUND AND KNIFE   45

* * * * *

"I GOT you a hi-octane French Roast," Maeve said at the little sidewalk table she'd been holding.

"Just what I wanted, hon."

One table over, two gay men in muscle-Ts were having what looked like a bitter argument with abrupt head bobs and death glares. One wore a bristly New York beard and the other had Maori tattoos on his cheek like Mike Tyson.

"You found it," Maeve said.

He cranked around in his chair for a moment. The only one of the Cesar Pelli buildings in sight was the newest red one. "Moby red is right there," he said. "My landmark."

Maeve smiled. "Dad, I used to worry so much about what symbols like Moby Dick were all about. But then I saw it wasn't some silly rebus puzzle that I was too stupid to understand. It has to represent something that comes right out of your unconscious."

"I had the same feeling with *Waiting for Godot* back in the fifties," Jack Liffey said, sipping his coffee and enjoying his daughter immensely. "Godot. Waiting for play-dough. Waiting for dodo." The coffee was damn good, almost Turkish. "Sorry, hon. That play used to seem so incomprehensible, and now it's so utterly clear."

"Remember you took me to see it in Long Beach? It was a student play at the college but I was thirteen and I was really blown away."

"What did it mean to you?"

"I guess I felt it was about something I wanted out of life but couldn't have. Like a dad who was around."

"Oooh. Remember, I was thrown out. Damn, sorry—so for you it was *Waiting for Dad*."

She shook her head and her tone changed. "Still waiting. I need help now. I guess I'm not as smart as I thought I was."

"Nobody is."

The bearded arguer nearby gave up and began to weep out loud, and his companion took both his hands.

"You heard my pathetic story," Maeve said. "What's my step two?"

He'd been struggling with this all the way over. Should he hit her hard and hopefully dispatch her back to college where she belonged, or go easy and wait for her native good sense to take over? Perhaps something of a performance was called for.

"You looked under the mattress? Notes on the magazines? Pockets in his clothes. Poked in his shoes. A CD in the computer. Patted the underside of the drawers. Looked inside the radio."

"He had an expensive Bose."

"Two screws open it up. That's the first place guys hide stuff."

She looked crestfallen. "I'm amateur city, dad. My bad."

He rested his hand on hers. "You have instincts, or judgment. Did you like his roommate?"

Both men over Maeve's shoulder were weeping, one of them hitting his forehead with both hands like a silent film actor emoting.

"I did. He's an architect. Do architects go bad?"

"Never," Jack Liffey said, smiling.

"I guess I'm like a math major going out for football."

"Maeve, I'm sorry." He couldn't let it slide. "Step one is still on the table. Can I have your contact information?"

"Thanks for not patronizing me. I'll give you everything I have."

Abruptly Mr. Beard seemed to be miming masturbation under the table. "You rat!"

Maeve did her best not to look over obviously, and he tried pretty hard himself. "We can work the case together," Jack Liffey offered.

"Really?" She brightened.

"On weekends. Back to class during the week."

"You're such a hardcore. I have trouble feeling worthy, you know?"

"I have real trouble believing something as wonderful and smart as you came from one of my sperm."

Abruptly the guys tried to storm away in opposite directions, both of them tripping over chairs at nearby tables, almost too tidy a comic event for reality.

Jack Liffey turned a big laugh at the slapstick into a coughing fit. "Swallowed wrong, sorry."

I AM BOTH WOUND AND KNIFE

The disputants got themselves up and ran off to their fates.

"Thank you, dad. My brain is probably average. If I were running things I'd have God make everybody feel smart."

"Einstein, you've got to stop telling God what to do."

She giggled. "Your sentences are getting longer and have less goop," she told him.

"That last was a quote—Niels Bohr."

* * * * *

THE Gusev workers sat on plastic chairs in the corner of the forecourt, a big cable spool as their table. They were eating from the lunch trucks for a change. Down the block a large cubicle-farm of trendy techies in a glassy rhombus attracted a lot of the new food coaches—Sushi High Noon, The Sheikh of Pita, Greenz on Weelz, Tandooristan. Zeke took a bite of his Atilla the Bun sandwich, spit on the ground and glared at the innards of a pink lambburger, the closest thing he could find to a hamburger.

"The fuckers ain't even cooked it."

"Put it on a shelf and hit it with the torch," Charlie Beck said.

Zeke tossed it down in disgust. "Tastes like armadillo roadkill. Foreigners do weird shit."

Talbot Denny tried not to smile as he pried the lid off his cardboard-partitioned bento box of weird shit—two sushi rolls, a rice disk, pickled ginger, glazed meatball, half a hardboiled egg and two winged apple slices.

"Jesus H. Christ," Zeke said, peering close at the bento box. "Any of that meant to be et?"

"This is seaweed," Talbot said mischievously. He used the chopsticks to point out the *nori* wrap on the *onigiri* disk. Then he poked at the core of the first sushi. "Raw octopus. And this one is the pickled maidenhead of a twelve-year-old virgin."

"Huh?"

Charlie Beck smiled, but Zeke was frowning pretty hard, and Talbot was afraid he might have gone too far.

"Shut them stupid pie-holes." Belkin arrived with some chunky microwaved sausage of his own. He rapped Zeke softly on top of his head. "You ain't in East Butt-Fuck no more, boy. Look around the big city. Enjoy. I'm a poor convict from badland and I try to grab all this great country I can."

That brought a laugh from all but Zeke. "Don't be hittin' my head, Russky."

Belkin sat, absolutely unmoved by threats. "I ain't Russian. Don't be shooting no people when I'm around, *Amerikashka*. I like to make my own trouble."

Charlie gave a brief clap to try to head off a dispute. "Belkin, you're a damn smart guy for all your pretend. You speak that sloppy English at ten words a second, with gusts up to fifty. Why don't you go to community college and get a real skill? A year and a half—you could be a toolmaker or draftsman. Whatever."

Belkin scowled. "Sit in a baby chair and listen to some shit-for-brains talk at me? No, *Jose*. I been to trade school long ago. *Posle draki kulakami ne mashut.* I don't swing no fists after the fight is over. I am who I am, Belkin the Conqueror."

Talbot ate the octopus roll in small bites, watching the petty feuding on and on. He realized every one of his co-workers was either a different class, a different nationality, or a different sexual orientation from him. He felt he ought to have some fellow feeling for others, but he didn't; they shared nothing at all with him. He could have written a new chapter of his dissertation about exile and the modern predicament on any one of them. That was the deal: lost among strangers.

The only real compensation for being an outsider, he had once concluded, had to be the way serious discomfort boosted the intensity of experience.

* * * * *

"I NEED comfort food, my darling. Can you make me beef *pelmeni*?" Petro Ivanchuk sighed as he lay back, his leg throbbing. She smiled. "*Konechno*, of course. I know how you love them."

Every culture had something similar down at the baseline of its food—gyoza, *pierogi*, tacos, *samosas*—ground meat and grease sealed into dough and fried. Do-it-yourself heart attacks. But basically he wanted his wife out of the way for a while. As soon as he heard her banging in the kitchen, he laboriously levered himself erect, then Frankenstein-walked to the phone on the dresser and dialed.

"DMV, Hollywood West. How may I direct your call?"

"May I speak to Olga Nikolayevna, please? Sorry, Olga Kuchin." Patronymics threw Americans into confusion.

It took a bit of waiting, tormented by electronic pop music, but soon she came on.

"This is Olga."

"This is Petya, my *droog*." They switched to Ukrainian. "Will you take an earring out of your ear for me?"

"Will you come see me?"

"When I can. I'm badly hurt right now and can't walk."

She sighed. "Ah, Petya, you always want the moon from me. Not just my *pizda*. This is my life you play with. Doing favors in the American DMV is very forbidden. I run from the wolf and hurry straight into a bear."

"This is very very easy, what I ask, Olya."

"Go ahead."

Reluctantly she agreed to look up the owner of the black Chevy Suburban with the license number he gave her. "Please come to me in the flesh, Petya. I long for you."

"Me, too, my darling."

* * * * *

"T HAT was my daughter," Jack Liffey said to the boy in the living room. "Do you know Mike Lewis?" He hated to namedrop, but maybe it would shortcut things with an architect. Mike was an old friend who had written two classics on LA social history that included a lot of critique of LA architecture, but had paid for it dearly by losing academic jobs to the rabid onslaught of the boosters and real estate interests.

"Know of. He and urban theory are a fixture at Sci-Arc where I studied."

"He's a close friend of mine."

"Good for you."

"What *is* urban theory anyway?"

"It's not as strange as it sounds—not like UFOs or deep tissue massage. I was into it for a while. It's about the importance of cities in history. How this meeting place of cultures has changed humankind." He smiled ruefully, and his voice became flatter. "It's also about good architecture."

"Fascinating."

Jack Liffey was worried about a resurgence of his sputtering speech problems. "Please call Mike if you need to. He'll say you can trust me."

"And you want?"

"I need to see Benjy's room. Without chaperone. It's important to help find him."

Earl scowled. "I don't think so."

"After three days, a missing person—the odds get much worse. Please." Jack Liffey gave him a phone number and the boy sighed and left the living room, which had that dorm-room look, used and temporary furniture, makeshift bookcases, items ready to be abandoned at any moment. A thick pamphlet on the coffee table was titled *Plant Closures: Myths, Realities and Responses*, by Gilda Haas.

He didn't get up to inspect the books, not wanting to look too inquisitive. He didn't want to let this turn into a combat.

Earl came back after a few minutes. "Jack Liffey—my apologies for the suspicion. I'm told you're one of the very good guys. And thanks for introducing me to Mike. He wants to meet me. Walk this way." Earl minced a bit. "If you could walk this way, you wouldn't need the talcum powder. Don't say it."

Jack Liffey smiled at the old vaudeville—was it Marx Brothers joke—or was it David Letterman? And followed.

I AM BOTH WOUND AND KNIFE

Earl opened the door to a smallish back bedroom, dim and cramped like so many of the bedrooms in these old bungalows. A painting that said *Did It Already* against bright orange assaulted his eye. Okay, why not?

"Please don't disturb things too much."

"You'll never know I was here. Here. Fear, dear, tear." Thank god he caught himself before 'queer' blurted out. "Sorry, a temporary quirk."

Earl shut the door on him with a grimace and Jack Liffey took stock. Pretty much as Maeve had described, but what was amiss? Something was always amiss. He set out methodically to check everything Maeve hadn't—under the mattress, the pockets of the clothes in the tiny closet, including a tuxedo in a plastic garment bag, the underside of the drawers. There was no CD in the computer. The little Bose was set to KUSC, the classical station. It actually took three screws that seemed factory tight against his Swiss Army knife to open the panel but there was nothing suspicious within.

He'd almost given up on the desk when he noticed a little notepad from a local realtor named Ruth Zinsky and decided to try a hoary old Dick Tracy Crimestopper trick. He tilted the pad to the window and saw faint depressions on the surface. It was always some absurdity, the payoff. He plucked a pencil out of a ceramic cup and rubbed the side of the lead lightly across the memo paper to bring up a phone number and an initial. He struggled with the initial until he realized it was a backwards R. Which letter was that? He'd tried to teach himself the Cyrillic alphabet once, just as he'd learned the Greek alphabet, but had failed miserably on Arabic. Я was *ya*, he remembered.

He spent another half hour communing with Benjamin Walker's belongings, then made sure all was tidy before stepping out of the room. "I'm gone," he called when Earl didn't appear.

"Good," a voice emanated from another room. "I'm busy now. Let yourself out, guy."

"Thank you so much, Earl. Duke-duke-duke of earl." He could tell he'd relaxed too much, but he fled for the front door before his inner demon could possess his voice box again. As I walk through this world, nothing can stop the duke of earl—

* * * * *

T ALBOT dozed off in his bedroom as mild revelry was going on in the rest of the house. Not too loud yet. His consciousness dipped in and out. He'd met Alvis's music-biz friends and liked them despite their rough-and-ready look—overflowing tattoos, either ultra chic or ultra unchic clothes, strange hair or no hair. He supposed they were all exemplars of post-modernism—a term so elastic these days that he'd seen it used to refer to Scrooge McDuck. His own intellectual roots were in old school modernism—the conviction that there just might be objective truth in science, instead of every belief being a narrative constructed on some prejudice. Yet he'd become a lot less assured about truth these days.

Eventually curiosity got him out of bed. Alvis had told him he was mixing a song about post-modernism. Talbot wanted to poke into that while Alvis was busy elsewhere.

The adjacent studio was dark with a starfield of flashing indicator lights across the broad console, sleeping monitor screens, speakers, electronic keyboards and mysterious metal boxes. He figured it would all come back to life if he just hit a random key on the main keyboard, and sure enough. One by one, the equipment blinked and hiccupped awake. Luckily the prominent upper right key said MUTE and he managed to kill a sudden hiss.

Before touching a thing he put on the big Klipsch headphones, then found what appeared the most recent CD with *Bengali Bump* scrawled on it in felt pen. Drums started up a catchy rhythm, and he dialed up the volume on his earphones. One monitor showed a complex array of bobbing vertical lines. A mildly Indian-accented voice rapped away in his ears.

Who's that man showing off the baby with the floppy head?
Beggars are frauds who just want another bottle.

I AM BOTH WOUND AND KNIFE

Buddha said the problem is caring, so let's pretend we're all dead,
Enlightenment won't come at all for years and then a lot'll

Hey, let's all get metaphysical!
Let's spin 'round 'till we get dizzycal!

Jesus, what was this awful stuff? he wondered.

We can all learn to levitate and fly up to the sky
Or stand with the cows in grass in rows and rows
'till we convert to vegan all those lions and tigers, oh my
and Shakespeare's in the alley with bells on his toes

Hey, let's all get metaphysical!
And chant 'till we're sure we're busycal!

Light flared into the room, and Talbot snapped his head around to see Alvis and two of the Gen Z partiers staring in at him from the door. He yanked off the earphones and realized immediately that the sound hadn't been muted at all. He hit the space bar to stop everything.

"Sorry, sorry, folks!"

"Don't be sorry—get even," a young woman with a Mohawk said and giggled.

"So?" Alvis asked. "Did you like it so far?"

"I'm not sure about so many layers of irony. I actually like Buddhism. Any religion that doesn't need a god is okay with me."

"Stop intellectualizing," Alvis said. "Feel."

"The mind is part of my picture permanently, Alv."

"This dude is deep," the other guy in the door said through the gold hoop piercing his nose.

Talbot realized he wasn't even sure how many layers of irony he was facing with these people. "I am both wound and knife," he said, trying to get with the spirit. Would any of them know it was Baudelaire?

B ELKIN had been home for several hours, worked out, eaten a dinner of cabbage soup and kidneys, and watched a little TV, but he hadn't heard from Cat and he was worried. The McDonald's bag of fillet-o-fish and French fries was undisturbed on the stoop.

Finally he went out with a flashlight, pried out the screening of the crawl space and peered under the house, in case she was down there already. Nothing but a few shadowy mounds of her findings. He could tell her bed of rags was empty. She usually left it made up better.

Something was not right. It would be hard, maybe impossible, to sleep tonight until she came home and he could greet her. When he flicked the flashlight off, he was startled by the utter darkness, like a terrible blot on the world.

Belkin watched meaningless American TV until he heard a faint noise in back. When he opened the door slowly he was relieved to see Cat devouring the cold sandwich and fistfuls of cold fries. She had cuts on her lip and a bruised cheek. *Shit.*

"Cat, I'm real happy to see you."

She looked up with a fearful expression, and he sat down in the doorway to appear less threatening.

"Go ahead and eat, my sweet. You know I won't bother you. Did somebody hurt you?"

She didn't acknowledge the question, just went on shoveling in food. As she was running out of food, he got up and fetched the chocolate chip cookies he'd bought. He tore open the bag as he sat to try one himself, but didn't like it much. Too sicky sweet, too weird.

She took handfuls of the cookies and shoved them into her mouth and chewed.

"Cat, you need a doctor. I know a guy."

She shook her head hard.

"I don't like to see you beat up."

"Fuck off," she snapped. It was almost all she ever said.

He liked to think this was her form of thank you. His life had been crazy and hard in Kiev, but it was nothing to the freak show in

I AM BOTH WOUND AND KNIFE

America, so much stranger and more unpredictable than Ukraine. He couldn't get over people thinking the cops might actually help you out. Finally she finished the cookies and seemed satisfied. She lowered her head and he did his best to stroke her snarled reddish dreadlocks, the happiest moment of his day.

* * * * *

VICTOR Antonenkovich Gorbenko parked his modified Ford van in the alley behind Romanie Street from the address he'd been given. The driver's seat had been specially formed for his kyphosis, a genetic condition that made his upper spine jut out like a mini-me that he had to carry around on his back. You hunchback, don't touch me. All his life—a demanding, ungrateful infant twin strapped to him who'd made him take the hard way all the time. He was seventy now, had buried his wife, and was beginning to welcome the approach of the long night.

This street was shoulder-to-shoulder cheap apartments built to topple in earthquakes, with only spindly pillars supporting a continuous parking bay at alley level. The dense neighborhood on the far east side of West Hollywood overlooked a sea of bungalows farther south.

The black Suburban was half under the parking overhang, blocked from getting farther in by a motorcycle. The license number was right. The call from Petro Ivanchuk had come in on his cell that afternoon while he'd been playing *preferans* in the park.

All Petro had asked him to do was check if that car was at that address—but good-hearted Petya had befriended him fifty years ago when no one else would, and he and mini-me weren't going to stop there. The park gossip had been very definite. Somebody had shot Petya and he could barely walk.

Victor had been an eight-year-old in the middle of the Great Patriotic War and the Young Pioneers had taught him how a gang of children could blind a fearsome German Tiger tank with smoke and then run up and hit its engine deck in back with gasoline bombs covered with sticky tar. The Finns had called them Molotov cocktails—an insult to the man, not a tribute. He'd never had the chance to fight, of course, but life offers its surprises.

Two big pickled beet jars contained gasoline and kerosene from Chevron and were wrapped in rags then covered with a tar-pitch emulsion.

All for one, one for all, he thought. *The Three Musketeers* had been his favorite childhood book. Dumas, the son of a Haitian slave. And now Milady was in distress.

It was far too late to make the world have a rational meaning, as the Young Pioneers had insisted. But he could make his own life mean something, and not leave a good friend wounded and helpless.

Victor Antonenkovich grasped one of his beet-jar fire-bombs, and smiled at the black Suburban that waited so innocently.

Chto pnyom ob sovu, chto sovoy ob pen' vsyo odno sove ne sladko, he thought. Whether you hit an owl with a log, or a log with an owl, it's the owl who suffers.

FIVE

Sometimes You Have to Suffer Along the Way

"Roski!" Captain Al Torres hailed him over the roof of the red fire chief's car. It was two A.M. and the fire crews had left. "Thanks for coming so fast."

The big black grease-spot under the cremated remains of an SUV lay in county jurisdiction by about fifty yards, just inside West Hollywood. Roski could see that the building above the vehicle had nearly given up the fight, too. A tall scorch was burned into the stucco above the parking and some had spalled away to show bubbly charred studs.

"Hello, Al. I hear you still run a station with no bonehead pranks against women or blacks."

"Just lucky I guess."

"On the phone you uttered the word arson."

Al Torres smiled. "Remember when you tried to explain the expression overdetermination to me?"

"Actually, no."

"Something about a woman standing on Hollywood Boulevard late at night waving at cars, wearing a tiny miniskirt and bandeau top. Overdetermination was when she turns on a neon hat saying 'Wanna fuck?'"

A ragged local crowd, murmuring and tentative, had gathered at the rim of some ill-defined perimeter that felt safely distant from authority.

58   *BOYSTOWN*

Roski nodded, but tried not to acknowledge it as an acceptance of any investigation he might have to mount. The boys from the local station hadn't mopped up the garage, probably at Torres' orders. He was head of Batallion 1 and could declare it a crime scene. "Why over-determination?" Roski said.

"Ever seen a vehicle burn up so fast without ...?" He flapped his hand at the charred building. "The woman living there said she heard a 'whomp!' as she put it. And over here." He pointed to a big fragment of broken glass that had to be from a jar. "Smells like pinetar."

"Got it. Go back to San Vicente and finish your pinochle."

Blue light flashed across the buildings as a sheriff's car pulled in fast with one of those self-important squeals at the last.

"You want yellow tape?" Al Torres asked.

"Tidy up and go home. If I need more, I'll ask the dick."

"Please copy me." Al Torres drove away and the deputy sauntered toward him, looking like a million other young recruits with tidy moustaches.

"I'm Captain Roski, head of arson, deputy," Roski said. "Can you hold the civvies back?" Mostly to keep him away from the fire. Nobody could mess up an arson scene faster than a patrol cop.

"Gotcha, sir. Just lay it out and I'll do it."

"Okay, when you can, find me the manager here or anybody who can name the days of the week."

"I'll do my best for you, sir."

"That would be a fucking new experience."

* * * * *

"**B**UN! Don't scare me like this."

Maeve found Bunny at last in a horse stable that she frequented farther up Topanga. She was sitting out of sight on a bale of hay right beside Mickey, a lovely black thoroughbred. She wasn't crying, but she obviously had been.

SOMETIMES YOU HAVE TO SUFFER ALONG THE WAY 59

"Sorry, Maevie. I come to big animals because they comfort me. They got no duplicity at all, and they try so hard to understand what you want from them."

Her voice was weary and on the edge of more crying. Mick belonged to one of Bunny's friends, a cast-off from a famous breeder because he'd never worked out at the track and was kept now as a trail horse. She knew Bunny rode him from time to time, especially when she felt disconsolate. A big horse but she was big enough to ride a big horse, Maeve thought.

"I started looking for Benjy," Maeve said. "I did my best but I had to ask my dad for help." Bunny was wearing a checked cowboy shirt with tear-open snaps. Maeve wanted to sink to her knees, rip it open and make love to Bunny on the hay. It scared her sometimes, the intensity of her desire.

Bunny perked up. "Find anything?"

"I met Benjy's roommate. But I didn't really think I was cutting it as a detective so I sent up a distress flare, and my dad's on the job."

"I thought he was disabled."

"Even disabled, he's worth a dozen me's. Trust me."

"Slow, please," Bunny said. Maeve had reached down to caress her cheek. "My mood is pretty fragile."

"I'm a little shaken, too." It was a lie that didn't matter. Maeve was so full of desire her thighs were trembling.

"I worry so much about Benjy, M. I didn't know it 'til he vanished. I hardly ever saw him across town, but he was my god back home in Grand Rapids. I followed him around like a kitten when we were preteens. Big brothers are so special. Right, Mick?" She stroked the horse's lowered forehead and he nuzzled her.

Maeve settled gently beside Bunny. "When did our lives become so dramatic?"

"That's easy, girl. For me, it was when I decided I might be college material. But for you, it was when you punched your way out of the womb, ready to take on the world."

Maeve smiled nervously. "Am I so whatever that is?" Maeve was starting to wonder if her passions were taking her down too many defiant and wayward paths.

"Hon, don't go there. You're the smartest woman I've ever met. But one of the scariest. You sit on this dynamite. I bet all your real dangers are inside you. Mine are mostly on the outside."

Maeve didn't want to talk about herself. "Which of your problems is eating at you?" Maeve asked.

"Things come out of nowhere, don't they? Like Benjy disappearing. Benjy was always a little dangerous, like you."

Tears rolled down her puffy cheeks again and Maeve turned to hug her awkwardly. Suddenly, with her face against Bunny's, she felt the amazing warm bristly weight of a horse's nose pressing into both their faces, as if to separate them. Jealousy?

Bunny clasped the horse's neck and it was as if the three of them wept together or felt something together as lovers.

* * * * *

"WHO's on top here?" Petro said. He had crutched his way to the picnic table in Plummer Park, where Victor the Hunchback sat on a small booster box to get him up near the level of the fixed table. They were surrounded by other tables where an endless supply of elderly Ukrainian men played the national game, *preferans*, a complex East European variant of Whist and Bridge.

"We just ended a six-of-spades round with closed hands—the Stalingrad game, the one with nowhere to retreat."

"Victor the clever one is up twenty-two thousand rubles on us," a gruff bearded man said. Like poker, horse-racing or craps, it was a game that could not exist without betting, but most had been so poor after emigrating that they simply kept a running account which would never be collected.

Petro readjusted his throbbing leg as he sat down at the end of the table. His wound hurt like hell, but he was totally in charge of his willpower now and could deal with that.

SOMETIMES YOU HAVE TO SUFFER ALONG THE WAY

"Might I speak to you?" the hunchback said.

He handed off the thirty-two-card Piquet deck to the bearded man and Petro sighed and followed to a quiet area in the park.

"You're grinning like a rascally penguin, my friend," Petro said. "I need to hear it, please."

"Petya, do you remember the Young Pioneer training when the Germans were coming?"

"I'm too young. I know those blockhead commissars taught a hundred ways for children to commit suicide. The doom of the proletariat was upon us, so history called for total self-sacrifice."

"I avenged you, Petya," Victor said abruptly. "I found the car you said and used what the commissar told us about victory cocktails. The black Chevrolet panther tank no longer exists. And no one was hurt."

"I didn't ask for that."

"I know."

Petro Ivanchuk eyed the hunchback with annoyance. In the end, the Great Eastern Soul might just be too volcanic for anyone's comfort. The pain in his leg was getting fierce, and he uncapped a vial and swallowed one of the tiny pink pills Dr. Trachtenberg had given him.

"No one saw you?"

"What am I—a *shmendrick*?"

There was a roar from the basketball courts nearby, a full-court game between two West Hollywood pickup teams. Petro was struck once again by the stocky high-fiving Ukrainian and Russian players, muscular and flat-footed. They looked like American wrestlers forced to play basketball.

"You're sure there were no security cameras?"

"What is this, Beverly Hills? We get sixty-year-old security guards: 'Stop or I'll shoot ... *maybe*.'"

Petro Ivanchuk scowled.

"I did fine, Petya. Please relax. The Three Musketeers must be who they are. Call me a pot all you want, just don't put me in the oven."

* * * * *

62 BOYSTOWN

"MAN, I almost didn't get here," Jack Liffey said excitedly at the door.

"I bet you tried to turn down Baxter Street off Alvarado?"

Jack Liffey nodded. "Jesus, I slammed on the brakes and even the parking brake. I couldn't see the pavement in front of me. It was like driving off a cliff. Cliff, get-a-whiff, diffidy-doo-dah. Sorry."

Roski ignored the outburst. "Don't feel bad. It's a thirty-two percent grade. On trash days they have to use a baby garbage truck and back it up the street so it won't tip over at the top." He beckoned Jack Liffey in. "We had a moving van get stuck up there once, rocking on its belly on the crest with all its wheels off the ground and the movers bailing out in panic. Welcome to Echo Park adjacent."

It was a newly trendy hilly area of old cottages not far from downtown LA that still contained a fair number of untrendy homes, including Roski's tiny bungalow where big flaps of white paint curled off the clapboards and an old refrigerator thrummed on the side porch. Inside, Jack Liffey sat next to a rusted swamp cooler at a side window. It probably hadn't worked since Roosevelt.

"Sorry about the unhappy circumstances, Jack. This is my divorce house. Defeat central. I can't get up the fire to fix it up."

Jack Liffey waved the apology away. "Been there, done that." He'd had an equivalent divorce condo in Culver City. "Wall-to-wall wretched."

"Let's not go there," Roski said. "To get a grip, I think you have to look inward from time to time, but this just isn't my time."

"So you work out instead," Jack Liffey suggested. Half the living room was filled with an impressive set of barbells, a rack of one-hand dumbbells and a big complex multi-machine.

"The best I can do these days is a healthy body and a healthy body inside. Strength does come in handy. One day I'll tell you how I took down that huge bucko who killed the Chinese girl you were looking for last year."

Jack Liffey held up his hand to ward off any inconvenient news.

SOMETIMES YOU HAVE TO SUFFER ALONG THE WAY 63

"I got some breakfast burritos from the Taco Flojo truck, if you're interested. Beats most roach coaches around."

"Great." Jack Liffey wasn't that interested in an intravenous bolus of cholesterol, but he followed Roski into his dilapidated breakfast nook off the kitchen. What once were blue leatherette benches were rejecting their tape repairs beside a blue Formica countertop with flying yellow kidneys. Roski had coffee ready and poured him a mug.

"That lunch truck is part of our legend up here. Hipster heaven mixed with dive cantinas."

"I can sightsee later," Jack Liffey said before sipping. "Report, please."

"Okay. I have to get to work myself. I need a friend, Jack. That's a very big truth. Something bad is hovering over me."

Jack Liffey started to stand up to comfort him, but Roski motioned him back down.

"Just take it under advisement. You carry around that aura of I-can-help, you know. I'll relax into chronic crisis. Let me pass on what I know about your Benjamin Walker."

Walter Roski served them both large puffy burritos from the microwave. Roski sat opposite and dug into his with a fork. Between bites he told Jack Liffey about visiting the apartment in Silverlake to talk to Karen Bustros. Before Benjy went missing, he and she had been beaten up after some ugly encounter at a café. The girl had told Roski that the assailant was some stringy quick-tempered character who she said was probably driven macho mad by Benjy trying to proposition him.

"That's a clue, Jack," Roski added portentously. "She said the guy sounded foreign. Another clue. Tons of Ukrainians and Russians in West Hollywood. But most are Jewish and not many of them have SS tattoos, I'd bet."

"Can I talk to her?"

"I'd rather you didn't right now, Jack. It took all my wiles to dig the tattoo bit out. I'm pretty sure I got all there was from her. I have enemies in the department and this is all very *ex officio*."

Jack Liffey assented. He tried a bite of the egg, bean, rice, cheese and lard concoction. He wondered how close he could let himself come to Roski? He liked the man a lot, but the fireman was obviously riding a razor edge in his emotional life."

"Do you know what your speech problem is?" Roski asked.

"No fucking clue, friend. It follows a brain-bleed, as they tell you when they think 'hemorrhagic stroke' would freak you out."

"Let's let it rest."

"Fuckin'-A. AAA."

Roski shoveled in the stuffing of the burrito for a few moments and then seemed to come up with an idea. "Can I try something out on you, Jack? There's no connection to your case. I just need to think out loud on this."

"Whatever." Jack Liffey was consumed by his own worries, but he pledged to himself to listen.

"Late last night I caught a fresh arson case, a firebomb on a car parked under a carport. I could see right away it was a bottle job with gasoline, but they knew somehow to put pitch in the gasoline to make the fire stick to whatever. That's an old Eastern European trick."

Roski told him the location of the arson and what else he'd learned— the car owner lived in the building but had made himself scarce along with his family. It got stranger. Right after the noise that alerted her, an old woman at her bedroom window saw a hunchback running away to a white van. "The lab is working on the evidence, but let me tell you what makes my inner ear perk up here," Roski said. "Do you know the social history of arson?"

"Uh, no." It was always simpler to assent to these self-invitations to lecture. Jack Liffey scooted the cold remains of his burrito aside and got up to refill his own coffee mug.

"Long before arson became the big tool of insurance fraud, it was a very common weapon in what you could call rural class struggle—starting back to the Middle Ages. Angry peasants could always torch some vicious landowner in the middle of the night and disappear. European peasants did it for centuries."

SOMETIMES YOU HAVE TO SUFFER ALONG THE WAY 65

In America, Roski carried on, farm laborers had always struck back at the cruelest of rich farmers by setting fire to their barns in the night, until "barn-burning" became a common expression for rebellion. The Indians in California had been dragged down from the hills and forced into farm work and fought back with fires. Faulkner wrote about barn-burning as part of the fight against sharecropping bosses and Jim Crow. "Down below the Smith-and-Wesson line," as Roski put it.

"It makes sense. The Mau-Mau in Kenya did it, Earth First! Arson really hurts, it's midnight easy, it's anonymous, and it's great advertising for your cause. Sometimes I wish I was on the other side it's so powerful, but I've seen saintly firefighters die of arson. Fire is my sworn enemy as you know."

"The fire last night?" Jack Liffey put in, trying to get him back to the present century.

"It fails the smell test, Jack. Oh, I know, boo-the-fuck-hoo, says my boss, nobody was hurt. But it could have taken down a whole building with all its sleeping tenants."

"Do you know what it's about?"

"No," Roski said. "That's what I'm trying to figure. Who would know about making a Molotov Cocktail with pitch tar? *Think* with me here."

"You and me may be too convoluted, Rosk. Maybe it's a total nutter who reads the internet. They got instructions for making an atom bomb now. Maybe it's a private feud. Hatfield and McCoy. Maybe just a total loon."

"If I think that, Jack, I'm utterly lost. For me everything has to signify, it's my job. I hate the bizarre special cases. It's a kind of mischief against reason."

"You've got a hole in your world the size of a caring god, don't you?"

Roski smiled grimly. "And you don't?" His eyes narrowed fiercely. "I don't think I absolutely *need* meaning—I just need the possibility of meaning."

Jack Liffey didn't have much to offer. Roski was stuck fast in his own dark, decaying universe.

*   *   *   *   *

"I LOVE naked bikes," Zeke said, watching Charlie Beck pull up on his Ducati Monster at lunchtime. "Screw all that plastic ninja shit the Japs wrap around rice bikes."

Beck rarely drove his bike to work, and he looked half way to a rage as he squealed to a stop. Talbot had to admit to himself that he liked the look of the plain street bike, too, without the wraparound cowlings and fairings.

Beck swung his leg off and kicked the stand down angrily.

"Here's a guy lives his big dreams," Belkin said.

"Fuck you," Beck said.

"Very witty."

"Wit this," Beck said, grabbing his crotch as he approached. They'd bought lunch off the coaches again, but nobody'd got anything for Beck.

"Have half my sandwich," Talbot offered.

"When I want raw fish, I'll let you know, Joe. Shut up, all of you." He plopped down. "Trouble's found us. You boys got to trust me now."

"You got the lead, Mr. Fighting-Soldier-From-the-Sky," Belkin said.

"Trust me as if you had a choice, Russky. I can hold up my end. That ain't bragging, if you can hack it." He glanced into the corners of the workshop, as if spies might be crouching there, but the other workers were out at lunch. "Some shitfuck burned up the Suburban last night. I stuck around long enough to hear the firemen talking arson. Here we are, pals. We know the butterfly man's got to have saw my license plate. It's got personal."

Talbot wondered if he should just stand up right now, jump on his brother's old bicycle and flee from these dangerous creeps. This was precisely what his mother had meant by "avoiding bad companions"— at least until he'd come out to the family and her fears had mutated in another direction.

"It ain't personal for you alone," Belkin said. "Mr. Big Beck. Far as the motherfucker knows, it was all and each of us that shot at him."

SOMETIMES YOU HAVE TO SUFFER ALONG THE WAY 67

Beck glared for a moment and then went on. "We know the man likes butterflies. He's over sixty, overweight, and if he come back at me so fast, he ain't stupid. He's wounded. We saw the blood on the trail. We should have tracked him all the way and finished him off but we didn't. We're up to the second floor now, the men's department. Plan B."

* * * * *

THE two glum-faced chesty men in their dark suits and ties were quite conspicuous as they pushed into the DMV office, amongst the afternoon crowd of Latinos and Asians who were mainly there to register old cars or take driving exams.

It was Olga Nikolayevna's turn to be cashier, but Mr. Butthead waggled his finger at her and sent Sylvia to take her place.

"Hold tight, Olga," Sylvia whispered. "Butthead's in a fizz."

"Thank you, dearheart."

The dark suits—cops of some sort, of course—led her to the break room and Mr. Greggs, her super, backed out to leave them alone. She heard the hallway bench slide against the door. No visitors. Okay, full alert. Soviet rules.

One of the cops wore $500 alligator shoes. She noticed things like that. And the other had a cheap Cassio watch. Mr. Alligator Shoes set a small digital recorder on the break table. "You're Olga Kushin."

"Olga Nikolayevna Kushin," she said. "What's this concerning?"

"That'll become clear, Miss Kushin," he said with an audible sneer. "My name is Lieutenant Plunkett and I'm with the West Hollywood sheriff's office. This is Sheriff's Detective O'Ryan. Sit down please. If all goes well, this will just be a little chat and nothing more."

"Then I guess I'll have me a little sit." They think I'm afraid, she thought, with some surprise. She'd been taken in three times to the KGB offices in Volodimirskaya Street in Kiev. She should now be afraid of these American *putzes*—hah! Mouth shut. Legs shut. Mind shut.

"At lunch hour yesterday, Miss Kuchin, you went online to the Sacramento DMV."

She stared back at him.

"Is that a yes?"

"I didn't hear a question."

Plunkett took out a pack of American Eagles with a sigh and adjusted them square in front of himself, like some weird threat to blow smoke in her face if she didn't talk. "Have it your way. We know you downloaded a page of California car licenses on your lunch hour. Toward the top of that list was a car that burned up last night. The DMV has an alert on that kind of coincidence. They call it a *terrorism* alert. Or maybe just coincidence, with cooperation."

"—"

"What we call it depends on you, of course. As an immigrant to our shores, you probably wouldn't want to lose your job and have your citizenship revoked for a minor offense."

"—"

"Do you like being an American, Miss Kuchin?" He took a cigarette out of the pack and toyed with it.

"It's had its moments," she said. She knew she shouldn't say a word, but he was such a loser compared to the inquisitors she'd faced that she couldn't help it. "Could I make a citizen's arrest if you light that?" she asked. Smoking was illegal in all public places in West Hollywood.

The cop might have grinned for just an instant. "You could try it, Olga, but I wouldn't recommend it. On the other hand, I'd recommend talking to us. We can make life pretty miserable for you if you don't."

"Can I slap her a bit now?" the second deputy said.

"Not yet. Miss Olga, we *are* going to get to the bottom of this. We need to know who asked you to make the records search. If you refuse to be helpful, it will go on your record and I promise we can find ways to crucify you. You could be sent back to the land of vodka and deep snow."

Oh, boo-hoo, she thought. We could hurt you—maybe. She'd been beaten and strip-searched and all-but-raped in the KGB office, just for being photographed watching a protest demonstration. Defiance became a second skin.

SOMETIMES YOU HAVE TO SUFFER ALONG THE WAY

"This is your last chance today, Olga. Who asked you to get that information?"

Kiss my ass, she thought. Petro Ivanchuk is my soulmate. Despite the difference in our years, I am going to snag him away from that horrible wife of his. I wouldn't betray him if you dropped me in boiling oil; in fact, I wouldn't even betray his wife to you limp dicks. Pucker up and lick my butt.

"So you're ready to be deported, Miss Kuchin?"

"*Terpi kazak, atamanom budesh.*"

"What the fuck is that?" the second dark suit blurted.

She tried not to smile.

"It means, Put up with it, *Cossack*, and you'll be an ataman." You useless pussies. Go on, scribble it down and get somebody to work it out for you.

It only meant, in effect, sometimes you have to suffer along the way.

SIX

Shoot Everything

SERGEI tapped lightly on the keys of his laptop on the kitchen table, vulturing off his neighbor's wi-fi signal. The furniture wasn't his either. He'd rented a furnished apartment in an anonymous part of mid-city LA, rented under the non-existent name on a phony driver's license. Most of his possessions—both owned and liberated—were five kilometers away in a storage locker. Never leave a footprint. It was the rule he lived by.

Living off the grid had been both easier and more difficult back in the Soviet days. Easier because he'd grown up alert and knew which authorities to avoid. Harder, because being off the grid there had been almost inconceivable with bureaucrats tracking you from birth. He'd managed only because an ex-Spetznaz hacker *banda* had helped erase his entire life track.

Tonight he'd typed out an SOS message to that same *banda* in two-key PGP through an e-postbox in Tajikistan—www.xyz.tj. Nobody in America gave a damn if a place called Tajikistan even existed. The ultimate recipients would be members of his old Alfa *grom* team. All resided in the United States now, many of them in Coney Island, but a few near West Hollywood.

He'd laid out the problem: an unprovoked attack on a countryman and friend. A few would take the appeal as a bat-signal and drop everything. Others would just stay tuned. That was as it should be. The response would come fast. These were men who could be relied upon. In 1993, his closest comrade, Vasili T, had been ordered by one of the slimiest Soviet *apparatchiks* to kill Boris Yeltsin. He'd only pretended that he would comply. How history might be different!

Sergei folded up the laptop. Never stay online more than five minutes. Call from the cheapest prepaid cellphones. Never use a phone with GPS in it. Never lick an envelope—it left DNA. Obey all traffic laws.

He knew there was a fundamental conflict between action and anonymity. Every act left a trace. But he was the near-perfect outsider now, as close as life would allow, and it gave him opportunities not open to others. He'd entered America off the books through Canada, had no genuine records on file that he knew of. Only once in the past few years had he been tempted to have a real life—a wife, a sensible career, a public circle of friends. But in the end he'd decided it was too late—his soul had long ago become void. He'd won the freedom of total absence.

Along the way he'd mastered the skills of history—the use of personal weapons and heavy weapons, hand-to-hand combat, stealth movement, quick entry, the quick cold-read of an opponent. And, most of all, how to bear suffering and loneliness.

He used his cell to call a number he kept only in memory, the Escort Zone. "This is Jim K-three-one-four-seven. I want to visit a blonde within three miles of Crenshaw and Olympic Boulevard tonight."

"Sure thing, Jim. Wouldn't you prefer to have the blonde visit you?"

"You heard me. And make sure she's a *white* woman with real blonde hair." They'd once sent him to a black woman who was dyed blonde, too damned odd. He couldn't bear the shrewd eyes of American black women, the vigilance they'd mastered to survive in a hostile world.

"Yes, sir. Take down this number and you can arrange it with Donna direct."

* * * * *

SHOOT EVERYTHING 73

W HEN Jack Liffey got home, Gloria was a curled-up heap under the sheet, the rest of the covers thrown off, snoring away loudly. She'd slept nine hours the night before but obviously needed more. Depression did that, Jack Liffey thought. And inactivity. He certainly hoped she could get back to the Department.

He pulled a chair over and sat with his hand resting on her thigh, on the theory that her unconscious could probably feel the affection. Woman, what's the matter deep down inside? We could get professional help from someone a lot smarter than me. He heard a whimper and a small outcry, then felt a shiver.

"Shhhh," he said softly. "It's fine."

An eye cracked open for a moment and might have recognized him before shutting again.

"Jack." Her voice was rough and wavery like a stream of beer running over rocks. "My service piece is in the top right drawer. Please get it out and shoot me."

"What's the password?"

"Fuck you."

"That's it." The eye popped open, fiercer. It was always a risk to joke.

"My soul is good at resisting happiness, Jack. Misery finds a way."

"Was there something today?"

She opened the other eye and rolled onto her back. "I'm so weary of this damn bed. I'm like a beaten alley cat licking my wounds. Or the old people when they finally knew the buffalo were all gone. Am I being a drama queen?"

Yes. "No. You're depressed. I just don't know how to help."

They'd been here before. She was terrified of the least hint of mental instability making it back to her superiors in the Department. He knew it wasn't paranoia. She would end up at a desk in the basement, filing unpaid parking tickets. "Can I find you somebody outside the loop? Nobody will know. Go with the flow." Do-si-do. Damn. The rhyme helped it sneak past his guard.

"We'll see. I'm sorry, Jack, how are you doing? You got as much right to moan and groan as me. You got a zipper down your chest now. And you had that brain thing."

He smiled. She didn't like to use the word *stroke*, and he could live without it, too. "I'm pretty okay."

Cognitive distortion was what his last annoying doctor called the mental wrinkle of speech eruptions after his stroke. He was supposed to slow down and try to catch flare-ups inside his brain before they escaped. A random error of data retrieval, he thought of it.

"You're a lot better, you know?" she said. "For a while I thought I was living with all the Marx brothers on amphetamines."

"I've had a perfectly wonderful day, but this wasn't it," he said, quoting Groucho.

She frowned at him, then waggled a finger at him.

"Jack, come closer."

Was she inviting intimacy? That would really be something. He leaned forward for a kiss. Instead of pecking his cheek, she snatched the folded slip of paper from his shirt pocket—the graphite-rubbed note from Benjy Walker's desk. She seemed to know immediately what it was. "You *are* on the job, Jackie. Why is the R backwards?"

"It might be Russian. If it is, it's called *Ya*." He held out his hand for the note.

"I bet you haven't called that number yet. Your phone technique sucks these days. If you tell me what you know, I'll call *Ya* for you. I'm your secretary and you can be anybody you want. Cop, FBI, insurance salesman."

"Terrific. Tell them I'm the Serbian Secret Police."

* * * * *

VICTOR Gorbenko fought his way up the cracked cement staircase, no longer an easy climb for an aging hunchback with a touch of diabetes. He saw that his apartment door was unlocked, unusual for him. He wasn't usually a sloppy Ivan.

SHOOT EVERYTHING

Gorbenko patted around inside gingerly for the light switch and filled the front room with illumination. He pressed the door open gently. The flimsy coffee table jutted away from the sofa at a strange angle but *maybe* he'd kicked it on the way out. He was none too graceful. Why did the room worry him so? Gorbenko didn't like the world of *why*. If you started that way, it never let go.

But he was worried as he toddled toward the bedroom. The apartment was far too warm, and he knew that virtually everything in America, even Maine, was below the southernmost latitudes of Ukraine. The Black Sea holiday spots in Odessa and Yalta were both north of Montreal. Los Angeles was down somewhere with Persia. He was trying to keep his wandery mind off the thought that something was wrong.

The dreary apartment suddenly felt like a place where you got hit in the head and lay there until somebody stuck a gun in your ear.

He snapped the bedroom light switch, but no light came. His irises were bouncing large and small, leaving the curtained room a mass of dangerous shadows. There was a smell of apple, salt and rust. In a weak trapezoid of light on the floor there was a shower of thin glass. The light bulbs in the wall fixture had been broken.

As Gorbenko's eyes adjusted, they went to the print of a village scene he loved by *Pryanishnikov*, the first Russian painter to embrace peasant life. The print showed an old peasant being forced to dance a clumsy *kazachok* by drunken landlords in top-hats. Gorbenko had always had a sentimental streak for the victims of bullies.

Half his mind had already seen the thing on the bed, but he didn't want to acknowledge it. Then he had to. The body wore an ugly bathrobe. He lit a matchbook match and saw his ex-neighbor Ruslan Grankin Jakov, eyes and mouth open horribly.

Halfway to the bed he felt someone come into the room behind him and his heart thundered. The match went out and he fumbled and lit another. He turned with a feeling of doom. But no one was behind him after all.

Gorbenko sighed and turned back to the bed. His mind ran through memories of Rusya, whom he'd known in Odessa. Quiet and non-political, but kindly and solicitous to a hunchback friend. The two of them had moved a big menorah from the Jewish Culture Society to the Duc de Richelieu monument on Primorskiy Boulevard, facing the famous Potemkin Steps. The Ukraine Jewish community had decided to risk a public celebration of Hanukkah.

A third lighted match, and he moved closer to Rusya. He saw that a lot of his face and one ear were gone, with no sign of blood on the bed linen. Gorbenko leaned in to see better, unable to help himself, putting the match near the man's face.

"*Braht!*" he demanded. Brother. He couldn't help noticing the old acne scars that had brought them together—two who'd been cruelly wounded by life at High School Number 52.

Despite his fear, Gorbenko felt a curious exhilaration. A man with a hunchback could outlive even a strong upright specimen like this. Then he saw a slip of paper tucked into the breast pocket of the bathrobe. He shuffled closer and plucked it out.

You want more, Russky bastards? Bring it on.

* * * * *

C HARLIE Beck's man-cave smelled of gun-oil and the metallic tang of the parts of a Browning over-and-under 12-gauge shotgun that rested on a card table. Eight empty Coors cans were stacked on the table and Beck rocked back in his chair, slightly tipsy, as the other two watched the last gasp of an amateurish program about shooting ducks on Hunt TV.

Belkin strode to the TV and hit the kill button so the guy in the red Pendleton jacket disappeared. There were a few moments of pleasantries in the room. Everybody was on edge.

Beck pointed a gun-finger at Zeke Tomlin who had groused about being called away from his home. "You're in this because you started it, Z." The aim shifted. "Belkin, you're in because I like your fuck-you attitude. The Talbot kid is out. We haven't known him long enough. So the grown-ups are all here." He rocked back again.

SHOOT EVERYTHING 77

"Come on, cap, get to it."

He seemed to grow philosophical. "You know, all the shit that used to scare me just pisses me off now. So I called my best friends together."

"Boo-hoo," Belkin said, taking a beer out of the fridge. He glared at the beer can. "Get some vodka, pussy. Standard or Stoli. Not the American crap."

"Drink your Coors and like it, Commie. It's that Rocky Mountain water."

"I hear people piss in it."

"Come on, Charlie," Zeke insisted. "I was just sittin' down to my pork roast. And I don't like to see that shotgun layin' there like a big dead hound dog. Are we gettin' into some bad shit?"

Charlie Beck stared at him for a few moments. "You're getting into some shit for sure. You're already enrolled."

"I don't know what the fuck you're all arguing about," Belkin said. "Maybe it's my crap English. Use little words."

"You speak better than half the guys at Gusev, convict. You're the guy who said he takes his morning dump on law and order."

"You're working on getting me worried, boss man," Belkin said.

"Me, too," Zeke said. "Charlie, come *on.*"

"I got some friends told me some stuff." He began reassembling the shotgun. "Get me a beer."

Zeke went to the fridge.

"You got friends, shit," Belkin said. "Congratulations."

Beck gave him the finger. "Shut up for a minute. These friends was Intel in Eye-raq. I know, Army Intel—lots of hoofprints going in but none coming out. Whatever. These guys are DEA now and like that and they know how to find shit out. The fool who burned up my fine car is now taking a long dirt nap."

"You wasted him?" Zeke said, rocked.

"No, I made him take his Nembutal and go beddie-bye. Nobody fucks with me and mine. That's the way it is. I told you the elevator is up in the men's department now. The guy was a waddling old peasant and he blundered in while I was searching his apartment. He tried to pretend he was somebody else, but he's over and done now. Nobody saw me, but whoever they are did find me before so I got to stay on my toes. Are Russians big on payback, Comrade Belkin?"

"How many times I got to say? I ain't a Russian."

A car braked noisily outside and then rocketed away, squealing its tires. When there was no explosion or gunfire, they relaxed.

"Hey, shithead." Belkin put his hand on Charlie Beck's rising beer can and pushed it down on the table. "On most volunteer patrols, you know—they give you a chance to take a step back and say no, even if they make you go, anyway. You couldn't of scared this old man enough to make you happy? You had to kill him?"

Beck rocked a little in his chair, and they could see he was a sheet or two to the wind. "How much space you got to stand on, Russky?" Beck said. "I got about a square foot. I can buy another fucking Suburban, sure. I don't know if I can get another square foot."

"Man, payback ain't the half," Belkin said. " There's plenty of emigres out there who got fucked up in Afghanistan and Chechnya. And there's a big old mafia, too. Nothing like the Dago mafia maybe. Mainly guys like me who learned to laugh in the bear's face and build a whole underground black market against the baddest-ass cops you got no idea of."

Belkin unbuttoned his khaki shirt and held it open. His hollow chest was a blue-black carnival of prison tattoos. At the center was a large onion-dome cathedral, flanked by Madonna and Jesus with haloes over their heads. On the sides were spider webs and burning candles and a couple of swastikas and lightning bolts. There were mottos all over in Cyrillic letters that neither of the Americans could read. They had caught glimpses of all this before, mostly the arms, but nothing like this.

"Fuckin'-A hog wire," Zeke said. "Didn't that shit hurt?"

Belkin gave his mocking smile. "You think? The needle was stuck to an electric shaver. The ink was burned shoe leather and piss. I'll show you what it felt like one day, crackerbread, I'll put a Dixie flag on your dick."

SHOOT EVERYTHING

Then to Beck: "You get a Abrams tank inked somewhere you won't like."

"What's that there thing say?" Zeke asked. He pointed to the biggest motto, across Belkin's stomach, just over a flock of seagulls flying above a sun that was low on the ocean.

"You won't get it. It says, 'My mother taught me to steal in the industrial zones.'"

"This show-and-tell is a whole lot of nothing," Charlie Beck put in. "We all of us got pails of our own shit to carry around. I want us on our toes now. Listen hard for twigs cracking in the forest. And keep your cellphones charged. Maybe this mess ain't over."

"I don't like the way you look at things, cap," Belkin said. "I like a world in control—not some poor cava-lary with Indians all 'round the fort."

"Okay, convict, suppose we're surrounded. As the Marines say, it simplifies the fuckin' problem—you just shoot everything."

* * * * *

JACK Liffey parked across the street from *Ya*'s apartment in a ragged part of the Westside he didn't even know what to call, probably Palms. After calling the phone number for him, Gloria had told him the phone belonged to a girl improbably named Yana Slutsky who was happy to talk about Benjy.

The two-story beige apartment building was south of the Santa Monica Freeway on the street called Motor Avenue that meandered seven miles directly from the gates of Twentieth Century Fox Studios in the north to the gates of what used to be MGM in the south—now Sony-Columbia. He wondered if they'd built it to lure away each other's stars and directors.

Half-way along it was a nondescript mixture of take-out pizzas, nail spas and cheap apartments, one of the many zipcodes of LA that had fallen into the ugly sulk of transience. Nobody but the poorest would be staying.

80 BOYSTOWN

He wondered who Yana was to the gay young man. Old friend? He wondered what it might have been like as a teenager to discover gradually that you carried a big social stigma. He'd often felt—rightly or wrongly—that the discovery was far more disturbing for a boy than a girl.

Back in junior high in the 1950s, with everybody in the closet, homosexuality had been almost inconceivable to him, though he knew theoretically that it existed somewhere. The only openly gay male he'd encountered had been Jay something, an extremely troubled and dramatically effeminate boy who'd arrived at Dana Junior High mid semester one day and soon started dancing for cruelly tossed pennies after gym class. The boy had fixated for a week or two on the young Jack Liffey, who had been alone in refusing to thrust him away. Rigid good manners mainly. He'd tried to get the boy to calm down, if not openly befriend him, but he'd been terrified of getting himself subsumed into ostracism.

Very soon Jay something had been yanked out of school, and nobody knew what became of him. Since then, the whole country had grown up a lot, of course. But Jack Liffey thought of Jay from time to time and wondered if young Jack Liffey had acquitted himself all that well on one of his first big life tests.

As he got out of his pickup, the angry street noise on Motor Avenue stirred at his interior funk. A vehicle siren offered its double-urgent *wooeep wooeep* from behind and he waited on the curb as a phalanx of police cars, flashing away like UFOs, crept past at a walking pace, followed by a pilot truck with a sign:

Stay Back. Radiation danger.

Behind the police escort a ridiculously large truck cab towed an astounding piece of machinery on at least thirty wheels.

Men in yellow jumpsuits walked ahead of the truck cab thrusting tall poles upward to boost dangling power wires a foot or so to make sure the whatever-it-was would clear them. On the lowboy truck was a huge

SHOOT EVERYTHING 81

finned mass of machinery with rods extending front and back where men slowly cranked away with other men standing by to take over. He wondered what on earth would happen if they stopped cranking.

How far could they get a load like this? There had to be a big handbook that listed the exact road clearances at every intersection. An inflexible inch too low—a cement bridge—would send a load like this miles out of its way.

Then the chimera was gone. Maybe it had never existed. Yana's apartment was up a walkway to the second floor. Beside the door was a large ceramic frog with a horrified expression on its face. The frog was reading a ceramic book with the title *Cookbook For Herons.* He didn't have time to appreciate the wit because a young woman opened the door immediately. She was in her mid twenties, a thin boyish blonde with pale skin and lank hair.

"You must be Jack Liffey?"

"Yes—and you're Yana."

"Go on. Say the whole thing, Yana Slutsky. I've lived with it all my life. Come in."

The living room was full of potted succulents.

"You know, the word 'slut' doesn't even mean what people think it does. It means somebody who doesn't clean up. A blob of dust under the bed is called a 'slutball.' I could have changed my name, but I decided it was a poor thing but mine own."

A young woman Maeve would have liked. "Good for you. Are you off work today?"

She grimaced as they sat. "I was lucky to get a job with the county library, but they've cut back like crazy. The branch is closed today and Friday, just when poor kids need it. So the millionaires can have their tax cuts."

Jack Liffey raised a palm. "I like the editorial ... but let's talk about Benjy?"

"Can I get you some coffee or something?"

"No, but please have anything you want." He was a little surprised at how smoothly the words had slid out of him without puns or song lyrics. Of course, he had little emotion engaged right now. And maybe the book-reading frog had put him at ease. Or the patchouli oil perfume he could make out fifteen feet away—plucking him straight back to the era of long straight hair, leather sandals, and wraparound Indian skirts at Long Beach State.

"I don't need anything, Mr. Liffey. Sit please. I met Benjy at the library desk. He was one disturbed boy, but, man, was he pretty, wow. I work at the West Hollywood branch and he was asking me all kinds of things about Russians and Ukrainians. My parents are poor Jewish shopkeepers from Ukraine with a mini-market down the boulevard. It's hard to know what he was after, he was so angry and not very coherent. He'd clearly just been in a fight. He needed help and I hate to say it, he was so handsome, I let him stay with me for a day. He tried getting it on a little but couldn't."

"Did you know ... he was gay?"

"I sort of figured it out. In WeHo it's good to keep the gaydar on. He wept and wept and he told me about all the pain he'd gone through to come out to his family. At first only his sister Bunny had been decent to him. Life can be tough, can't it, Mr. Liffey?"

"Call me Jack, please."

"You're not gay, are you?"

"If they ever start ... rounding up gays for concentration camps I will be. But no, I don't seem to be."

"Can you tell me why you have that hitch in your speech? I don't mean to be rude."

He sighed, thinking he'd been beating it. She really was a kindly and direct young woman. He told her about the heart attack and stroke. "I should be dead several times over. It's left a few marks. If I don't slow down my talk ... silly babble just bursts out."

"I think I might like that."

He smiled. "I guess I like it, too. Do-be-do, do-be-do."

"Let it out, man."

"A man's got to doooo what a man's got to doooo."

He stepped on his brakes. Change the subject, man.

SHOOT EVERYTHING 83

She applauded gaily, and he almost wept. He hadn't realized how much tension he'd accumulated fighting the urges.

"I can tell you're a very sweet man."

"Thank you." He felt himself blush. "Can you tell me more about Benjy?"

As she talked, Jack Liffey looked away from her, afraid he'd finally become a dirty old man. He realized that the moment a woman became real to him, he couldn't help evaluating her breasts. Small and boyish in this case.

"Benjy was looking for some rough character that he'd had a run-in with, but couldn't tell me enough so I could help. I just told him to hang out at Plummer Park for a while and he'd see some rough characters that he could ask."

He nodded and stayed quiet.

"Benjy left and I never saw him again. I gave him my number. I'm a sucker for needy."

She fell silent, brooding over something. "Mr. Liffey, do you know if something happened to him?"

"When I find out you'll know."

She seemed to be getting more and more choked up and emotional. All of a sudden, she walked across the intervening space and kissed him startlingly on the mouth.

"I'm an emotional mess. You'd better go now."

SEVEN

Worse Is Yet to Come

P ETRO Ivanchuk waited until he was certain his wife would be gone for a few hours—tea with an old friend and a Macy's shoe sale—before he invited Sergei to come.

"I know you're careful," Petro said, as the big man came cautiously in the back and waited in silence near the door, declining to sit. His eyes were like lasers boring into everything they aimed at. "I've been careful. I thank you for coming."

Petro assumed the nondescript Toyota he'd seen park out front had a license plate that belonged to some other crushed car on its way to Japan as scrap. He knew about Sergei and the man did not leave traces. And that he had often slipped out of his Alfa Group *osnova* in Chechnya at night by himself and had killed numberless mujahedeen silently with a knife. There was a leopard-like restlessness in the man that suggested that despite his size he could move very fast indeed.

"Dr. Trachtenberg is my blood brother, sir," Sergei said softly in Russian. "He asked me to assist you. I am at your service."

"Thank you. Don't tell me any more. Your reputation precedes you. With ten of you, the Soviets would have ended up ruling the world."

The thickset man did not smile. "There *were* ten of us. A nation's future is not about individual prowess. The strongest mouse in history cannot defeat a pride of lions. The end result comes from a country's political will, its resources, its population, and the impulse of history. The Soviet Union was eclipsed. In thirty years, America will be eclipsed by China and worse still will come—as we all know in our hearts."

"Our dark souls. You're the man I want as my champion."

"Sir, before we talk—may I please see your butterflies? I have heard about them since arriving in Los Angeles."

"Really?"

"Tell no one please. A butterfly saved my life once."

"Truly?"

Sergei flashed a smile so quick he almost missed it. "An old joke amongst warriors, sir. The insignificant thing that is significant because it saved my life. The butter knife, the untied shoe, the cowardly mess sergeant. But I do love butterflies." He said his uncle in Nizhny Novgorod had taken him butterflying every spring—a brief reprieve from an otherwise dismal childhood.

Petro Ivanchuk led him upstairs along the narrow staircase, and the man grew visibly uncomfortable, glancing back. "Is there another way out of the house, sir?"

"All the windows are barred, but one window upstairs has an emergency release. You could get onto the first floor roof and jump."

He could see Sergei making a difficult decision to enter what could be entrapping. "Carry on."

The big room didn't seem to fit the arts-and-crafts house at all. The entire upstairs had had its inner walls torn out and was now a very Russian library, paneled in white mahogany, suited to one of the less boorish *shlyakhtych* houses. It had cost Petro the last of his smuggled patrimony. He flipped on the subdued lighting to show that the walls of the big room were lined with slim wooden cases of butterflies.

"Are you familiar with California species?" Petro asked.

"My poor knowledge is only of the Volga basin."

"Pity. My *metelyky* are left behind in Odessa. Allow me to show you some you don't know."

"Please."

WORSE IS YET TO COME 87

"These two panels are swallowtails, the largest butterflies found in California. Look at this wonderful anise with its two glorious red spots. And my giant, *Heraclides cresphontes*, almost fifteen centimeters. Yes—I bought this specimen mounted.

"These two are a blue pipevine. The back and the underwing. See the rainbow of red dots it shows while feeding. The pipevines are poisonous to birds though many other species have evolved to ride their reputation, to copy the pattern to keep off birds—Batesian mimicry. But you know about that."

Sergei gave an appreciative sound, almost a purr.

"Come see my prize beyond prizes. I can't stop looking at it myself. I caught this specimen on the lower slopes of the Eastern Sierra, and it's been in dozens of journals."

Sergei appeared mesmerized. It looked like a butterfly assembled from spare parts, divided precisely down the center line. The left was bold black stripes on ghostly white like an albino tiger, and the right was deep night-sky purple.

"It's a pure bilateral gynandromorph. The left side is a male tiger swallowtail—*Papilio euremedon*—and the right half is a female swallowtail in every way. At the first cell division of its zygote, the left cell got the XX chromosome and the right got only X. It's a rare freak, of course, but what a glorious freak."

The man's fierce dark eyes found Petro's. Petro Ivanchuk heard another odd gurgle in the man's throat. "If it's both sexes can it breed with itself?"

Petro shrugged. "I doubt a gynandromorph can breed at all, but who knows?"

Then he heard a Siberian chill in the man's voice. "Do other butterflies kill them for being different?"

"How would a butterfly kill, man? They have no weapons? This is a stray cosmic ray striking the egg after fertilization. If you prefer, God looks away for an instant."

The stocky man's eyes went back to the gynandromorph. He accepted the magnifier Petro held out to him, leaning close to peer at it. "Sad," Sergei said finally. "An outsider to his kind."

Petro smiled. "The Dostoyevsky of butterflies."

Whether it was that comment or some other impulse, the man seemed to disengage from the study of butterflies. Sergei reached into in inner pocket in his coat. Petro almost expected a weapon, but it was a small cardboard frame with cutouts that displayed five passport-like photos, face-on, grim and cheerless.

"How did you get these?"

"Shhh. These were your hunters?"

"Not this one." He pointed to one who was definitely not one of the four he'd watched from the port-a-potty door. The rest were.

"Which one shot you?"

Petro tapped the flattop haircut and caved-in jaw. "The way they were talking, I'm sure this is the one."

"*Zhizn korotka, a del mnogo,*" Sergei said. Life is short but there's a lot to be done.

"What will you do?"

"Shhh. He will not be dancing in a meadow."

"*Chyort poberi!* You mean—?"

"Shhh. You want me to avenge you or not, sir? Yes or no."

Did he really want to launch this deadly missile? Just then the gods decided to put his weight on his leg to give him a searing pain. The word was almost a reflex: "Yes."

Petro wondered if he would regret that word. But these fools had shot him for no reason. They were a menace to the world. He was far more afraid of disappointing Sergei, even for a moment, than of any consequences.

"Are you lonely in America?" Petro asked him as they trudged back down the staircase.

"Would it make any difference to you?"

* * * * *

WORSE IS YET TO COME

89

"**H**OLY jumping cheeses!" Maeve said as he opened the door. She had no idea where that comicbook oath came from. "That hill almost made me pee my pants."

Walt Roski was unkempt and baggy-eyed with a big book in his hand. He smiled. "That's like what your father said. Baxter Street."

She nodded, still shaken by seeming to go over a cliff.

"I'll have to start telling people to come in roundabout, off Park."

An hour earlier, she'd called the number she'd swiped from her dad's crude Rolodex and Roski had invited her. She sat across from where he'd obviously been reading on a broken sofa that was leaking its stuffing.

"Sorry about the dire look of things. This is my divorce house. I can't get up the energy to spiff it up."

"You're home mid-week?" she asked.

"I took a mental health day to nap and read. I might be clinically depressed." He showed her the book—Hegel. "Maybe not the best remedy. Maybe I'll commit suicide before you leave."

Maeve sat up quickly. "No!"

"You *are* like your dad. Don't worry, hon. That was joshing, and I know it was too raw."

She settled back uneasily. It was indeed a sad bungalow, one side of the front room dominated by old barbells where a dining table should have been. A rusted swamp cooler projected from the window, supported by wobbly-looking legs.

Change the subject, Maeve thought. "I hated driving past that lumber yard with all those men waiting hopelessly for day jobs. The *mosca*." Showing off her idiomatic Spanish a little. "It's almost noon and they're not going to get any work today."

"Nothing to feed a family. Their simple presence here keeps jabbing at a big rotten spot in our political culture, though they only see the consequences."

"That's a thought."

"Maeve, I have endless sympathy for outsiders, I hope you know that. I'm running hard but I find I'm getting winded. I need your father as a friend, and I'm starting to worry I might lose him. By the way, dear, how did you get my home number?"

Amazing how quickly a cloud had scurried in to shadow his face. She didn't want to say she'd snooped her dad's desk. "Everybody's on the Internet, Mr. Roski."

He nodded skeptically. "Please call me Walt. I don't want to feel like my own granddad."

"Walt," she said tentatively. It was difficult for her to use first names with an older person. When would she ever grow up? "I hope I didn't get my dad in danger. Could you tell *me* what you've told him about Benjy?"

"Only if you'll be a princess and share a special drink with an old man." He headed for the kitchen.

Her sympathy was engaged by his obvious neediness. The last time she'd shared a strange drink—absinthe—she'd acquired her first female lover. No no no. He came back in with two bulbous glass snifters and a strange porcelain book that turned out to be a bottle with a picture of a Renoir nude on the cover. Too weird.

"Just a midday sip with my friend's grown-up daughter. I collect cognacs. This one is called Camus and I absolutely worship Albert Camus. No relation to the booze, really. And you'll like the Renoir painting. This bottle cost me two weeks' salary."

"It's a little early in the day for me," she demurred.

"As Bukowski said, 'It's five o'clock somewhere.' Humor me and have a sip. No lovely ladies ever come to visit."

Some of her lower innards were thrumming away. Walt Roski was obviously very needy and he was buff and attractive for a middle-aged guy—a dangerous combination. "I'm incorruptible, dude."

"The only real sin in life is optimism," he announced as he twisted the gold cap off the decanter and splashed some into both snifters. His got a second and third splash. "In the era of Auschwitz, optimism is moral cowardice. It's refusing to open your eyes."

WORSE IS YET TO COME   91

She knew the plump Renoir woman on the decanter—"Woman after the Bath." She wrinkled her nose at the snifter. "What is it you love about Albert Camus?"

Roski sipped, and he apparently didn't have to think about his answer. "He's da man. He says when life is going to hell, your duty is to push on. I love it. The French are so dramatic, though burdened by a culture that's lost its authority in the world. Bless 'em." He knocked the rest of his snifter back in two goes, and she took another sip. It scorched her throat, and a buzziness came over her. Whoa. Enough.

"I don't follow," she said.

"Me neither, dear. Ignore my outbursts." He poured himself more cognac. "I think I need some kind of vitality in my life, against the big fadeout. You're way too young to appreciate that. Don't work yourself up. I know you have an excess of sympathy. Some day you'll pay dear for that. Pretend I'm an opaque old fart. Pretend pain is the world's normal. Pretend we two can share what we know about this missing young man. This is an entirely professional chat."

"Pretend?"

"As you wish."

Emboldened by something that she wanted to go away, she finished off her snifter in a long gulp. "I'd like to talk about Benjy, please. And have another drop."

"Are you sure?"

"I'm sure," she said, meeting his intense milky blue eyes. Girl, calm yourself.

He held out the porcelain book-bottle, and she crossed the space between them and poised her snifter for a refill. "What's really troubling you? You're such a good man inside. That's why my dad likes you."

He poured her a too-generous portion. "Do you know that William Blake said if the sun or moon ever began to doubt, they would immediately go out. Blake was wrong. They get dimmer and dimmer first."

As if to prove something, she drank her new portion right down and choked and coughed. She was still standing beside him, though teetery. "Walt, would it help you right now if I make tender love to you?"

"Ah, a charity fuck," he said.

"Oh, God. I'm experiencing too much sensation. You're such a dear man."

"Somebody would end up crying," he said. "I'm fifty-two years old, sweetheart."

"Let it be me who cries, then. I'm a hundred and four."

"Lousy math. Worse idea. But thank you very much."

* * * * *

TALBOT had phoned into Gusev sick, faking a raspy throat. Toward the end of the workday before, Charlie Beck had received a hysterical call from his wife that someone had fired a shot into their bedroom, and he had taken off on his bike for home like a rat on fire. Talbot had just about had it with all these low-lifes. Why was he even working there?

For years he'd slogged away in various libraries so doggedly, seven days a week, that he almost didn't know what to do with a free day. He lazed in Alvis's party-cluttered living room, savoring his coffee and a croissant from down the block. Plastic cups and soiled paper plates had been discarded throughout the room, like the remains of some sordid game. It had been days since the party, but he didn't really care about the mess and hadn't run into his brother since then. He must have got lucky.

He thumbed idly through a fat sound equipment catalogue. A little peek into a self-contained world. Twenty-four channel audio snake. IF receiver field unit. Uh-huh.

The bedroom door surprised him coming open.

"You looking to steal my life, Tal?"

"Not a chance." He tossed the catalogue down. "I don't know what any of this electro-shit is. Looks like the party went nuclear."

Alvis wore a lovely orange kimono reconfigured to a man's bathrobe. "I don't remember, bro. I went home with Gina, I think. You'd have been very welcome, you know. At the height of things, we had a whole bunch of gay guys. And not an even number."

WORSE IS YET TO COME 93

"I'm not trolling, Alv. Every relationship is extra trouble."

"Man, you said it. I think I'm gradually emerging from the teenage sheepdip of hormones."

Talbot laughed.

"Any extra coffee in the kitchen?" Alvis asked.

Talbot nodded, and Alvis fetched himself a mug and another croissant. He sank into a crunchy red bean-bag chair opposite the sofa.

"I hope my mind hasn't atrophied. Or my soul. You were the bravest person I ever knew, Tal. I don't think I ever said this to you, but I never had the guts that you did."

"Thanks."

"I remember that terrible day in junior high."

Talbot held up a palm "Please."

"There's such cruelty. People are so terrified of difference."

Talbot nodded. "That's pretty much what my dissertation is about, Al. Being the Other." Or not. It was certainly one aspect of it, of calling exile the essence of modernism. "I really don't know what's happened to America. When we grew up, didn't America used to be proud of liking the underdog? Alvis, you know, I never once worried about you turning on me."

"If this country ever liked underdogs, I can't remember it." He took a long sip. "My brother, I want to ask you something deep."

"Nothing is off limits. Not even what we boys *do* in bed."

"That's off *my* limits, dude." Alvis took a big bite of the croissant and frowned. "I always wondered if being gay is, like, a decision you made based on your experiences, or if it's not even a choice, just a fact of life you were born with. I mean, did you decide it or find it out?"

Talbot laughed in relief. "I thought you wanted to know where mom's pearl necklace was hidden."

"Hell, I know *that*."

Talbot sat up in astonishment, but quickly decided his brother was kidding. The disappearance of her necklace had been the colossal trauma of their childhood—with everyone a suspect. Almost worse than his coming out.

"First, here's the PC answer. Take notes, Alv. Most people say it could be any combination of genes, hormones, environment and early uterine development. That answer boils away pretty fast to nothing, but here's mine. I think I came out of the birth canal liking dicks, to be straightup about it. A lot of people I respect say sexuality can go either way, but I don't buy it. Pussies never interested me. Tell me—do you spend a lot of time thinking about sucking dicks?"

"Don't be on the warpath, Tal. I'm on your side."

"Sorry, there's a lot of explosive emotion in that very issue. But I wouldn't be staying here if I didn't trust you."

Alvis finished off the roll with a grimace. "Amazing what you'll eat when you get lazy," he said. "What makes anybody think you can make a croissant out of whole wheat?"

"We avoided it a lot in high school, didn't we? Believe it or not, this is only the second time I've talked about it directly with somebody who's cis. My thesis chairman brought it up one day in his office. An old man, rather prissy, who was never ever going to change his ideas. What he said actually surprised me. Wait for it. He said he didn't really believe in homosexuality. What could I say, for god's sake? I got mad and told him his belief wasn't necessary. Being a fag wasn't like the Easter Bunny."

Alvis burst out laughing. "Wonderful! You're still my hero. Can I read your dissertation on outsiders, man?"

"Of course you can. Do you really know where mom's pearls were? Maybe it's your turn to be outed."

* * * * *

VICTOR Gorbenko held his fingers spread before his face, as if inspecting nail polish, and saw how they trembled. Ever since he'd found his neighbor dead, he'd been pushing himself forward on adrenalin, with little sleep. And cursing the damn Mini-Me strapped to his back—how many times had he joked to himself about going to Paris to jump off Notre Dame.

WORSE IS YET TO COME 95

He stared at the old World War I Springfield rifle on the motel bed. He couldn't go home again, not with poor Ruslan's body on the bed.

He knew the gun shop had sold him a piece of junk meant for a loser. The bluing was wearing off the rifle barrel, the stock looked like a chewed pencil, and he'd already forgot how to disassemble the damn thing to clean it. It was the only weapon the gun store salesman would sell him cheap without a waiting period. But still—it was $288, plus the $100 for no paperwork.

All Victor really knew about Petro's enemies was the address of the apartment where he'd firebombed the Suburban. That morning he'd slyly driven past to work out the number of the charred parking stall, located the apartment of the same number and then fired a round into what was probably the bedroom. He secretly hoped he hadn't hurt anyone. He simply had to lash out to prove he was as good as anyone. And he'd got poor innocent Ruslan killed, even if he was a big bore.

A wave of loneliness overwhelmed him. He'd been keeping to himself for more than a decade in America, not even seeing acquaintances like Ruslan much. Victor had been working at home on his computer, translating advertising blurbs into a stylish and humorous Russian, first for a print catalogue and then a web site that specialized in bilking Russia's nouveau riche with items of fake Americana—Billy-the-Kid's real six-gun, Apache arrows, Buddy Holly 45s—all made in a plant in China. Working alone he'd gradually grown more timid than ever, a scurrying shadowy existence.

More than ever he treasured the Dostoyevsky quote he'd carried in memory since his adolescence.

We are all cripples, each of us, more or less.

* * * * *

"GINGER ale, Jack?"

"You remembered."

He popped the can. Somebody had swiped a bus bench off the roads and plopped it down above a wild and shrubby stretch of the LA River in Frogtown. It was a weedy dirt riverbed here, even with its concrete banks, though downstream it became the notoriously all-concrete channel meant to drain floodwaters out to sea fast.

In the cool early evening, he and Roski could hear frogs croaking away below, occasionally drowned out by the hum of traffic from the Golden State Freeway, the I-5, a quarter mile behind them.

"What are friends for?" Roski said. "Don't answer that. Where would we be without rhetorical questions?"

"You mean hypothetically? Hip-hopically. Topically. Sorry."

Roski smiled and chugged a Tecate from his little cooler. "I have the deepest sympathy for the former river down there. Imagine we're sitting on the remains of an Indian village called Yaangna. What's sadder than something wiped off the face of the earth? We're Romans bemoaning what our ancestors did to Carthage."

Jack Liffey glanced at him, and Roski made a wry face.

"Angst later, friend," Jack Liffey said. "I need a report."

Roski shrugged. "You first."

To control his affliction, Jack Liffey told him very slowly that he'd talked with a girl, Yana Slutsky, who said Benjy had been beat up and was trying to find the guy who hit him. He described a skinny foreign thug.

Roski nodded and clucked.

A couple trying to walk four tugging and lunging dalmatians came along the river path.

"I can't hardly hold on, Tommy."

"Dominate. You ain't got a hundred and one of 'em."

The woman had to unwind from tangled leashes.

"I've got nothing new about Benjy today," Roski said. "I have to do my own job once in a while. Let me pass this by you. It's about the arson case I'm stuck with." He reminded Jack Liffey about the gasoline-bomb attack on the Chevy Suburban in West Hollywood, a pitch-tar-added bomb that he'd found out was more-or-less a signature of Soviet training.

"So you figure that narrows it down a lot in West Hollywood. What, a third of the population?"

*WORSE IS YET TO COME*97

Roski frowned. "Don't mock. I'm thinking out loud—maybe we can help each other here. Your daughter is reporting to me on her investigations, by the way."

"Really?" That perked him up.

"She feels she's got a bit over her head. You're a tough role model, Jack."

"What's going on here?" He heard his voice becoming querulous.

Along the path one Dalmatian broke free and ran, the leash flailing behind. The man took off after the dog, shouting.

"And when she saw how lonely I was, she offered to sleep with me."

"Walt!"

"She's a really sexy girl, Jack. Who wouldn't jump her bones to pretend to be young again."

"What!" Jack Liffey leapt to his feet.

"Jesus Christ, sit down! I'm sorry, Jack. We're both so morose. I was joshing, for Chrissake. Hear what I'm saying. Maeve and I were teasing each other with taboos that's all. I'm telling you this for your own good. Look at the big picture. What brought Maeve to talk to me in the first place was she's worried about you. Calm yourself, man. You and I are friends, and to her I stand for you in a way. I said, *sit down*."

Jack Liffey's innards had been stirred to where he felt ill. "Walt, stuff like that—it isn't funny."

"Listen to me. She's in love with *you*, you asshole," Roski said. "Whatever the Greek word for that is. I suspect that her being lesbian is half about trying to run away from her feelings for you. She came to see me—I'm a surrogate for you—because she wanted to stay close to you. But she's really a together girl, Jack. And like the best of us, a little bit of her isn't. I wouldn't have touched her, man. I'm not insane. I'm sorry I joked about it."

Jack Liffey very nearly reached for a beer, but stopped himself and had another ginger ale. He felt himself on the edge of tears. How many times had he failed to provide what Maeve needed? And he couldn't forget Yana's unanticipated and terrifying kiss.

The sensation (and the possibilities) had stayed with him all day. It had been a long time since he'd been able to share any tenderness with Gloria.

EIGHT

The Missing Pearls

C AT sat stiffly on the back stoop, waiting out in the open for him to come home, which had never happened before. She usually hid out of sight and surprised him with a gentle knock.

"Cat! What up?" He came in the back gate, holding up the white McDonalds bag of food, but she was impassive.

Her sleeves were rolled up, and for the first time he got a good look at the monstrous scars on her right forearm. Self-mutilation? Torture? It was so reminiscent of his father's lost hand. Vitaliy Fedorenko Belkin had caught his arm in an unfamiliar corn husker imported to a collective farm near Kalusk—growing American sweetcorn throughout Ukraine being a brainstorm of Khrushchev's, after his visit to Iowa in 1959, but like most top-down bright ideas it hadn't worked out very well. The manager had come running, but his father's hand had been torn to shreds and he'd eventually had to be fitted with a crude snapping turtle of a hand. Bad for work but still good for punishing sons.

"Two fish sandwiches for you," Belkin said. He'd splurged because he had no idea how much she'd had to eat that day.

She growled softly and held out a hand.

"If you wait a minute or two, I'll bring my food out and eat with you," he said, but she practically inhaled the first Filet-O-Fish, then gagged a little.

"Okay, Cat. I got no problem with nothing about you. Do you want to tell me what happened to your arm?"

She glanced momentarily and then rolled down the sleeve. "Nuh."

Late at night his father had woken up in the cottage screaming, "The hand! Where's my *hand*?"

Belkin knew he'd probably never find out much more about Cat and he didn't care. "I'll protect you from everything, girl. You just let me know what you need."

* * * * *

THE second-floor window that Victor Gorbenko had shot out the day before was taped over with cardboard. Not bare cardboard though. **BACK AT YOU!** had been written in marker pen, and he felt a mild chill.

He knew it was dangerous for him to be seen anywhere near this location, but he had returned, drawn by a tremendous tug of something like sideways gravity. He had to avenge Petro—or whatever the itch was. What sort of honor would the world ever grant a hunchback? The big people would let you dance for kopeks, like the *Pryanishnikov* painting in his bedroom. That was about it.

His friends at the park reassured themselves with the notion that forced exiles were often the bravest and most resilient souls of their generation. But he couldn't see himself in that observation. He was a man people stared right through rather than acknowledge. The chance to avenge Petro had been a beckoning to gain self-respect.

He knew if the police discovered his papers were flawed, no country would take him in. Did hunchbacks have a homeland? He was as illegal as any Mexican who'd trekked here across the Sonoran Desert, except he couldn't turn back. Every country on earth would turn him away, except some bumfuck Pacific Island nation that was sinking into the ocean because of global warming. Luckily the police here—like everybody else—never even noticed a cripple like him.

His rifle and two more firebombs were in the back of the van, but there were far too many innocent people in the building for that. He

THE MISSING PEARLS 101

had his principles. Suddenly a powerful motorcycle pulled up over the scorched asphalt and parked where the big SUV had once been.

* * * * *

WHEN Jack Liffey got home he heard a thumping and hurried upstairs, astonished to find Gloria in a gray sports bra and panties doing the exercise that his high school gym coach had called burpees but everyone these days seemed to call squat-thrusts. He watched for a moment and something about her energy (and undress) reminded him he had a sex drive.

She stopped finally and gasped for breath with her hands on her hips. "'Malingering' means you're pretending so you got an illness and can shirk your duty, doesn't it? I looked it up."

"Yes."

"Fuck Captain Hanson and the horse he rode in on. It's time I sucked it up and got into healing my body before they drag me out to pasture."

"You can't do it all in one day."

"Just watch me."

"Oh, I'll watch. Less exercise. More body, please."

"Knock it off, Jack. I'm about as sexy as an old brick."

He came around behind her and gently cupped her breasts. "I like old bricks."

She slapped his hands away but not too hard. "The right one is pure rubber and about as sensitive as meatloaf." He knew about the mastectomy and reconstruction. That was before he'd even met her. "The other one does say hello. You've been good to wait on me, you been good all around, but I still need time. By the way, your daughter called to say she's coming in a little while to show us something important."

"Something bad?"

"I don't know. Shoo. Go start dinner. Play in a busy street. Let me finish up here without all the crotch peeks."

He laughed as he headed out. She hadn't sounded this frisky in a long time. "Don't wait too long," he said. "It'll fall right off." Coherent

102   *BOYSTOWN*

speech, without rhyming or gaming, he thought cheerfully. Maybe he *was* improving.

When Maeve showed up a half hour later, she wasn't bearing news of catastrophe. "Help me in with these, Dad-o-mine."

The big paintings just barely wriggled out the back door of her Echo at an angle, and he did his best not to sneak a look at them before she wanted him to. He did get one foreshortened glimpse and thought he saw a slash of abstraction, unusual for her. He didn't believe the visit was just to show them her new paintings, but who could fathom a daughter like this? Roski's analysis of their relationship had thrown him a lot.

Gloria came down in work shirt and jeans, and Maeve turned the oils around in the living room one by one to a general hush. Of consternation? Awe?

"I know, I know," she said. "But it's the primal image of our time."

"Just our time?" Jack Liffey said.

"*Interesting*," Gloria said neutrally. Jack Liffey knew it was a private joke, meant for him. She'd told him before that she'd heard a journalist utter that word to the police chief at the unveiling of a truly revolting police-sponsored mosaic on the front of a local station—a grinning uniformed officer joining hands with two delighted little girls as birds and butterflies circled overhead. Gloria had fastened on the wonderful ambiguity of *interesting*, and she used it regularly.

All three of Maeve's canvases were of huge, minutely observed vaginas. One had an engorged clitoris. Another was shaved. Was he mature enough to handle this from a daughter?

"Brave," Jack Liffey said. "Anyone I know?"

"Dad! You know I've been fascinated by the body since I started painting. My generation is a lot less worried about the sex parts."

"We did the best we could with ours back in the day, hon," Gloria said. "I must say it makes me think. Why not look close at anything, right?"

"Yes, yes! That's it, Glor! Why not look close at whatever we want? Let's normalize every single thing that isn't cruel and hurtful."

THE MISSING PEARLS
103

"Doing any penises?" Jack Liffey asked. He was worried about seeing Roski's penis show up. But how the hell would he know whose it was?

"The ancients did that already. It's only in Forest Lawn that David has a fig leaf over his johnson."

He nodded sheepishly. How had he got himself to a place in life where he was discussing vaginas and penises with his daughter? And he was afraid he wasn't even coherent enough to answer her in full sentences without blurting out puns and rhymes. Life kept getting more confusing.

Eventually he and Gloria changed the subject to the missing boy and they all relaxed noticeably. He had tried to shield Maeve from the ragged side of life, but she had got pretty ragged herself, and she had initiated this one.

They talked about the Benjy hunt for a while and he figured he'd tell her that Benjy was probably still unsettled about his sexuality.

"You mean this girlie you talked to came on to him?"

"Maeve, shame on you. She's a young woman."

"Sorry, but I get so tired of people trying to save us, like it's a virus."

"She says he was the one who came on to her but it didn't get far. Could it have been a last spasm of some childhood panic at discovering he was an outcast. *What is it?*"

They were both staring hard at him, as if he had just grown a second nose.

"Jack, that speech was real good," Gloria said. "Maybe you're going right side up."

"Yeah. Bravo, dad. A thought cogently expressed, without any puns or rhymes."

But as if to dash their hopes, something tripped his hammer. "Right side up, Glor—which is that? The bright side? The far side. The beef side. Glide bide hide. Up—I like *up*. Sup, morning. Really up. Morning wood up."

"Don't wind your watch so hard, Jackie. We love you."

He wanted to collapse in a heap and cry. He took a few slow breaths. What had set him off? The women, in a kindly and sisterly mood, chatted among themselves for a while so he could recover without close attention.

"We'd better thaw some burritos," Gloria said. "Assuming we want to eat tonight and you haven't rustled anything up."

He nodded and sat solemnly, letting them get on with it. He enjoyed watching them work together. He loved them both and it seemed to stoke his libidinous feelings for Gloria.

* * * * *

"YOU better put that down," Zeke said darkly.

Carolina Sue stood there with her heavy-lidded eyes and stood him off with a couple sweeps of the spatula. "Zekie, back off, you're like a doggie in heat."

She whacked him on the neck with the greasy spatula but pulled the blow—like so many people not used to hurting. Zeke *was* used to it, and he knocked the spatula aside and slapped her so hard it spun her around. He pinned her against the stove, ass out, and yanked up her cotton skirt.

"Mom knowed you'd do me like a dog."

"What's your problem, woman? It's my right to take you for my pleasure. It's God's law." He ripped her baggy white panties down. "Wiggle your butt now."

"Make me."

He wondered if this was just her ordinary truculence or something else.

"Honey baby, what's the matter?" Zeke asked.

"You ain't let me get myself wet, not a little bit at all. You know it hurts all dry. Don't you got some sweet words?"

"Aw, if that's all, you can fetch the whole damn Crisco can. I just got home from a hard day at work with a needful woodie and there ain't no time to woo at you for an hour. I'll open a beer and give you a minute and then I want you starkers and ready."

THE MISSING PEARLS   105

Zeke got his beer and turned to the kitchen window in their duplex, saw weeds and used oil cans and potato chip wrappers in the back yard that they shared with a Mexican family that had a bunch of teenagers, and he wondered why Mexes dropped their shit like that everywhere. Hell, even West Virginians could put their beer cans in a barrel.

He reached out to a funny red spot wobbling on the glass. There was a light tinkling sound in the kitchen, like a wind-chime stirred unexpectedly, but there was no wind-chime. A small hole appeared in the kitchen window with a craze of cracks spreading outward. Zeke fell to the floor with a startled "Yikes," limp as a big gunny sack of doorknobs.

"Hon, whatchou up to? I'm gettin' it ready, I swear." Carolina Sue dropped to her knees beside him and didn't start screaming until she noticed the hole in his forehead.

* * * * *

"ALVIS, what're you cooking?" Talbot's brother was chopping vegetables on his big freestanding cutting block, bought used from a butcher-shop. It sat on sturdy legs and was rounded over by decades of being scraped and chopped on.

"Stir fry. I don't know if you like tofu. It's the hard kind."

"Don't worry about me. What's up?" He could tell Alvis was upset. Brothers were like that.

"I think I broke up with Gina. She broke up with me, I guess. Probably all for the good in the long run. Boy, *that's* hard to say." He chopped away at a head of some odd elongated cabbage. "She's been in analysis for years and she told me this morning, 'Hey, I know my problem now. *You're* my problem.'" Alvis laughed, but not convincingly.

"Ah, shit, man. It's *her* problem. You're worth ten of her and change." Alvis raised his palm to suggest Talbot back off. "Whatever."

All at once Talbot noticed that his brother had his cut-off jeans on inside out, the empty white pockets dangling outside. His talent for intense distraction, Talbot thought. Alvis had always been focused tight. He'd use a hand tool for something, set it down wherever he'd used it and forget it there for months.

106 *BOYSTOWN*

"Have a Campari-soda, Tal. I want to get blotto tonight."

"I'll keep you company halfway down."

"But let's don't talk of Gina, okay? Inform me what's going on with you."

"I went back to work today." Talbot measured out his own drink, keeping it pale enough to hold off the ambush of the liqueur a while. "I noticed I have this weird loyalty to the lead machinist, Charlie Becker. He's got that kind of hard-guy responsibility that Dad had. They were both army sergeants, maybe that's it.

"Charlie left sick midday and I actually missed him. You know, I even like that crazy hardbody I told you about, Belkin. He's got a kind of deep-core crumb of decency in him. Maybe I'm talking shit, I don't know. I've got this in-betweenness thing going on. I can walk away from my summer job any time. It lets me play at liking it."

"Go on, I love it."

"Zeke is another matter. The guy would use a death ray on blacks and Mexicans and me and Moslems if he could. I tried to be really obliging to all of them today, but they've obviously shut me out. Maybe they suspect what I am."

Talbot thought about the shooting in the mountains, and it brought back a kind of compacted loneliness he was feeling. "Alv, you deserve to know about this. The front end of all this is bad—on our hunting trip last weekend they shot a guy up in the mountains, or Zeke did. It was kind of a prank, one of those things that leaves your jaw hanging open when it goes bad. Any of your friends ever make you go cow-tipping out toward Liberty or playing mailbox baseball?"

"You were the adventurous brother."

"Adventurous," he scoffed. "I surely regret those dinner table shouting matches with dad. Like I had to lead the charge for a whole generation of sons."

Alvis brought out a paper basket of mushrooms and started slicing. "We know he was a good man, Tal, but he really wouldn't let himself be faced up to. He had so many self-protections. Neither of us would ever have had a bicycle if you hadn't stood up to him. 'Way too danger-

THE MISSING PEARLS 107

ous. Kids get brain damage every day.' Remember? We'd be wearing foam rubber suits without you. I think Vietnam really wrecked him."

"Wrecked a few million Vietnamese, too. *Alv!*" Talbot leapt to his feet.

Alvis froze at the cry and stared down with surprise at how close he'd come to chopping off some fingers. "Blow me down. I just about bit me on the see-gar." He set the knife down. "Remember that old fall-apart *Pogo* book dad had? I think it was Pogo who said, 'He who strikes the first blow loses the argument.' Then Albert wallops somebody really hard and runs away fast, shouting 'I lose, I lose!' I don't know why I thought of that. Gina hated Pogo."

"Don't you know Gina was off her rocker? Jeez, admit it to yourself."

"Who are you, the Grand Poobah?" Alvis was hiding his grief as always.

"Stop glaring to me," Talbot said. "We're all treading water in life the best we can. Now's the time, dude: tell me about the damn pearls. I'm certain now you know."

"You damn bushwhacker. You wait 'till I'm tipsy." It took a few moments for Alvis to seem to break through his last reserve. "Okay. Okay. Okay. I was playing dress-up with the damn string of pearls, Tal, and when dad came home early I hid them under my bed. I didn't get to sneak them back, and that weekend mom went on her big tantrum. I'd never seen her even frown before. I felt like I'd killed her. What could I do? I was eleven years old, for Chrissake. The folks were already in their tizz that you might be gay. When the necklace turned into such a big deal, I panicked and sneaked it outside and threw it down a gutter hard as I could. Mom's goddamn heirloom pearls are in the Missouri River silt, maybe all the way down to St. Loo. Can I please be forgiven? Now?"

Talbot started laughing, then stood up and bear-hugged his brother. So many years of recriminations and family rages. The terrible hovering mystery, all his teen-age years, complicating every other decision. All for an act by Alvis so innocent and frightened and tender.

"I guess all philosophy founders on a moment of childhood panic," Talbot suggested. "I love you a lot, man. I'll be here for you, whatever, about Gina. But I need you, too. I think I've got a shitstorm coming down with these summer soldiers."

* * * * *

VICTOR settled his back into the specially formed car seat. He felt rage against that American—a presumed brute—who had attacked Petro. His anger made no real sense, but it had swollen by incorporating all the hurts done to him and everyone weak. By all bullies, all petty bureaucrats, all lords and ladies. He would love nothing so much as joining an enraged crowd racing toward a manor house with torches and machetes. It was a time like *Notes from Underground*—the corrupt last days of the tsars. The people who cried out from their blood for justice. So many lost cripples and deformed and losers without hope, chickens and crybabies and befuddles, those left with half a nose. With the rich and cruel and arrogant beating all of us to serfs.

He had to hit out at someone, like the anarchists of 1905. He is sure that the past and the future communicate through the present—but only in a secret way, through your unconscious and behind your back. He might come back in the next life as an archduke. But now to see to a man with a big motorcycle who had injured his friend.

He could wait in the shade of a hedge and throw one of his bombs at the motorcycle. A human urge made him pause—it would be terrible to die that way and even to see it. But maybe a world-punisher like himself could go on a rampage and be excused.

Victor put the gasoline jars into a cloth gym-bag and stepped out of the van. He would watch close for the motorcycle man, keeping in shadows. He found a hedge that he could sink into, his ungainly hump pressing against a springy bough. He was almost comfortable. Finding a way to sit without pain had been such a constant issue—in movies, in school, in the doctor's waiting room. His servitude had been discomfort.

THE MISSING PEARLS

As he waited, he listened to the breathing of the city around him, different from other cities. Hoarse and dry and faraway, a whisper that issued from some deep cavern of thousands of machines. This city had marked him in new ways, made him even lonelier. And angrier—aware that his only future was novel forms of victimhood.

He would be avenging his neighbor, too—Ruslan the tiresome, though he could barely imagine the man's face. Ruslan, sorry, but I hardly knew you.

Hissing airliners in the sky unrolled their contrails, cars had no hurry, an old lady tugged a wire cart full of groceries and muttered.

Abruptly a dazzle of light shocked him alert. A voice bellowed, "Freeze! Move and you're dead!" He hadn't heard any police cars arrive.

Victor considered grabbing for one of the gasoline-bombs, but his eyes adjusted fast enough to see the barrel of a shotgun a few centimeters from his eyes. He realized he had no deep desire to do anything much about his predicament. I am who I am, and I am not James Bond. Don't hurt me.

"Mr. Small Man, interlock your fingers and place them on top of your head. If you don't spikka de English, God help you."

Victor could see now that the man wasn't in a police uniform.

"Yes, *boss*," Victor said. Americans always liked you to say 'boss.' He complied with everything the man demanded, abandoned his bag of weaponry and wedged out of the hedge to lie on the sidewalk and await his fate. The man held a short shotgun.

"A hunchback! You're one ugly little fucker. Who are you?"

"Victor Antonenkovich Gorbenko. Musketeer in Milady's service."

"A Russky! I could stomp your balls and be in my rights."

"Victor Antonenkovich—"

"Shut it." The man squatted and felt his pockets. "You're the guy that burned up my Suburban, aren't you? I should deal with you like a haji, but here in America we believe in the big picture. Don't move an inch."

Wailing police cars stopped nearby and shiny black shoes pounded into view. Victor didn't bother thinking about it. He would stick to the identification he'd offered. Even under torture he would never implicate Petro Ivanchuk.

* * * * *

"*CHERNYI—KRASNYI—BELYI—SERYI*," Sergei said, systematically indicating himself and each of the other three in his apartment. Mr. Black (himself), Mr. Red, Mr. White, Mr. Gray. They had all been *spetznaz alfas* and he was well aware of their birth names and their war *noms*, too. "No names, even if you have a fine new one you love."

"Mr. Black. I can't be Mr. Red. It's obvious why. I can be Zelyonyi." Mr. Green.

"No, Mr. Red. The plan is what it is. And lose that *telnyashka*." He was flaunting the horizontally striped blue-and-white undershirt of the Soviet navy, which had become a mark of honor for the special forces, too.

"Nobody in America recognizes this shirt, Mr. Black."

Sergei stared at the man for a long time, then he electrified the room by drawing a PSS silent pistol from a sling under his jacket and pressing the ungainly thing against the center of Mr. Red's forehead. "*Korosho*. You're out. Leave the room now, leave Los Angeles. *Bystro*."

The man didn't meet his eyes, but didn't seem to want to move.

"Are you deaf?"

"I hear you but it's unreasonable." A whiner, Sergei thought. He hadn't known him well in the service.

"You're finished here, Mr. Nothing," Sergei said. "If the bird's claw gets caught just once, the bird is lost."

"I'm sorry I didn't meet your expectations," the man said, the blunt nose of the small silenced pistol still hard against his forehead.

He walked straight out the door without looking back.

"Whatever a fool does, he does it wrong," Mr. White said.

Sergei turned to Mr. Gray, a small stringy man with dark deepset eyes, who was standing against the wall and hadn't said a word. He

THE MISSING PEARLS   111

never sat down. He had a scar across his eyebrow, a childhood incident that Sergei knew about. "Satisfied, Mr. Gray?"

"What falls off the cart is gone," Mr. Gray said. "We await what we need to know."

Sergei set a photograph of Zeke Tomlin on the coffee table between them, a grainy photo that showed off the man's scoop chin and puzzled expression. "This one is taken down already, and not by me. So beware, we have another actor in play. Here are the other targets." He slid Zeke's picture aside and then snapped down three others. "The job is not about money or doing the dirty work for unpleasant gangsters, as I told you. This one is for our honor as warriors. We're ronin now, are we not? We are highly trained samurai who have no master any longer, but we have our personal honor."

Another photo. "This is Charlie Becker, former US Marine. Trained as what they call recon, like us. This one is Arkady Belkin—yes, a countryman—but an ordinary jailbird from Vinnytsia and many other prisons, in for burglary, carjacking, and sodomy, etc. Odessa scum. And this is Talbot Denny, the odd man out. A college boy studying philosophy and a homosexual. He met the others at a summer job, and apparently they took him along on their hunting expedition. He probably did nothing. But we have to clear the table. We can't leave any eight-balls to accidentally scratch on."

Mr. Gray fingered the photograph of Charlie Becker and slid it toward himself on the table to stare hard, as if he could unlock the man's secrets with intense scrutiny.

"*Recon* Marine. *Da.* Pussies. *Ne tak strashen chort, kak ego malyuyut.*" The devil is never as scary as they paint him. "Mr. Recon goes first. Mr. White and I will take him."

NINE

A Tragic Clutter of Duty

Roski was drinking a latte and trying to clear his mind at 9 A.M. when his desk phone rang. Last night had been a glorkfest, as his ex-wife would say. He wondered if he was becoming an alcoholic, or just plain *was* an alcoholic.

"Roski," he answered.

"Morning, smoke-eater. You intellectual pervert. Just shutup and listen."

It was his old friend Len Mars at the LAPD Hollywood station, the ugly windowless box on Wilcox

"Last night we picked up a guy with a sack of gasoline bombs near your arson fire. Wait for it. He's a hunchback. Maybe a fucking orc from Mork. Hah! Too much, right? He only gives name, rank and serial number, but this guy ain't never had a rank and serial number. He says over and over that he's one of Milady's Musketeers, whatever the fuck. Grab a pen. The name is Victor Antonenkovich Gorbenko. Jesus, it's hard enough to remember *one* of these names."

"Hold on, hold on. Repeat." Mars spelled it for him.

"Thanks, Len. What more?"

"He had a beat-up rifle in his vehicle, fired recently and uncleaned. One of those crap war-one things that the gun shops sell assholes. The vehicle was a gimpvan, definitely his, the front seat curved back for his hump. They're questioning the guy now with no sleep, but he's not saying a damn thing. Gimps are loners. It's the extroverts that break down."

"If your guys are interested, the Milady stuff is from *The Three Musketeers*, by Alexandre Dumas. Want me to spell it?"

"Fuck you."

"What else you get from him?"

"You really want us to do all your work for you? We got his pocket phone book and there's a couple Russian names in it, and one of 'em's dead the night before, coincidentally, his face shot half off with a shotgun. Guy was shot through a pillow to keep the noise down. A pro? Want the name?"

"I want all the names. Can you fax me the book?"

"Man, why do any work at all? Just go play with your matches."

"It's too early for this shit, Len."

"I sense a hangover. I'm a bottomless pit of sympathy."

Roski didn't reply.

"Look for it in half an hour, Walt." He sighed. "The fax is *so* twentieth century."

* * * * *

MAEVE woke late, curled up against the substantial body of Bunny, noting that both of them were smelling of, well, both of them. Bunny was just stirring, too. They'd tested a teensy line of coke the night before and after the euphoria and the endless energetic track meet in bed, it had set them both down hard. Maeve could tell they were going to miss their morning classes, but she'd been skipping off and on for weeks. All but art, of course. Could she even go back now?

"My heart was thumping away last night," Bunny said. "You know, a lot of theater folk have trouble with tachycardia. I don't know if I want to try any more coke."

"I was buzzy, too. Is that like a panic attack?" Maeve rested a hand on Bunny's forehead and felt how warm she was.

A TRAGIC CLUTTER OF DUTY

"Popping an Inderal beta blocker right before curtain is a theater cliché. Right up there with never saying Macbeth inside the building."

"What's that?"

"I don't know where it started. It's supposed to be hideous luck to utter 'Macbeth' inside the theater except doing the play itself. Everybody just says 'the Scottish play.'"

"That's weird. I wonder if painters have superstitions like that. Can't use Prussian Blue before lunch. But painters aren't social enough for something like that."

Bunny rolled over and then lifted the sheet to kiss the big G tattooed on Maeve's breast. Maeve had told her the story of being forced to get the gang tattoo. "G is for gorgeous. You didn't tell me if you learned anything about Benjy yesterday."

"Sorry. Nothing new. My dad and this fireman are both working on it like crazy."

"It's upset me a lot, M. And, you know, to be real honest, I worry about Benjy, but a lot of the worry is really about me. The family always made me think it was my fault if I was unhappy. Mom was always, but always, pretending to be so cheerful when I *knew* she was on the verge of jumping off a tall building. Every generation, I bet the parents inflict come kind of pull-up-your-socks stuff on their kids. All the Puritan baggage. Be nice to your Aunt Vi, always think of others first—it accumulates around us like a tragic clutter of duty."

"Wow, is that Tennessee Williams?"

"It's just me."

Maeve leapt out of bed, grabbed a hairbrush and pushed Bunny around to work on her hair. "Here. No here."

"Ooh, that feels great."

"All through high school I was a nerd or a creep," Maeve said. "I felt like an outsider. I wasn't in the super in-group of girls. Weird, you know. There were only about twenty of them and three hundred of us."

"You weren't an in-girl? High school kids are soo stupid. But you *were* a smarty-pants."

116

BOYSTOWN

"And I didn't run with the jocks. I liked the smart guys. I wasn't into being L yet. But maybe, unbeknownst, it was happening."

Bunny chuckled. "It took a burning angel like you to jolt me over all the way."

Maeve grasped her and pressed against her back. "Bunny, I love you so much. Be happy now. Your theater world must be okay with the L word—there's so many gay men in it."

"But the guys into movies freak out. I think knowing you're into women takes away their permission to grope you."

"I'll issue you a passport for my private country," Maeve said.

* * * * *

T HE fax contained eight obviously Ukrainian or Russian names, retyped from the address book. He knew the police would never show him an original. Remarkably they'd already compiled short bios on the eight names and sent them along, too. The one who interested Roski the most was listed as a philosophy instructor at LA City College, plus: "noted butterfly collector." *Noted*, he thought. These days the noted celebrities were only famous for being famous. Cynicism would end up suffocating him in his own morbidity. Still, something in the man's bio resonated.

A heavyset man answered the door an hour later.

"Mr. Pogorelets?"

"Close enough."

"I'd really like to get your name right."

The man pronounced it slowly. "Don't bother, it's hard. The English language has only two levels of stress and most vowels reduce to the same unstressed 'uh.' We have two levels of vowel reduction."

"My name is *Wal*-ter *Ros*-ki, and all the stress is in my psyche."

The Russian smiled.

Roski explained that he was from the county fire department, investigating an arson. He noted it didn't seem to make the man nervous.

"Please come in, Mr. Roski. Were your ancestors from Russia?"

A TRAGIC CLUTTER OF DUTY 117

"Generations back we were Croatian, I believe. I'm an American mongrel. I like it that way. Hybrid vigor."

"Yes, good, but you know there is no evidence for hybrid vigor in mammals."

Oh dear, a literalist. Roski saw that the man limped as he moved away from the door, favoring his left leg.

"Have you hurt yourself?"

"A muscle pull. Would you like tea, Mr. Roski? The samovar is always going."

"No, thank you. Please don't stir yourself."

"Ignore my leg. Somebody somewhere is always pulling a muscle."

Roski sat on the nearest armchair which audibly poofed like a whoopee cushion.

"Would you prefer something stronger? A beer?"

"I'm fine. Please have what you like and sit with me."

"Of course." The big man settled directly on the end of the sofa and winced.

"Do you know a man named Victor Antonenkovich Gorbenko? He has a back deformity. Kyphosis, a hump."

"No."

Roski hadn't seen the fidget of a lie, nor was there a too-fulsome answer. "Do you know why your name was in his address book? He underlined *professor*."

"I'm not really a professor here, Mr. Roski, though I had a chair at the National University of Ukraine. I am at the bottom of your hierarchies—an adjunct instructor not on tenure track. I have had to teach many night classes in English to get that far. I'm very free with my telephone number if students need help. You'd think I'd remember a deformed man named Gorbenko, but I don't. I'll happily give you access to my class lists."

They went around the name Gorbenko again but got nowhere, and Roski didn't warn him that he was going to have to do it all again quite soon with the LAPD. "Do the Three Musketeers mean anything special to you?"

"Dumas, of course. We've always had an affinity for French culture and Dumas in particular. But in Soviet times we were forced to swallow our own crass romantic hero, Vasily Chapayev—the Red Army superman of the revolution. We have comic books and movies and games based on him, like your Davy Crockett maybe."

Roski wondered why the man was trying so hard to distract him with side-lying facts. Was it just a pompous streak? *Two levels of stress-reduction.* Like I give a shit. He pressed the issue of the Musketeers again, mainly so he could feel he'd done his duty, but he got nowhere.

Roski's evil twin within wanted to find a chink in the armor of this well-defended ego. Everybody from the former Soviet Union he'd ever questioned had been very practiced in fending off interrogation.

The look of the man's house didn't offer him much, a bland innocuous public face, ornate furniture chosen very well from thrift stores, the kind many Americans skipped over because it didn't suggest "modern." The frame house, maybe 1930s, had built-in glassfront bookcases. The few titles he could see were in Cyrillic. A few nondescript lithographs. There was a single mounted blue butterfly behind the man's head.

"I see you like butterflies."

"I don't want to talk any further until you tell me what your visit is about, Mr. *Ros*-ki."

Roski thought about it. Len Mars wouldn't like him giving anything away, but he could lump it. "Sir, one old man is dead, shot to death in bed. A car was burned to the ground with a Molotov Cocktail. There was another man killed by a gunshot through a window nearby." Roski wondered if it could all be mongrel Americans versus Russians or Ukrainians? Hatfields vs. McCoyskys?

"I know America seems a violent place, sir. But this isn't the usual and your name has come up. What do you think?"

The man ruminated. "May I speak from the heart?"

"That would be remarkable."

"Do you know what it's like to be in exile, having lost everything you've struggled for?" It wasn't really a question. "Some days I want

A TRAGIC CLUTTER OF DUTY

119

to tear off the stickers that other people slap all over me. Ukrainian. Russian. Jew. Exile. Foreigner. My own stickers say butterfly-lover, paradox-lover, teacher of ideas. Lover of paprika! I was a distinguished professor in Kiev, with many published books on the German philosophers. When I can, I still go to conferences. When I go it's like a track meet with *Ukraine* written in parentheses after my name. I give my talk, and I hear a voice on the Tannoy: 'Pogorelets, Ukraine, last place, thank you for coming.' Last year in Prague an old colleague showed he resented me for getting away to an American college. Ha. 'You sell Ukraine to America,' he said. 'Like a little spy kissing the butt of his new masters.'

"'Why would America spy on Ukraine?' I shouted. 'You have wheat, they have more wheat, more walnuts, more corn.' I told them selling information about Ukraine was like selling used Air Albania tickets. Mr. Roski, in exile, your true personality fades out, day by day. I'm unwanted everywhere. My colleagues wish me to die and disappear, but I won't."

"Professor," Roski said and pointed, "the muscle pull in your leg is starting to bleed badly." A deep red stain was spreading down his immaculate trousers.

"This needs tending."

Human feeling won out. "Take it easier on yourself, professor. I'll see myself out."

The man didn't say if he would or wouldn't take it easier on himself. Roski looked over the house as he left. Shabby chic, clapboard siding, burglar bars all around as usual for the area, an ample second story with barred windows there, too. He wondered if he could afford it.

* * * * *

J ACK Liffey noticed that Yana's dingy apartment building had a name—*Crapi Apartments* in big metal letters across the stucco. Either a goof for Capri or a sly gesture of contempt toward the tenants.

Nobody answered when he pushed her button at the garage gate.

120   *BOYSTOWN*

He waited and slid in behind a beige 1962 Mercury Comet. A venerable hulk, he thought, as he watched the big rectangular vehicle recede. Hulk. Bulk. Sulk. *Stop!*

A sad little swimming pool sat in the middle of the cement courtyard, surrounded by loungers with sagging plastic straps. The grounds crew must have gone AWOL. Paper plates and plastic cups were strewn everywhere. Yana Slutsky lay reading on one of the loungers. She wore a startlingly tiny blue bikini that nearly made him turn on his heel and flee. The skinny woman was such a pale blonde that he wondered if in some lights you might see through her.

"Excuse me, Yana. Jack Liffey." He sat down gingerly on the edge of a creaking chaise.

"I remember. You're that sweet man who liked my froggy."

She scootched herself up in the lounge and he glanced away hastily for a moment. There was so little to fill the top that one cup yawned open.

"I assume—you haven't heard—from Benjy," he said, when he could look back.

Her hand was pressing the bikini top shut, so she had registered the moment. "You haven't either?"

He tried to read the title of her book as she set it down but couldn't. "No. Let me ask you. Are you willing—to talk some more about Benjy."

"How about you calm down first? Maybe you can talk in whole sentences. Nothing to see here, move along." She tugged down her bikini top for a moment to display almost a boy's chest with tiny dark brown nipples.

He looked away again. Amazing how a boy's chest on a woman was still enticing.

"I'll tell you anything at all," she said. "I like your company."

"You told him to check Plummer Park to talk to some exiles. You're Russian—Ukrainian. I guess we're all aware of the distinction these days. Can you tell me about the community."

"My folks came here in the big exodus in the 1980s. For a Jew to leave before the collapse of socialism, you had to tell the bureaucrats

A TRAGIC CLUTTER OF DUTY 121

you were going to Israel—the *aliyah*. I guess that means the return. They spent about ten minutes in Israel. My folks hated all religion. Pretty common in the Soviet Union.

"I was either conceived in Odessa before they left or in transit. My dad had a brother in America who sponsored him and helped him for years with the Ukraina Mart on Fountain. I went to Bancroft Middle School and Fairfax High with a lot of the other new Americans. I speak a little Ukrainian brokenly. You don't absorb it from the womb."

He told her he wanted to try some names on her, and read the list Roski had shared over the phone, but none of the names registered, either consciously or not, as far as he could determine.

She touched his knee softly, an electrifying touch. "Mr. Liffey. You're in trouble, aren't you?"

"I don't think so."

"I beg to differ." Her voice shifted register. "This crappy courtyard is depressing and I'm going upstairs to have a drink. I think you told me you don't drink, but you can have tea or Diet Coke or some middle-grade dope if you want. Please join me. I want you to explain a video I just saw about Jean Baudrillard."

His insides were in turmoil for a lot of reasons, but he followed her docilely up the pebbled cement steps. He certainly hoped she was joking about Baudrillard or any other post-modern philosopher, but he had more questions.

* * * * *

TALBOT was asleep on the sofa, sent off by Hegel's *Philosophy of Right*, when the doorbell sounded. He woke up immediately and slapped his cheek, then hurried to open the door to pretend to himself he hadn't snoozed away an entire evening. Alvis leaned into the room from his studio.

"Are you sick, man, or was your call bogus?" Charlie Beck snapped from the porch without prologue. It was so rude and abrupt Talbot didn't know what to say. The scraggly Belkin stood behind Beck, looking amused as usual and they came right in.

"Gentlemen, come in."

"Don't call us that. You just like the way it sounds in your frat boy mouth. And you—!" Beck pointed at Alvis. "You come in here, too. Is anybody else here?"

Talbot saw they were armed, Beck with a big square pistol that glinted from a holster in his armpit, and Belkin with an untucked shirt and a lump in his waistband.

"This is my house." Alvis probably hadn't seen the guns, and Talbot hoped he didn't bristle.

"Shutup for now. Sit *there*. We'll deal with you later. Talbot, you called in sick two days running and we need to know why, what the fuck's going down."

"Sorry if I'm truant. I don't like the summer job much. I'm way over my head working with electronics, and I'm probably going to quit soon. Is that sufficient or are you going to shoot me?"

Belkin laughed and Charlie Beck gave him an angry frown and turned back to Talbot.

"Don't go self-righteous. People tried to kill both me and him. They burned up my Suburban and they put three rounds into Belkin's bed. Luckily he happened to be having a midnight hot bath or some Russian shit."

"Bathhouse is our culture. Don't dump on it."

"This has to be because of the butterfly man," Talbot said.

"Bet. Whatever Zeke stirred up, they're going to write you into the story, too, don't doubt it. They ain't making no exceptions for big IQs and good intentions." Beck looked around and seemed to settle into himself for a moment.

Alvis stirred, but Beck stilled him with a fierce finger, then came back at Talbot.

"Zeke is dead, kiddo. That big dumb Cletis was shot in the face right in front of his wife. We know it should be over with that, but it ain't. Somebody is tracking me. I bet they don't know shit about the hunt except the four of us were there and they're going to want all of us to cry."

A TRAGIC CLUTTER OF DUTY

"Holy Jesus."

"I'd like you to leave now," Alvis announced. "I don't know what you're talking about and I don't care. I'll vouch for me and my brother. We're from the heartland and we don't snitch, if that's what worries you."

"That's super duper, Heartland. We'll get to you. Talbot, man, has anybody hit you with *any* of this? Cops, phone breathers, guys with funny accents?"

"Only you two."

"Don't be no wiseass. This ain't no game. I assure you we're on top of our survival and that's going to include you, like it or not." He walked forward three paces and pressed his index finger against Talbot's forehead. "This is where the metal goes, right into the brain bucket. Just think of it as watching the rest of your life with the sound turned off.

"Now *you*." He turned to Alvis. "Has anybody contacted you about your fancy brother?"

Talbot could see his brother working himself up to a retort. He tried to send Alvis a fierce *don't* look.

"Nobody's contacted me. I'd like you guys to leave my house now."

"Mellow down, son," Beck said. "Your brother's life is in danger."

"You want me mellow so bad, shoot me."

No guns had come out but Talbot was terrified.

Belkin displayed his acid grin. "I challenge you all to a hundred push-ups."

* * * * *

"MR. Gray, your report?"

"I learned where the man goes and when, but he's spooked and he's staying away from home. There was no clear opportunity. You can't kill Yeltsin when he's inside a bank vault."

"Blow up the whole bank. I think you two need help." Sergei had never tolerated excuses.

"We don't need it or want it, Mr. Black."

"Mr. White, Mr. Gray, hit the Marine now."

Mr. White was almost as furious as Mr. Black—Sergei. "I accept your leadership, but I remind you that I was in charge at Buynaksk. We stopped the Arab terrorists from murdering the hostages from the 136th Motor Rifles. It was planning that stopped *Ibn al-Khattab*, not reckless action."

"If this American is too much for you, just indicate by nodding," Sergei said, his hand flat to the silent pistol under his jacket.

"Don't overdo it, Mr. Black. I served with valor. I will not stand for the heave-ho like Mr. Red. We will terminate this Recon Marine."

"Good," Sergei said.

Mr. White was not mollified. "And the innocent one?"

"I take him—no problem. No mid-course *Sputnik* corrections."

They had a stare-down for a while.

"I've heard," Mr. Black said, "that the American troops from Vietnam and Iraq were unhappy when they got home and nobody said, 'Thank you,' and 'Welcome home.' As we know, they have no clue about the depths of betrayal that's possible. A whole country collapsed while we were fighting for it. Is a country important? I no longer know."

"As you say, honor is all," Mr. White said.

"You are held in much respect by all, Mr. White," Sergei allowed. "Let's cut off the head of the snake and then we can see about the body."

"*Da*. Mr. Gray—you and me, we'll find this American Marine and finish off the head without doubt. I'm not sure the Belkin from our prisons is any normal snake body. Something about men like him worries me."

"Leave him to me," Sergei said. "The marine is now, college kid is for anytime."

* * * * *

"CAN you tell me why symbols of death undermine the capitalist economic exchange?" Yana asked after making him watch a bit of lecture on her laptop. She wasn't the least interested in an answer which helped.

A TRAGIC CLUTTER OF DUTY 125

"I don't have a clue." His eye caught on the book she'd set aside. "How are you—liking *Dalva*?"

"I think I like it, but I'm not sure she's convincing. She's a bit like a tough man in a woman's skin. But maybe I'm like that, too. Sex roles are *so* culturally determined."

"Up to a point," Jack Liffey said. "I've always had a hard time—getting pregnant."

She smiled. "Please relax into speaking in full sentences. You have no worries here at all, Jack. You are welcome to stay with me tonight or not. You'll find the world a lot less repressed about sex these days."

"It's still perplexing to me."

She smiled and headed down a hallway. "I'm going to make myself comfortable," she said. "I'll come to the Casbah very soon and have a stiff drink. There's two blunts in that ceramic box if you want to light up."

He did, but he didn't. So, ride your asceticism until the wheels fall off, he thought. He picked up *Dalva* and it fell open to a passage she'd marked.

I have never met a girl who made everyone she met feel more strongly that they liked to live, a fuzzy notion but true.

He wanted to live. But what on earth was he doing in this apartment? She was young and obviously willing. Gloria hadn't let him touch her in six months now. Was that all it was? His mind tried to come up with further questions to ask her about Benjy, but there really weren't any. Fuck you, guilt. Go away. I haven't done a thing here.

Luckily her comfortable only meant a tie-die T-shirt and sweatpants, not a transparent peignoir. It would be pretty easy to take off though. Stop it, Jack.

"I'm a Scotch man," she announced. "Single malts. No ice. That signifies I'm a tough broad, right? If you're still Mr. AA, I'll get you a Diet Coke."

"Sure, thanks."

At the portal to the kitchen, she turned back. "My college girl-friends used to laugh at how the guys always pushed drinks on us at parties. In their heads it was to loosen us up, but we all knew it was to work up their own courage. I wonder if that's what I'm doing." She laughed and went to the fridge.

He sat frozen, his deep alarm system making a horrible racket. Leave this place now, or don't blame the fates.

"Am I so intimidating you have to fortify your courage to seduce me?" he called out.

"Is the Pope a duck?" she called back. "Is a Catholic barefoot? Oh, dear, I got that really wrong."

Chuckling, she handed him a can of some generic cola and sat too near him. "Sure you're intimidating, Jack. You're old but you're tall, dark, handsome, fatherly, funny, and really in need of saving. You're smart and decent at heart. And you radiate bottomless horniness. Name me one more trait aimed straight at a girl's heart, just one, and I'll melt into a puddle of butter, I swear to god."

Time to run, Jack. "I have a swollen prostate."

She laughed hysterically for a few moments and then swilled a long drink. The peaty smell took him back a long ways. He'd been a Scotch man, too.

"Those frat guys with all the party alcohol, they didn't seem to know the girls wanted it more than they did," she said. "I know your generation was hung up about sex, but we're not. We're just not. It's a great release and it's fun. It's human contact. It's affection. What could be better? No guilt, no claims."

"And in my case, you get an unusual bonus," she said after a pause, and then cross-armed the T-shirt off grinning like mad. "As you know, I've got almost no breasts at all. So if you've got any latent gay in there, Mr. Butch Jack, you get to pretend I'm a boy."

TEN

Deep in the Funhouse

THE West Hollywood sheriff's office called Roski at eleven at night from the scene of the arson that they knew he was working. He headed straight to his car. If somebody had chalk-outlined the Suburban arson-scorch on the concrete, the two stiffly posed bodies would be pretty much in the exact center. Two dead tenpins, a hell of a message to somebody, Roski thought.

One was a bloody mess, missing a hand and foot, though there was no blood on the parking apron. Killed and brought here. They were aging males, no facial hair, not particularly foreign-looking, but something seemed amiss—other than unnatural death, of course. They were maybe too nondescript, including their clothing. Like men trying to go unnoticed.

"No IDs of course," the shift sergeant said. "But if this doesn't relate to your arson, I'll jump on Roseanne Barr."

"Spare me, Sergeant. Large loud women have their own charms. Has anybody talked to the residents?" He nodded to indicate the structure above them.

"Give us some credit. Nobody is home in the apartment that pertains, but the super is on his way. Anyway, it's a known fact that fat women are a sloppy fuck."

Roski gave the man the evil eye. "Never defend a bad joke, man. It just makes you seem defective. Who found these two?"

"You got any info to trade?"

Roski decided to give up on the deputy: he'd only know the obvious, anyway. "Sure. A day without sunshine is just like night." Roski walked away and knelt to look at the bodies, without touching anything.

He could see that the clothes were from Walmart or similar but the muscles weren't. These were men who'd needed and maybe used muscle once, and they'd gone to some trouble to keep themselves fit. The sheriff's crime lab might find out more, but somehow he doubted it. Something was really off base.

Being quick and careful, Roski got away with reaching out to brush the shorter man's eyebrow. Sure enough, he had a small scar across it so old that it was almost glacially healed, like a childhood scar.

Roski glanced around, and saw the deputy-sergeant had gone to bully some bystanders. He pried a shirt collar back and tugged in one quick movement. Sure enough the label had been removed. That gave him a chill. Nobody did that but spooks or some other kind of pro—a hitman, or in his own bailiwick, a hired torcher. He didn't like it at all, and he began to worry about the Liffeys, who might be up against something a lot more coldblooded than they knew.

A uniformed sheriff's deputy wandered up to him. "Sir, who are you, please?"

He showed his badge. "Walter Roski, County Arson. This was my crime scene three days ago. Obviously somebody's kicked that idea into the gutter."

"I understand. Please forgive Deputy McLaren, sir. He's a bit un-tucked today. If you give me your business card, I'll make sure you stay in the loop."

Roski handed him his card. "Your name is?"

"Rowell Davies. Not row-ool. R-O-W-E-L-L. It's Welsh. I think these two stiffs are Ukrainians or Russians, if it helps. Not a stunner in WeHo. I'll be in touch."

"Thank you, Deputy. I won't forget the professional courtesy."

DEEP IN THE FUNHOUSE 129

* * * * *

As the first gray light penetrated the room, Belkin emerged from his hideaway in the kitchen nook and began his normal wake-ups, largely meant for stretching and flexing, with a few yoga asanas thrown in—*king pigeon* and *wild thing*. Between finding his bed shot up the night before and his adventures with Beck last night, he'd had a wild ride. And he hadn't seen Cat in a while. When he thought about her in danger, his anxieties tended to swing way up into the top branches like spooked monkeys.

Charlie Beck had shown himself a lot more hotheaded than he'd realized. Belkin had seen a whole lot of rough stuff over his years, but he'd never seen a man let body parts be shot off him as he was being questioned, without a word. He wondered if Charlie had done that in Iraq. *Ohuyet!*

After five years of boredom in dead-end jobs in America, this mess had blasted him right out of his screw-it-all doldrums. In an earlier lifetime he'd helped rob a rural bank in Moldova and raced away on dirt tracks with bullets flying both ways. And he'd been arrested and questioned none too gently many times in Kiev and Odessa.

But Beck's interrogation was something else. The taller of the two men they'd surprised lying in wait had been a hard case for sure, not a word as his foot went away, just through-and-through defiance.

The scratching noise at the door froze his morning routine. Cat never came to visit in the morning. She prowled at night and slept the morning, always.

He tugged on sweatpants and opened to Cat, who was wide-eyed with fright. "What's wrong?" He tried to tug her in for her own safety but she was surprisingly resistant, so he sat down in the doorway as he usually did. "What is it, Cat? You look so *rastroena*. I mean—I don't know—*worried*."

She made a fierce face and he beckoned her again to sit. She finally did but shook off his attempt to stroke her dreadlocks.

"Ack. Man. A man," she squeezed out.

"It's okay, Cat. I'm here."

She shook her head hard. "Man. *Man!*"

He was pretty sure she was trying to warn him about a particular man. Just to be safe he went to the freezer and retrieved the pistol Charlie had given him. Her dark eyes followed the pistol back to the threshold as if it were a dangerous cobra. "Can you act it out?" he said.

There was a swelling of traffic noise that made her quail a little, but she nodded. She went out into the yard, gave one longing glance toward her refuge crawl-space, then went to his side window. He looked around and came close to guard her. "*Man.*" She peered wide-eyed into the bedroom window in an exaggeration of a man looking in.

"I had a peeper. What else?" He knew. The scorch-holes in his bed had kept him in a sleeping bag under the kitchen bench.

Cat asked in gestures to hold the pistol. He didn't think twice about trusting her. She aimed the pistol in the window and said "Poom, poom, poom." Luckily the covers had been rumpled enough to suggest a sleeper while he was at the bathhouse.

But she wasn't finished. She slapped herself in the chest several times before pointing the gun at herself. "*Cheee!*" She jumped in the air and mimed running away. He wondered if she'd tried to drive off the shooter to protect him.

Beck had taken two down but there was at least one more out there. Her devotion to him was overwhelming. Never in his life. What an amazing creature.

"Cat, I understand you. A bad man, a terrible man. Thank you from my heart. I will protect you, too."

She made a kind of grimace, maybe a stab at a smile. "Ack!"

"*Korosho.* You're a good girl. Can you come with me now to a safe place? Nobody will touch you."

She stared at him for a while, maybe considering, but finally shook her head hard. He knew there was no moving her and no time to waste. Mr. Peeper Man might be back at any moment. "Cat. This was a very bad man. Do you have a safe place to go for a while? Not here."

She nodded.

"Do you need a shower? I can wait outside."

DEEP IN THE FUNHOUSE 131

She shook her head, and patted herself in a way that demonstrated the limits of mime. What was it—I have no bedbugs?

"You can't stay here. Go to your other safe place. I have a safe place, too. When it's okay to come back, I'll move that big black rock next to the gate. Do you understand? Look for the rock. I won't leave you."

"Want," she said clearly.

* * * * *

JACK Liffey woke with the morning light leaking around Venetian blinds. In a moment or two, a blast of body electricity informed him that he wasn't at home. Oh, shit! This was going to be ugly, no matter what. He'd spent the whole night away from home, which hadn't happened since his time in intensive care.

Yana lay in a fetal clench on the mattress, talking now and then in her sleep, sometimes coherently. "Oh, priceless," or something like it. He pressed his knee gently against her firm buttocks to turn her face-down which seemed to stop her talking. Sleep-secrets were too intimate for a first date. He nearly laughed at the thought, but was too upset at himself.

Her body had indeed been like a boy's, but just as disturbing was his straying to a wayward previous life. The return of portable ethics. It wasn't that he hadn't had an affair or two, but he'd figured he was past all that now. His carefully constructed self-image was based on narrow bounds of decency, honor, kindness, concern, and loyalty to Gloria. He'd thought his new character would last him the rest of his allotted span. Right now he was doing his best to push away any vulgar satisfaction in bedding a lively young woman. Oh, Jack, Jack!

On the nightstand a little plastic robot with a clock in its belly stamped its metal feet in impotent fury until her slender arm snaked out and slapped the goofy thing down.

"School day, Yana," she mumbled to herself.

"Don't freak out," Jack Liffey said softly. "You have company."

"Mmmm. So it seems." She turned over and nuzzled against him. "No three A.M. man flit. Means I must have worn you out. Or maybe you even like me."

The pathos hit him hard. He'd already found out that Yana, despite the super-tough pose, had inner vaults of stored up humiliations. Don't we all?

"Yana, you're a lovely young woman with a lot of brain and energy and tenderness to offer some worthy young man."

"But no boobs to play with."

"Allow me to apologize for the fetishes of my gender. I hear Italian men adore big bottoms, and the French like legs, and for all I know German men like elbows. American men are mad for silicone boobs, obviously still longing to be breast-fed."

All at once, he noticed that she was gaping at him. "*What?* Do I look funny?"

"Did you listen to yourself, Jack?"

"Ohmigod." He realized he'd just got out several longish complete sentences, without puns or rhymes or lyrics. This was horrible. He not only had to account for a missing night, but how that night had blasted him back into his groove. Maybe he'd better go on with some pretend Asperger's for a while. Once before a guilty sexual encounter had jolted him out of a funk and he didn't want to think that was his deepest nature.

He rested his palm on Yana's warm cheek. "Last night's disorderly sex was delicious, Yana, and I'm going to be eternally grateful. I remember every affectionate moment with you. You're my heroine."

She smiled. "Thank you, Jack. You don't owe me a thing, but I like you a lot, too."

"If I were young and fearless—no, forget that. I'm old and *not*. But I'd be honored to stay your friend."

"Great, Jack. I have to get somewhere. If you need first shower, go."

"I have but recrimination awaiting me. You first."

He kissed her forehead, probably too aloof. In the heat of lovemaking, he'd toyed with what it would be like to run off with this

DEEP IN THE FUNHOUSE

child-woman—like a brief illusory reprieve from declining age—but the daydream fled. Supplanted in fact by a wave of genuine affection for her. And, of course, a mix of love and terror concerning Gloria. What a species we are, he thought, as she climbed out of bed in front of him, nude and boyish and nimble. Why do I deserve any peace at all in this mess I keep creating? Deep in the funhouse I have real ghosts.

* * * * *

"THOSE two you caught wasn't the bottom of it," Belkin said. He sat beside his little satchel on the old sofa in Charlie Beck's man-cave.

"I figured. The tall one wasn't no superman. The way we snuck on them wasn't some Apache wonder."

Man, you never had to live as an underman, Belkin thought. "You don't speak Russian, Beck. As you was killing him by pieces, he was telling the other guy to keep his mouth shut up tight."

"Wake up, Russky. It's a really hard rain outside. I see I like it hard, it keeps me sharp. They may not have been top of the league, but these guys acted like pros."

"Man. I worked with a lot of small-timers at home. The goofs your TV shows call the Russian Mafia. *Meh*. They're nothing special—not organized like the Dagos. More like kids on the street looking for loose hubcaps, selling a little crank. I'm talking about myself here. We had to deal with cops that hit you a lot, sure, but nobody I ran into got steel eyes on them like those guys last night. I'd guess they're *Spetsnaz*. Special Forces to you. We got a World War III waiting out there and you best call in any dirty dozen you got."

"I work alone." Beck got up and turned on both water taps in the little sink. "Covers sound," he explained. "You never know. I'll tell you this just once, Belkin. Pay attention. My war was always private. I'd picture those twin towers going down then paint up my face with camo and slip out of the firebase late at night, and I'd tiptoe into some sandbox village for payback. Any house with a weapon in it, I used the bad knife or the wire. I think I took out every *haji* in our area. I never took a dinar. Honor has its own honor."

Belkin didn't know what to say. He'd have taken a whole lot of dinars, happily, but would never have killed a guy with a garrote. Holy St. Andrew. He needed a little taste of crank, but he was all out. "What now, boss? You caught those two flat-footed. We know there's gotta be at least one more guy, and I bet he's sharper. He might be at the window now."

Charlie grinned. "You scared?"

"Man, you're *not*?"

"I read in *Parade* that sixteen years was the average lifespan for a caveman. Already we kicked those odds in the balls. And speaking of odds." There was a smallish whiteboard on the wall. Charlie Beck stood up and wrote *Standings* on top of it with a red felt pen, then drew a midline down.

Belkin watched the messy, jerky handwriting, like a child's. Oh, I'm really fucked with this goof, he thought. I got to start looking out for number one. And Cat.

The felt pen squawked like a parrot as Charlie Beck filled out the left side:

Good Guys
1
Zeke Offed

And then with a flourish he went to the right side:

Bad Guys
3
Humpback in jail
Tall guy Offed
Short guy Offed

DEEP IN THE FUNHOUSE

"Maybe they got one more troopie, and maybe the butterfly man himself. On our side, there's you and me. Forget Talbot, he's a discard. I'm worth ten of their best warrior assholes. So we still got eleven to one."

"The *one* was Zeke, man. A messy Joe for sure, but we ate lunch with him."

Charlie Beck shrugged. "Deal with it. Everybody's got to cry. Are you with the program? Anything you need to talk to me about?"

What could he say? "I'm with you, boss. I'd be happy to take down the guy who shot up my bedroom." Belkin would not add that the man terrified Cat. He would keep her out of it.

"Yeah. The wild card. We'll get him."

* * * * *

JACK Liffey didn't notice Maeve sitting in her little Echo down the block waiting at the turn, and she honked twice and nearly had to ram his pickup to get him to stop before he got to the house. *Now* what? he thought. He parked and walked to her car as a red sun was coming up over Greenwood Park where the gangbangers used to hang out. Yeah, and Maeve.

"What's up?"

"It's always nice to see you, too, dad. Good morning."

"Good morning, etcetera. I bet I'm in big trouble."

"You might say that. Climb in."

She drove them to a little to-go bakery nearby called *El Jato's* that had passable coffee and a plastic table in a corner that no one ever used. He picked out one of the hard Mexican sweetbreads that he thought he might tolerate.

"Your eyes look awful, dad."

"You should see them from inside. but enough about me."

She gaped, just as Yana had. "Dad, you just emitted, like, a whole coherent sentence. And I didn't have to hear the title of that Lee Marvin movie you're quoting."

"So why did you shortstop me?"

"Gloria called me about three A.M., in a tizz. I don't usually answer the phone in mid siesta, but I did. Basically because my intimate family is so given to domestic tragedies. I want to try one of those."

"Have the rest of this one." He pushed the sweetbread across. "It's like a three-year-old doughnut."

After a bite, she made a face and pushed it back. "That one's called a *novita*," she told him. "When she called me, Gloria asked if you were sleeping at my place." Her eyes were accusing.

"And you told her what?"

She sighed. "I said I had a bed-mate in the studio, which I did, but I thought you might be on the sofa in the main house and I'd let her know when I could."

"Wow. You actually lied for me."

"I guess I did. I thought I'd better leave all options open. Even if my poor dad was off messing up again. I've learned that we're all imperfect, even me."

"Bless."

The bell on the bakery door rattled and a group of day-laborers in work clothes came in and bought bags of tamales and some whitish liquid in bottles. The bottles were handed surreptitiously over the counter. Most of the men were quiet and dour, but one had a merry laugh up in a high register as they left.

"What's in the bottles?" he asked.

"*Pulque*," she said. "Fermented century plant. It's rough and hasn't been distilled like mescal or tequila. Those men were *Indios*. They weren't speaking Spanish. The guys I knew wouldn't touch *pulque*. They felt it was from way in the boonies."

He grimaced. He didn't particularly want to know any more than he already did about her year of living gangbangerly. She had survived it pretty well, and from her buoyancy you might think she had a completely untroubled past, except after she came out of that time she was never at rest, always very alert.

"Dad, what's going on with you? Did you have that trouble with your zipper again?"

DEEP IN THE FUNHOUSE 137

He managed a pained smile, and she rolled her eyes. That ought to be enough to get over, he thought, but it wouldn't be. Nor would it help to bat his eyes with a goofy grin. "There's a young naughty librarian who's involved in this mess because she knew Benjy. She's a good kid. Loneliness gets heavy for anyone." So who was he referring to?

"Golly, tell me about it."

"Don't be mean, hon. I've been through a whole cocktail of emotions. It would have been really cruel to skip out on her before dawn."

"Dad, you live like you're still twenty-five. What are we going to tell Gloria?"

"I guess that's the sixty-four dollar question."

She sighed. "Oh, Dad-o-mine. We're quite a pair, aren't we?"

He found her reactions oddly stylized, but less judgmental than usual. He was hardly in a position to complain.

"I don't know if it helps," he said, "but I actually felt and still feel real tenderness for the girl. Woman—she's probably thirty. Her name is Yana, the one I mentioned, the brief girlfriend of gay Benjy. I'm sure I did a little better at things than he did." He didn't mention her boyish looks. "On the positive side, I didn't drink and she was swilling a good Scotch, I didn't smoke her dope, I didn't do anything kinky."

A ripple of something like annoyance crossed Maeve's face. "Dad! *Kinky?*"

"Okay, hurtful. Cruel or destructive. I'm not pathological, just weak-willed."

Maeve finally smiled. "Oh, dad. The main problem with the truth, as I've found out to my shame, is timing. I don't want to tell Gloria something today that you're going to cave in on tomorrow, okay? I love Gloria and I don't want to be seen as a Quisling to womankind."

"*Quisling*, wow. Your history class is pretty good."

"Don't change the subject. What story are you going to cling to, or are you going to break down and spill all and risk nuclear war? Gloria was pretty upset."

He noticed that somebody in the back of the panaderia was actually playing classical music, maybe Bach, not *mariachi* or *banda* or *norteño*.

138   BOYSTOWN

Stereotypes were being violated everywhere—it's what made life worth-
while. Yes, he was avoiding.

He could feel the stiffness of his own smile. An insoluble dilemma,
really. Luckily, he thought, we get to go around a second time in life
and we'll know how to get it right next time. No, sir, you *do* not. He felt
a little light-headed with lack of sleep.

"I'll cover your ass to the death, hon," he said. "I guess I shouldn't
say 'ass' to my daughter. Tell Gloria one of your friends saw me at your
place, and I'll insist I was indeed there for a while. Under tortures. I'll
break down at some point."

"That's too damn clever. How many times have you finagled me
like that, dad?"

The heavyset clerk came out of the back room did a tiny stut-
ter-step and waited in neutral at the cash register, humming gently.

"You'd know my lies by now. The only real advantage to the truth
is you don't have to remember anything."

* * * * *

"So, bubba, you still into crazy philosophy and shit?" Len Mars
said from the fancy Aeron chair behind his desk.

"Mostly shit," Roski said.

The cop smiled, but his eyes didn't. He had a back office in the
Hollywood Division LAPD building with a beautiful view of absolutely
nothing. He'd put on quite a few pounds, but that was par for police sergeants. They just wouldn't look like police sergeants if they were slim.

"I caught the case on your murders," Mars said in his lifeless voice.
"For now anyway. Downtown will take it away if it looks good for pub-
licity and promotions. This thing is either connected to your arson or
somebody is trying damn hard to make it look that way."

With nowhere to sit, Roski tipped a chair forward harshly so a foot
of papers balanced on it sprayed to the floor, then he sat. Mars pretended not to care. The place was a deliberate mess, like a Freshman
drunk's dorm room. Apparently Mars' captain wasn't a neat-freak, and

DEEP IN THE FUNHOUSE 139

Mars was sinking into aging-cop bitterness. A bad place to go in any world. "What do I get to know?" Roski asked.

"The Mouseketeer hunchback claims he ain't never seen the dead guys. Funny—them all being Russkies. He took a good look at the mugs and didn't flinch. But what do I know about Russians and their reactions? I've Mirand-ized plenty of them, and they laugh in my face because they know I'm not going to sap them to the floor like their own cops used to. I should go over there. Sounds like a lot more fun."

"Trust me. Whoop-ass is a very inefficient crime-solving technique. Have you found out where these men were killed?"

"No. And as you seen, one of them was messed up pretty bad. Missing a hand, a foot, and most of his boy jewels. Wherever that went down, there'd be a bloody mess, right? It wasn't in the apartment upstairs, or anywhere we know that the drips would show."

"Fingerprints?"

"These guys ain't in IAFIS. Surprise, surprise. A hundred million fingerprints, including all legal immigrants plus 30 million law-abiding civilians, and still nobody's home to the FBI."

"Did you find any weapons?"

"Negative, and you can bet they was strapped when they left mommy's that morning. You never seen clothes more sanitized. No labels, no little nametags from scout camp, nothing in the pockets, not even a Chapstick or a car key or even a cold credit card to grab a plane in a emergency."

"Abandoned vehicles in the neighborhood?"

"The ground troops got all the license plates and they'll check again this afternoon. Don't hold your breath. My thought here is we got some pros. But unless the Mouseketeer is a lot smarter than he seems, he is just some kind of asshole that just fell into this."

"Can I talk to him?"

"No. You got to see the DA about that. It's gone sensitive. Why don't you give it a rest for a few days?"

"I don't rest," Roski said.

"You're so full of shit, man. You remember you told me once that any idiot could stand up to a crisis—it was the daily living that wore you down."

"That was a long time ago, Len. You've got the memory of an elephant. It's Chekhov."

"That little dipshit on *Star Trek*? Man, you come see me and you always talk this deep shit about your own problems. You never ask about mine."

"Tell me about your problems," Roski said glumly.

"Thanks for asking. Last year I did a roughish cuff-and-stuff on a tattooed Mex who was wearing a wifebeater shirt, fat chinos—you know—looked like any bean drywaller on his day off, but his dad turns out to be a city councilman. They're trying to push me out of the department. I got enough time in to retire half-size and maybe I'll go quietly, up to Idaho with all the LAPD, who knows? Do you remember me putting you up for a night in my own bed after your wife left you?"

"No, Len, I'm sorry."

"Well that's good, then I don't have to remember you."

"Man, I do care."

"You think people should *care*? Wow. I find that really moving."

Roski didn't want the dick-waving to drag on. "Sergeant Len Mars, my friend, please tell me one thing I didn't know when I came in the door. For old times."

"California Penal Code 219 means trying to wreck a train."

"About the dead guys, please."

Mars seemed to consider. "The guy holding the paper on the burned-up Chevy was a Recon Marine hellballer. Tough as stumps, they say. Seems there was a kind of gray area of unauthorized killings out in Hajiland, but they let him out honorably. Charles Beck is the name. He's some sort of machinist at a place called Gusev Emergency Power on Chattus Street, which is, by the way, also owned by a Russian. Duh. And yet another guy who works at Gusev is a lowlife named Arkady Belkin. Just coincidentally, all these guys called in sick this

DEEP IN THE FUNHOUSE 141

morning. Though the owner almost never comes in anyway. Happy now? Tell poppa."

"Thanks, Len."

"Now we can all care so much. No question about it."

* * * * *

H E waited for White and Gray to call, then hang up after two rings and call again, but they didn't so Sergei knew something was wrong. No matter how professional you were, things could always go wrong. Look at the Moscow theater mess in 2002. He'd been on the team. The Alfas had been told absolutely positively by the *apparatchiks* that fentanyl gas would send everybody inside into deep sleep. Sure, just like the triumph of Communism. It killed 150 of the hostages while the terrorists went on shooting back. Later he'd read on his own that fentanyl was 100 times more potent than morphine, not a sleeping gas.

What they didn't expect was that he tracked down the two assholes who'd lectured them on fentanyl and killed them both. It's a random world at the best of times, but you had to pay for outright stupidity. *Da*, he knew sometimes children could bicycle into the kill zone at the wrong moment, or dirt clog a moving part. That's the bad. There was no such thing as innocence for a warrior. If you didn't want accountability, stay out of the game.

Sergei double-checked his throwaway cellphone—battery charged up, no calls. He had to assume that Mr. Gray and Mr. White had failed. And so had he in a way, he thought. He was sure Belkin hadn't been in his bed. But Belkin was nothing, less than nothing, a null in the universe. He could be ignored. It was the big American Recon Marine, Sergei's true opposite number, who was the bump in the road. Deep inside, Sergei knew he shouldn't have sent the other two. Beck was for him. Wolf to wolf.

ELEVEN

Colorless Green Ideas Sleep Furiously

R OSKI stood at the driveway entrance to the Gusev parking lot, watching two workers prodding and poking things inside tall metal cabinets. There were seven or eight work stations along the back wall of the open building, but only three men were there. He couldn't see an obvious foreman but he was drawn to a young man wearing a T-shirt that said "Colorless Green Ideas Sleep Furiously." You and me, kid, he thought.

The boy saw him coming and didn't like it, but he set down a hammer and center punch. "Can I help you?"

Roski showed his ID. "County Arson. Could you take a few minutes to talk?"

The young man seemed to consider and then nodded toward the plastic chairs in the far corner of the parking lot, far enough to be private.

"Could I ask your name?" Roski said as they walked.

"Talbot Denny. I don't know why you want me. I'm the littlest kahuna here, one might say."

One *might* say? he thought. Mightn't I not?

A police helicopter passed low overhead and began to make its big circle over Santa Monica Boulevard—"orbit" as the cops called it. An awful lot of expensive technology to nab a purse-snatcher, he thought.

144   *BOYSTOWN*

"This is just a summer job," the young man said.

"Going back to college in the fall?"

He shrugged. "I've got the magic letters—the P, H, and D. I'll go to a half dozen modern philosophy conferences in the spring, and then I can take up my natural profession of saying 'Do you want fries with that?'"

Roski chuckled dutifully. "What was your dissertation? Broad or narrow?"

The boy cocked his head a little and looked at Roski differently. "Maybe broad. The state of exile as the essence of modernism. What did you do?"

"Philosophy, Berkeley."

"I'm Columbia. Wow—Berkeley is top five. What was your focus?"

Roski held up a palm. "Dropping out. I need to ask you some questions. I take it Charlie Beck isn't at work today."

"I almost didn't come myself. I need the cash. Is this about what happened to Charlie's car?"

"You mightst say," Roski allowed. "I am arson."

The helicopter came over again and they both winced. Something was worrying the kid.

"Could you tell me about Beck? I haven't been able to get in touch with him."

"Mr. Beck is a master machinist, and he helped me out when I started. He's grumpy, but he didn't have to help me and he did. I knew power tools from my dad but not these digital CNCs. I only got hired because I was a friend of a friend."

"Arkady Belkin is off today, too?"

His eyebrows went up. "I never heard the first name. He's just Belkin here. One look and you'd think he's a real lowlife, but underneath he's a nice guy and funny. I'm not being a snitch, am I?"

The helicopter came around yet again annoying them both.

"Does that possibility worry you?" Roski watched the young man carefully.

"I just want to be sure it's all good."

COLORLESS GREEN IDEAS SLEEP FURIOUSLY 145

"Do you have some reason to think it's *not* all good?"

"You," the boy said. "Coming here. Isn't it reason to be concerned when an investigator shows up?"

"Ah, concerned. Broadly speaking, you're a student of the human mind, Mr. Denny. I'd like to get your take on those two workmates."

Running steps passed outside a wall, the helicopter came around waggling the intense light beam from its sun-gun, and sirens wound up around the compass. "Hollywood just can't resist drama," Roski offered.

"I guess," the boy said neutrally. The commotion receded a block or two.

Roski worked on him a while longer, but he was becoming reticent.

"Colorless green ideas," Roski said, staring at the T-shirt.

The boy stopped in the middle of some evasion and glanced down at his shirt. "You know it?"

"Sure, Chomsky."

"A sentence that's absolutely perfect in syntax, but has no meaning at all."

"Like so much of life," Roski said.

"I won this shirt." Talbot Denny plucked at the cloth. "The *Daily Spectator* at school ran a contest to write a flash fiction, five hundred words tops, that would end with this sentence and the context would force a meaning. I came in second."

"Go for it, sounds interesting," Roski said.

"Some other time, sir."

Don't cat-and-mouse me, son. "Mr. Denny, what if I told you that two unidentified men were murdered last night and laid out on the spot where Mr. Beck's car was incinerated? Left there just like green ideas sleeping furiously."

Something was going on behind the boy's eyes. "I need to get back to work, sir."

"Are you glad we had this little talk?"

From not too far came the sound of a mangling crash, a vehicle ramming into something immovable. Roski hoped it was one of the police cars.

"What does that mean?" the boy said.

"It means you've told me what I need to know," Roski said mischievously. "You were part of whatever's going down, or you know about it, just like you were the bright and favored child in a split-level home, the place where you always got away with things."

Roski set his business card on the cable-reel table. "I'm a lot nicer than the cops will be. The sooner you clue me in, the better it'll be for everybody."

The young man walked away without touching the card. The young were so prone to bravado, Roski thought sadly.

* * * * *

A T the top of the driveway, Jack Liffey wondered what would be the best initial attitude. Contrite? Imperturbable? Preoccupied? It really depended on the excuse that he didn't have.

Lying was ultimately futile because he knew he'd break down later, but he had to protect Maeve's lie, too.

As he came in the front door, he heard a rhythmic thumping upstairs, heavy, on and on. Gloria was working out in her angry way, possibly a return-to-work mania, or a rage at her absconded mate, or unspoken grief at life wounds. Or all of the above.

It was a question of getting through the morning with a minimum of damage. The rest would play out.

When he finally went upstairs she was doing jumping jacks, suited up with one of his T-shirts and shiny purple Laker trunks, long and floppy. He loved the way young black men had gradually imposed their culture on a minstrel-sport owned by old rich white men.

"Hi, good morning," he said.

A flick of her eyes acknowledged him, barely. "I have trouble with names, but I never forget a face," she said.

Replying almost anything would be a serious mistake.

"Last night," she added evenly.

COLORLESS GREEN IDEAS SLEEP FURIOUSLY 147

I was busy burying a dog, he thought, but Loco was still downstairs. I was driving Robert De Niro around in a taxi. She held her laser focus on him.

"A mess, sorry. I was at Maeve's for a while and then I wasn't. I was chasing down leads and I ran out of gas out in the valley. Not the car. Me." Keep it simple, she's the expert at this.

"I didn't know you had a girlfriend in the valley."

"I tried to watch a house, but I fell asleep in the truck. Look at me. I'm a mess."

"You're talking pretty good all of a sudden. Does getting laid do that?"

"Probably sleep deprivation." Come on, Jack, you're tough enough to just shutup. "How are your ribs and hip?"

"The last thing I want is an organ recital." She finished the jumping jacks and paused only a moment before she went into what'd been called "wings" in high school—holding your arms straight out and making tight circles.

"You're my hero," he said.

"I'm just looking the big rat in the eye. I'm getting pretty old to fight my way back."

He hoped she was referring to mortality as the big rat, not him. He watched her exercise with real grit for a while. "Why don't we go on a trip together, Glor. We never have. Get away from all the craziness in the city, sit around a campfire and look up at the stars."

She stopped and glared hard at him. "Jack, Indians don't go *camping*. We didn't come out west on no covered wagons, okay. We're the ones the campers shot to shit. You want to come scalp some rednecks that keep their hounds under the porch, we can talk about it."

"I could get with that."

She gave out a big breath and let her arms droop. "Just drop it, Jack. Let the rough end drag for a while, okay? Get me a beer."

As he went to the door, she went down into pushup mode. He froze there for a moment then stepped back and said, "You're right, Glor. It was a girl. It was really really stupid."

* * * * *

C HARLIE Beck flipped open the chest in his man-cave and started dragging out armament.

"What the hell is that?" Belkin asked. A stubby plastic rifle that looked like it was from *Star Wars.*

"That's an XM8, a prototype. It won the Army tests for the next generation weapon, but fucking politicians killed it. Just having the ammo magazine is a felony." He tucked it into a big duffle and then pulled out pistols in web holsters. "These are SIG Sauers. And this is an M203 grenade launcher. Happy?"

Belkin peered down into the chest. There was enough angular martial junk still in there to take down a small country, but Beck was picking it over carefully. *This* one, not this. Finally he took out three curved rectangles of dark green about the size of books. *Front Toward Enemy* was embossed on one side, and Belkin knew what those were—Claymore mines. *Chyort poberi!* "How did you get all this stuff?"

Beck gave him a dark look. "Why would you want to know?"

"Oh, man, sorry. I don't give no shit nohow."

"Take this." He tossed a lumpy duffle to Belkin. "We go in your car unless you want to shoulder both bags on the back of my bike."

Belkin felt spent and anxious, the way he had in the *militsiya* stations he'd been dragged into all through his youth. Something to do with his life force had gone away. The raging rebellious boy he'd once been was no longer present, but other feelings were. He worried about Cat as he carried the duffle outside.

"Fuck." The imperturbable Charlie Beck was perturbed by the sight of Belkin's car. It was a classic lo-rider he'd bought cheap off a guy headed for forever prison. "You got us riding around in a neon zebra."

It was a candy-apple purple 1950 Mercury, chopped and decked, with a red-and-orange flame job billowing around the front fenders from a chrome shark-tooth grill implanted from a De Soto. Belkin had loved it at first sight.

"It's what it is," he said.

"No shit. Like bad weather."

COLORLESS GREEN IDEAS SLEEP FURIOUSLY 149

"The guy called it a lead sled. It makes me feel good."

"Open the trunk, Russky. Let's not get us killed arguing out here like a couple of faggots."

"I don't want to kill nobody. I'm not wired that way."

"Open the fucking trunk before we draw a crowd."

* * * * *

R OSKI had told her a little of what he'd discovered looking for Benjy, but Maeve figured he was holding back. Not counting what her dad had from the girl he'd slept with, the only lead she had was from Roski—about two brothers living in West Hollywood who had to be completely innocuous or he wouldn't have mentioned them. She sat in her car watching the spick-and-span done-up house, bigger but almost as clean as the one where Benjy had lived a half mile away. The whole area was just too tidy. When the gays come, she thought, count on your property values soaring. Boystown was unlike any neighborhood she'd known—in Redondo with her mom, Culver City with her dad, East LA with Gloria. Something about the place seemed unreal, almost a movie set. The atmosphere too thin to support real life.

The doorbell nailed it by chiming "The Witch is Dead" from *Wizard of Oz*.

A chiseled handsome young man answered warily. "We don't do business at the door."

"We don't either," she said. "I'm looking for Benjamin Walker. You've heard of him?"

His brows furrowed. "His picture's on every phone pole that doesn't have a missing poodle. You don't look like a detective."

"I'm working with my dad who's a detective."

"I like your—I don't know—*chutzpah*. Who are you really?"

Something about her presence could often get people to open up. "Could I ask are you Talbot or Alvis?" she said.

"Talbot. My younger brother Alvis is the main man here. You may notice that we're both named for antique British cars. If you were a detective, you could have fun checking into that."

She told him that she was in fact an art student at UCLA, but she was helping her dad. In exchange, he told her he'd recently done a difficult defense of his dissertation at Columbia and was taking a summer break. He was tired of describing the dissertation, but when she asked, he said it was about exile being a distillation of the modern condition.

"Like a permanent outsider, you mean?"

"Yeah. The French philosophers love the idea but Americans desperately want everybody to feel at home. Aren't we all so happy?"

Maeve smiled. "I like the way you think. Could I have some tea, please?"

"Not really. But sit down and tell me why a lesbian art student is coming on to a queer philosophy student at ten in the morning."

She laughed out loud in her nervousness. "Hey, one of us could solve it all by having a sex-change operation. Or is it both of us? I'm confused. Talbot, man, I'm sorry but you're as beautiful and graceful as a Degas figure."

He mimicked a bashful recoil with a hand to his chest. "Golly, no one's ever said that to me."

"Bullshit. What was a Talbot car?"

He cocked his head oddly. "It was a rich-man's toy before World War II—a bit like the old MG. The brand died and was resurrected several times. Chrysler bought it and destroyed it for good. Like the Hotchkiss and Delahaye and Packard. Oh, yeah, and the Alvis—little bro."

"I didn't have my gaydar on," Maeve said. "And I didn't realize I broadcast the L."

"It's not open and shut, at least with you."

"What are the tell-tales?" She looked herself over. "No short hair, no lumberjack shirt, no Doc Martens."

"How many people knew Sonny Liston was gay?"

"*What?*"

"Kidding, Ms Maeve. I *will* make you some tea after all—green tea, I bet."

"Any kind. I think I'm learning to love people without labels."

COLORLESS GREEN IDEAS SLEEP FURIOUSLY

He smiled in a doubting way and straggled into the kitchen. They talked long-distance about their discomforts in high school and their tastes in music, swapping favorite singers and groups. She wondered why he'd suddenly lightened up on her.

Talbot brought her a steaming cup on a saucer and set it down with a loony hand flourish. "Madame will be pleased."

"Madame is not often pleased," Maeve said. "If I must choose between nothingness and grief, I will choose grief."

He fetched his own cup and sat opposite her with a grin. "Who?

"Kate Chopin in *The Awakening*. Yes, it's a Spanish Moss gothic but it was proto-feminist. She was interrogating a woman's enforced self-image and the obligations of motherhood. Almost an American *A Doll's House*."

He cocked his head again in his wry pantomime of appreciation. "Big praise. I confess I've never heard of her."

"Heard-of is pretty elastic in a world of greats run by old white men. I'm sure you know *Death in Venice*, *Giovanni's Room* and *Billy Budd*. Male gay issues, right."

"To be sure."

"They're in the pantheon and we get segregated twice. How many of these do you know? *The Price of Salt*, *The Well of Loneliness*, *Nightwood*?" Something was weird about the tea.

"*Nightwood* is Djuna Barnes, a Bohemian novel in Paris, but I don't know the others. I guess nothing in life is fair. Are we going to split hairs about who's worse off—the cocksuckers or the carpet-eaters?"

"Don't, please. Words can still wound. If I really have to choose between nothingness and grief, I'll take over-medium eggs. I do have a question for you, Mr. Talbot Denny. About Benjy Walker."

"Shoot."

"You didn't know him. Not all gays in WeHo know one another."

"For sure."

She watched him for a moment. "So, why is your name coming up in the investigation?"

"I was just starting to relax. Maybe they found out I mooned the Bishop of Kansas City." He made a face.

"Please—not attitude," Maeve said.

"Here in LA, I fell into a rat-cage full of jerks in a summer job. It hasn't been fun but I have nothing to do with this Benjy on the milk carton. Neither do my workmates."

"Could you tell me more about these jerks?"

"No. I have to live with my discretion. I'm sure they have nothing to do with your missing guy."

"What are you hiding?"

His face fell. "Maeve, I'd just like to get out of this summer alive."

TWELVE

Too Small to Be Big

PETRO hobbled up the wooden steps to Olga's apartment from the back parking lot, carrying the bottle in a paper bag, a very good Stoli Gold. He'd have preferred one of his Belugas, but at a hundred fifty bucks a bottle, it wasn't for mistresses.

The place was a wreck, the straitened circumstance of so many of his compatriots in exile. Olga had grown up in a grand Odessa manor overlooking the Black Sea, a spoiled daughter of one of the local *nomenklatura*. And now she was living alone in a shabby apartment above the shop of a nail painter and hair plucker.

"Petya!" She smothered him with pecks. "I was so worried. Fear has large eyes."

"I am making a remarkable recovery, so Dr. Trachtenberg says. The old fossil better be right. I have vast powers of retribution."

"No, you don't. You're a sweetie-pie," she said.

"Only with you, my darling."

"Shall we go straight to the bedroom?"

"I need a drink. I brought the vodka you love."

She went to the kitchenette and came back right away with a small platter of frozen sliced bacon, pickles, crackers, roe, salami and herring.

"I stood up to the cops for you, Petya. I told them I would turn the seas to fire before telling them a thing."

"Yes, light up the seas. But why did the cops come?"

She sat down against his thigh as he poured two juice glasses full.

She sighed melodramatically. "I processed that license number. They seem to flag an inquiry like that. Is 'flag' the word?"

"Did the cops reveal anything?"

"Only that they operate under the rules of a very constrained society, God bless. They didn't hit me once. And one of them wore $500 alligator shoes."

Not so good, he thought. But the feud was over and he was avenged, or so Sergei had assured him and who was Petro Ivanchuk to doubt the word of a great warrior. "Forget them, dear, they won't be back."

But then where was his hapless friend Victor the damaged who usually phoned incessantly for a game of *preferans*. Petro had called him over and over for the twenty dollars he was owed but no answer. It was worrisome.

Olga pressed closer, leg to leg. He liked the comfort that she offered, though her attentions were ultimately cold-hearted—which only helped diminish any feeling of responsibility. He ran his eyes surreptitiously over her welcoming full body and wondered if she knew that he knew she was scheming every minute to take him away from Alina Abramova. Some day he might tell her how little status an American community college instructor carried. Her father would have bellowed—no, no, the owner of a department store or a distinguished surgeon. Petro downed the glass at one go, almost tossing the drained glass at the decorative fireplace.

"Darling Olga. I've missed you so much."

"So you say. I have a new trick for the bedroom, *mylashka*. I can be so shameless. It makes a lot of noise and will release you from a thousand prisons."

"Well, then, let's learn this wonderful trick."

She grinned. "Yet I can be as fierce as a commissar."

"So, your new trick is to interrogate me under torture."

"No, no. Petya, I just need to ask you a tiny favor."

Oh dear, he thought.

TOO SMALL TO BE BIG

"I know your wife is planning a surprise sixtieth birthday for you in a week. You must know it, too. Dozens of your friends and our countrymen are invited. She's planning to divert you with a walk somewhere while people gather in your back yard and stand in a large six and zero. She will bring you home and take you upstairs and ask you to look out the window. But God is far away and the tsar is busy." Her voice wavered a little. "The great secret love of your life is not invited."

The birthday party actually was news to him, but he didn't show it. Alina Abramova had kept it secret, and Olga was certainly spoiling it on purpose. But now he had the sly prospect of not letting on and dancing around the subject to tease Alina. Perhaps he would suggest other plans for the day.

"You will be invited, Olga." But how?

"I'm going to lie down and die a second time," she exclaimed happily. "Come, my big man. Upside-down we go."

* * * * *

"THE man I bought it from said it was the main feature in a magazine called *Rat Rods from Hell*," Belkin said. Charlie Beck hunched down in the tuck-and-roll bench seat of the absurd vehicle. "He did admit the chassis was once in an accident. At speed it wants to go sideways like a crab, but who gives a shit?"

He double-clutched down a gear. The shifter was a three-foot tall mast with a crystal skull on top. The steering wheel was a chromed chain welded into a circle.

"Stay a couple days in this safe house out of the way," Beck insisted. "Just hold onto the weaponry and keep it ready."

As directed, Belkin drove far up Vine into the Hollywood Hills.

"Sure, man. What's all this you got going on?"

"It's all covered. I'm a great planner. There will be no mistakes."

"I gotta believe it. How you gonna get back down the hill now, Charlie?"

"I'm going to borrow this neon dirigible. It's perfect for the next tactic."

"Hey, you can't!"

"Don't sweat it. Nobody will beat recon. Your precious car's not going off a cliff, and you'll be snug as a bug up here watching videos. I'll park your baby under cover."

The minute he'd seen Belkin's giant trout lure, the big purple Davy Davis, the idea had come to him. He never got out of the baddies who they were and who else was after him but they definitely knew where he lived and there were going to be more. He'd left the bodies right there to keep them interested. Now he would park the flying purple people eater in his carport to signal that he was ready and waiting.

* * * * *

H E waited until he was sure none of the hikers on the abandoned hill road were watching him. Sergei stepped quickly off old Runyon Canyon Road. The road had been closed to everything but walkers since the 1980s and its pavement nibbled away by whatever it was that ate asphalt.

He high-stepped through chaparral and then down a barely perceptible deer trail for a quarter mile to a shrub-and-outcrop profile that was burned into his memory. Twenty-one paces due left through the sage and toyon, he found a forbidding patch of poison oak. Red-leaves-in-three, leave-it-be. He thrust his hand through the poison oak into the loose soil and found the buried steel handle.

Sergei wasn't immune to poison oak, but he was mildly resistant and he could tolerate anything life had. Before lifting, he dragged a finger through the soil and found the switch a few centimeters to the side. If left on, it would have blown an accidental treasure-hunter into next week.

He propped the lid up with its pole. Back home he might have had a better selection of weaponry, but he had what he had, and it had served him well. In the back of the storage tub were the superior weapons, two small RPG32 *Hashims* that could take out tanks, a *Dragunov* sniper rifle with a flash suppressor and a live optical sight, two PD-19 *Bizon* submachine guns, folded to the size of a computer keyboard. To

TOO SMALL TO BE BIG 157

the right side was the ammunition ready in magazines, R60 grenades and some *trotyl* plastic explosive blocks in wax paper. There was more, but there was never any sense overdoing a withdrawal. In front were the real tools of his trade. A dozen cheap .25-caliber pistols, Saturday night throwaways. They were as effective as any weapon on earth shoved unexpectedly in someone's ear.

As the last century came to its ugly end, he had decided he could become a killer for hire as long as he made sure his target deserved to die. There was little of honor else for a ronin in this chilly world. He was not about to sell encyclopedias door-to-door.

This time, he gave some thought to the capabilities of his enemy. His police sources told him that Mr. White and Mr. Gray had been caught off-guard, interrogated cruelly, then killed and left in an alley in a way that mocked them and him. Nobody could foresee everything unexpected, but Mr. White and especially Mr. Gray had been very good.

He smiled a little inside. A worthy opponent added zest to the hunt. He plucked out two of the throwaway pistols, and just in case, the sniper rifle that he disassembled to get into a sports bag. He shouldn't need any exotics.

He returned the rest to hidden status and sat on his haunches for a moment, his wrist beginning to ache from the poison oak. Everybody lived in some relation to emptiness inside, he thought. His own parents had been secretly Russian Orthodox, and their worship had grown more fanatical and rigid as they aged.

Sergei had grown up hating religious belief as much as he'd hated the prating communists. Only expertise mattered. Belief was childish, and unmanly. The only thing left for a man of honor was a kind of life that was led moment-to-moment in opposition to what you could do something about.

* * * * *

MAEVE insisted that the young Latino at the entrance kiosk call Roski's number to confirm her invitation into the County Fire offices in the hills of City Terrace. Everything was so over-defended now, she thought, as if Al Qaeda or Isis squads were fanning out for assaults on fire stations, city halls, banks and McDonald's restaurants. The terrorists have won.

"Park over there," the guard said. "He'll come out."

"Take it easy, *ese*. I'm no *problema*."

He shrugged. "It's a job, *ruca*."

"*Sale-vale*."

He gave a sly double-take at the slang, okey-dokey. She parked in an empty row that overlooked Monterey Park where smog was accumulating over the whole San Gabriel Valley, as usual.

Before long Roski dragged out of a low office building. There was something about the man's gait that reminded her of her father's absent-minded shamble. What if she fell through some strange hole in her comfort zone and did make love to this likable man? Yikes!

"Maeve. Come on."

"You've got a hell of a lot of security," she said.

"Yeah. I can't offer you cognac here, but we have a break room with awesome iced tea."

He was breezier and more distant than she remembered. Yes, he was at work, but it saddened her. "Have you heard from my dad?"

"A bit. Is he in woman trouble? Men—you know, just can't live with 'em, and you can't kill 'em."

"He'll be okay. How about Benjy? Find out anything?"

He punched at a code-box beside the door. Inside, he greeted passers-by with a few words or a nod, most of whom eyed Maeve with curiosity, wondering whether she might be his daughter or even a lover. A few lone men tried to peek into her blouse. Nothing unusual.

"My information about the missing boy is indirect. Sorry, Maeve, I haven't really been on that job full time. I've had to concentrate on an arson case." He went quiet as a fierce-looking older woman in a Mixmaster hairdo bore down on them.

"See you at three," she challenged.

"Muriel."

TOO SMALL TO BE BIG 159

They sat down in a quiet corner of the Spartan break room and he didn't bother offering iced tea again.

"I think it's best to back off Benjy right now," he said. "Two men who are still unidentified were murdered, and it might be connected. The ME says their dental work is Eastern European. This may be turning into a big international feud."

Maeve was about to answer when the break room filled with an alarming braying sound from a nearby table.

"I have recently had the opportunity to observe Mr. Dudamel from the front rows," a stringbean of a man bawled. "I was devastated by the energy arrayed in front of me."

"So you enjoy great music," a woman wearing too much makeup replied. "I adore it myself—symphonies, divertimenti, opuses."

"Did you come of age in a tuneful household?"

Maeve glanced at Roski who was covering his mouth hard with his hand. "Is there something wrong with me?" Maeve whispered.

Roski's back was to the couple but he bobbed his eyebrows twice like Groucho Marx.

"We must be kindred spirits!" the string bean cried out. "Let us continue our trenchant discussion." Roski nodded toward a sliding door and escorted Maeve out to a patio. Ice-cream chairs had a view of little but parking lot.

"I have to work with her on a daily basis," Roski explained.

"That man is going to lose his hairpiece any minute."

"It's loneliness," Roski said. "Don't be too hard. It does terrible things to people."

Maeve turned her back to the glass door. "I talked to a young man named Talbot and I think you did, too."

"You're a good kid, Maeve. Please back off and tell your dad the same. There's some kind of vicious firefight playing itself out, and it's out of our league. It may not even relate directly to Benjy Walker."

"Are you sure of anything at all in this?"

160 BOYSTOWN

Roski frowned. "I always want an unmistakable context, but it's a weakness in me. Life is a terrible muddle. That's an important philosophical principle, I believe. What do you think?"

"Despite everything, I believe that people are really good at heart."

"That's Anne Frank. Do you really believe that?"

"I'd like to." There was more racket from inside. "I read once about Freud thinking there might be an innate death drive. I can't believe it, but where does all this violence and hatred come from? I can't even control my own hates."

She liked the way his face softened when he let it. "I wish my daughters were as thoughtful as you. All they cared about was which celebrity would get booted off the island. I don't get to see them anymore. Their mother broke a court order and moved out of state."

"I'm sorry."

"I'll tell you anything I learn about your Benjy, but stay away from it, please." His watch buzzed softly. "Meeting."

"Uh-oh." Back in the lunchroom, the man and woman were locked in a desperate, wriggling, hip-to-hip kiss.

"Follow me," Roski said.

He took her hand and led her over a low railing onto a narrow bed of African daisies and then along the side of the building, laughing softly. "My mother always said there's a lid for every pot," Roski said.

"I wish my mom could find a good fit." For the first time she realized Roski and her mother might just hit it off. Kindred spirits. Ha. She wondered what her father would think of *that*.

* * * * *

CHARLIE Beck pulled the purple Mercury into the parking lot off Sunset at what had been called for two generations Rock 'n' Roll Ralphs. After midnight it would fill with the odd night-dwellers. His purple beast wouldn't be too conspicuous here while he gathered a few supplies. He had a lazy moment before getting out of the comfortable sedan and thought of the busty bottle blonde he'd picked up in the bar two nights ago after his wife had cursed at him about the fire and

TOO SMALL TO BE BIG   161

the cops and the general uproar and taken their daughter off to her mother's in Oakland. The chunky blonde cooze had brainy airs and made it clear she was slumming in taking him home. Jasmine or maybe Yasmine turned out to be a big believer in the new age or anything off the wall—every crow she saw out the window signified something. He didn't say a word, hoping it meant he'd grabbed onto some wild inventive sex but the useless woman fucked like she'd been dead for a week. You moved, bitch. Did I hurt you?

Beck wondered what possessed people to believe that some God overseeing seven billion people could arrange omens just for *them*. His new troopie Belkin was even more twisted than any of the wild cards he'd picked up in bars or trained in his platoon. But Belkin wouldn't be snitching, he wouldn't give him the chance. Musing away, Beck wondered just who those men were he'd driven to the old warehouse and questioned. They were no ordinary civilians for sure. No wallets, throwaway pistols and the one he'd worked on first had a kill-knife strapped to his ankle. They'd said hardly a word. The second man had watched him shoot the first and then held on through a hell of a lot himself. In that situation there was nothing you could offer but pain. He wasn't going to let them walk away and they knew it.

They were obviously pros of some kind and he really wanted to know. He didn't want to have taken off some DEA or ATF undercovers running a sting.

A weasely Latino kid with an acne-scarred face rapped on his far side window and Beck jumped out. "Back off," he snapped.

"Cherry Merc, *esse*. I saw another guy in this sled yesterday. You win it off him?"

"Beat it."

"Doo wa diddy," the kid said. "Turn around, *gabacho*, meet my. Big. Brah."

It was a set-up, he thought without concern, and behind him was a guy the size of a bear who was mad-dogging him. If Beck hadn't had his mind on other things, it would have been funny.

162   *BOYSTOWN*

The acne kid went on chattering. "Oh, yeah, meet up with Double-D, old man. Double-D is the stuff of legend—if he talk to you once, you remember the day forever. D-D be above God. Better make an offering to God, you know. Don't need much, *esse*, maybe bread for a couple sixes."

Beck stuck a five in the big man's T-shirt pocket. "Get some Cheetos on me, *amigo*. I got no beef with you."

Nothing happened.

"In five seconds, you're still in my face, you will cease to exist. One ... two ..."

The man stood like a sumo wrestler posing bowlegged for a portrait, truly a stupid way to go. It was so tempting to kick him in the crotch, he decided not to. Of course, Beck didn't wait for *five*. He hit him several times very fast. The first few didn't have much effect, so he knew the man was actually toned. The next was a kick to his knee that snapped audibly, and then a knuckle hard to his windpipe. The big man sagged to the pavement as if all his bones had evaporated.

Beck turned to the weasel kid, who was running away. Great stuff, Charlie. Attention is just what you want. Well, maybe it was. The car was going to be mad bait, after all.

* * * * *

JACK Liffey was throwing together a pasta from what the kitchen had available. Luckily there was a little hard parmesan and some sausage. He would load it up with garlic and a big plump jalapeño for Gloria. After he'd made enough noise in the kitchen, she clumped down wearing sweat pants and a Sitting Bull T-shirt. Warpath time, but he knew better than say that. She grabbed a beer and complained about the clutter in the fridge, complained about some smell of rot, complained about the burned out bulb in the fixture above the breakfast nook. Nothing would be acceptable that night. Silent burns were not Gloria's thing.

"No fucking girlfriends hanging out, at least. Maybe I better check the pantry."

TOO SMALL TO BE BIG

"You've got a right to complain."

"A right? A fucking right? This is my house, Jack. Don't forget that."

"You want me out?"

"I said, don't forget it. I didn't say *leave*. If you left, I wouldn't get to bitch at you."

He glanced at her, hoping for the ripple of a smile, but got only an unreadable expression.

"Jack. You been damn good since I got all my bones broke. You been nurse and cook and all that shit. I know all the yada, yada. And we both know my sex drive is so shut down I won't even give you a blow job like some little *chiflada*. There's an old Paiute saying—you want somebody to hate you, do them a big favor."

"I bet that's not a Paiute saying."

"You're right, but it's true. And shut up, I don't want to know what famous writer said it. I want you to know that I'm a hundred percent aware that I owe you big time, and that owing you pours acid over all the feelings I got. And then you did this *chingadera* with the young stuff— yeah, it pissed me off a little."

"I get it. It was a mistake."

"Jack, *shut up*. I'm telling you something." She finished off the beer in one pull. He nodded toward the fridge and when she agreed, he got her another.

"You're too good to throw away, *hombre*. I ain't crazy. Indians survived a lot of bad shit, and we got magic endurance. So if you want to poke my dried-up cookie bad, I'll grease it up and lie back and salute the flag. I want you to stay with me, Jackie. There, I said it."

He wanted to rush over and hug her, but she held up the flat of her hand.

"Gloria, that's the only cookie I want right there under your sweat pants, and only when you feel like it. What's the Paiute for pussy?"

"Things are very modest on the rez. We used the polite Spanish word—*el funciete*—or sometimes the really rude *la chocha*. I don't even know a Paiute word."

He smelled the chopped chili starting to burn and slid the frying pan off the fire. "You took care of me through my heart bypass and a lot of bad stuff, and we know it."

"Jack, I'm getting better. I promise. This will all pass."

"Of course it will. Anyway, what's *chiflada*? You and Maeve both hit me with your *Cholo* slang whenever you feel you need an edge."

At last she smiled a little. "It means pricktease."

THIRTEEN

Survival Is What Life Is About

TACTICAL adjustments, Charlie Beck thought. He parked the conspicuous car conspicuously directly over the scorch left by his old car and carried his duffle next door and in through the gate to the garage man-cave. He'd already given the terrain a once over and begun preparations, including breaking all the nearby light bulbs. His wife and daughter were safe and away in O-town, and the neighbors would just have to take care of themselves if all hell broke loose. It was Firebase Hurricane in Al Anbar all over again. The Ramadi Inn, they'd called it. In his mind's binoculars he saw rubble and dust, walls of rough clay brick, a disabled Humvee under a palm tree, and the open garage of a big smashed house where somebody had spray-painted: *Jiffy Lube—No Waiting.* The mind-image had him tensing up. Nothing quite like being in command and ordered to respect every citizen when every citizen was trying to kill you.

He surveyed the grassy yard again, the entries, focal points, options for flex, defensive retreats. He posted two Claymores aimed at the back gate and a third pointed toward the side fence, though he hadn't armed any of them yet, not wanting an unexpected red meaty rain of alley cat. The raised garden bed bordered by railroad ties had gone to weed long ago. It would be a good fighting hole after a little more digging with the E-tool.

166   BOYSTOWN

He retrieved some night vigil munchies from his man cave, dried fruit, string cheese and jerky, nothing crunchy, plus two water bottles and some recon popcorn—orange amphetamine pills. He dug out a kneel trench behind the railroad ties and strung a decoy tripline from the back gate latch to a cello wrapper in the weeds below that would crackle and alert him. No tripwires to detonators. Collateral kills here would be bad news.

He wired the three Claymores to hand clickers that he set out on the railroad tie. Then he positioned a handful of grenades beside his knees in the trench and settled in with a Mossberg 590 shotgun across his lap. An Israeli Tavor assault rifle was nearby. It was fading twilight, but he never underestimated how soon the enemy would be on him. He'd spent enough nights guarding the FOB. He had to assume he was up against a pro now, and probably angry as a hornet after losing his pals.

Beck got out the paint sticks that looked like dark green deodorant cylinders. He daubed his face with black and woodland green. And as he rubbed the camo paint onto his cheeks and brow, his forebrain reprised one of the chants they'd sung on forced marches.

I paint my face black and green;
You wont see me, I'm a Recon Marine.
I slipped and slithered in through the night.
You won't see me till I'm ready to fight.
You'll run in the bushes, you'll try to hide,
That's why you're sure to die.

* * * * *

PETRO Ivanchuk hobbled across his living room, playing it a bit more Frankensteinish than his wound required. He would keep any extra consideration he could get from Alina Abramovna.

"I just remembered that it's my sixtieth birthday in a week," he said. "Maybe we should fly off somewhere special for butterflies, like

SURVIVAL IS WHAT LIFE IS ABOUT

central Mexico to see the monarchs." He enjoyed the moment of panic in her eyes.

She set down her *Oprah* Magazine. "I haven't forgot your birthday, my sweet commissar. I think we can do something special right here."

"Oh, probably." He wasn't a sadist. "Let's both think about it."

"I've been thinking of an idea, Petya, but I can't say it just yet."

"There can be a holiday in our home street." It was an old proverb. "Tell me your idea when you can, because there's some people I work with at the college you don't know, and I'd like them to be with us."

"Of course, Petya. Please sit down. That stumbling around makes me uncomfortable."

Not as uncomfortable as Olga Nikolayevna will try to make you at the party, he thought. But everybody knows that everybody knows.

* * * * *

"I CAN'T stand this junk," Talbot said, as Alvis dug into the party mix watching TV. "If you really want to watch it, I'll go off and read."

"Shit, no." Alvis snapped off the *Mad Men* rerun.

"They say it's a critique of the fifties," Talbot said, "but really it's inviting us to reinhabit those values."

"Sure, Tal."

"You can't have it both ways."

"I guess. Archie Bunker back in KC, remember? All the old guys in the neighborhood wanted to *be* him. '*Stifle!*'"

"Nostalgia for a time of guilt-free cruelty."

"I'm glad you came for summer, Tal." He squirreled around on the sofa. "I really love remembering how you always challenged me and dad's lame ideas."

"I don't know about calling them lame, Alv. Those feelings are probably pretty complicated."

"Aren't they just prejudices you outgrow?"

Talbot shrugged amiably. "I do think the country is actually killing itself hating or fearing anybody who's different."

168   *BOYSTOWN*

"Whoa," Alvis said. "Americans love the underdog, don't we?"

Talbot smiled. "Allegedly. Nobody watches Charlie Chaplin anymore. Look at our teen comedies. We like the bullies. We mock the crippled and fat and weak. Ack, enough rant."

"Want a beer, bro?"

"Go for it."

Alvis headed for the kitchen just as there were bellows and screams of outrage from the cottage that was too close next door, back and forth—two shrill male voices.

Talbot sighed. "There's gay life for you. Shit."

"Don't be mean to yourself, Tal." Alvis hovered halfway to the kitchen as the screams turned into a smashing of breakables.

"Some people say the wall-to-wall cat-fight in *Who's Afraid of Virginia Wolf* was modeled on a gay relationship," Talbot said.

"I can top that. My English teacher said it was based on a professor named Ray Ginger who was blacklisted by Harvard in 1954."

"The biographer of Gene Debs. It could be both, you know. Commies and gays are classic outsiders."

Alvis scowled. "Do you really think the country is doomed?"

"Did somebody say beer? Don't take me too seriously. I'm going to end up blathering away at the North Dakota School of Animal Husbandry."

"You're really smart, bro."

"Philosophy is a privilege of the overeducated. I cogitate on things that are of absolutely no interest to anybody else."

* * * * *

B UNNY waited until she was snuggled up in bed before asking about her brother. In the main house their three roommates were partying away noisily with some frat boys and other girls. "You said your dad was on it, M."

Maeve tried not to stiffen with guilt, she'd done so little. "I talked to that arson guy again, and he says to stay away. He thinks Ben might

SURVIVAL IS WHAT LIFE IS ABOUT 169

have run off for a while because of some big feud going on." A comforting lie, but possible.

"Do you think so?"

"I really don't know anything, Bunny. I'll give you your miracle if I can. *Ooooh!*"

Bunny had begun massaging Maeve's nipples with intent. "Good, isn't it? My stepmom was Cuban. She used to say never let a man touch your *tetas* or you'll go out of control."

"Oh, have your way with me."

It was hard to ignore the uproar of the party in the big house. "The world's definitely getting better, Bun. A decade ago those chanting frat boys would have stormed in here to try to save us from unnatural acts like *this*."

"Oooh! You know what else my stepmom said?" Bunny bucked a little as Maeve wriggled under the sheet. "She said only touch the pink-meat to wash it, but don't wash it too much."

"Like this?"

* * * * *

E MERGENCY sirens had cranked up a few minutes ago, swelled and then receded, leaving only faint hip-hop sounds far up the alley.

Charlie Beck reached for a dried apricot gently. Even those you had to chew very slowly. M&Ms were okay, too, if you let your saliva melt the sugar coat off. Radio silence. Any sound above fifteen decibels could be heard a car-length away, and breathing was already ten.

The water bottle was open and he shot a little into his mouth instead of sucking on the bottle. The Mosburg shotgun on his lap was a comfort. Come to me, comrade, and we will have fireworks. Your pals were careless and assumed I was an idiot.

When he'd first come home from OIF, Beck nearly agreed to muling a car-trunk of lorazepam across from Mexicali to Oceanside for one big score to set him up, but something had held him back. What if he'd been Russian and *that* Russia didn't exist anymore when he got home? Wouldn't everyone try to skim something before it was too late? He pointed a finger toward the gate like a weapon. One orange stay-on-top pill was making him jumpy.

A bird chirped and chirped. Do they chirp at night without being disturbed? Iraq birds hadn't. You couldn't fill an American alley with crinkly foil. Every stray dog would be a cattle-prod up your ass. To calm his pounding heart, he stared at the constellations he'd once known well.

Watcha doing down in that hole, Marine?

Controlling the access point, sir.

You afraid?

Negative, sir.

What kind of place is this?

It's my home retreat. I've got me a close ambush. Green forever.

Adapt and overcome, Marine. Be flexible. Semper Gumby.

Roger that, sir. It's all attitude.

Charlie Beck's heart slowed gradually. That pattern overhead was Orion. Everybody knew Orion. South of it, out of sight, would be Sirius, the brightest star in the sky. His mind snapped back at a tiny scrape-scrape in the alley.

Spooky. The Arab kids had mocked their patrols in Iraq, applauding very softly from around a corner and then breaking into American gangsta rap.

Watch out for the hajis
Mr. Marine.
Ain't no rematchies.

* * * * *

AT midnight Talbot lay snoring on the sofa like a ripsaw. Alvis rode a tall unicycle into the living room and came to a stop in the middle, racking the pedals forward and back to balance.

"Wakey-wakey, Tal. Your snore is too damn loud."

There was a gargle and a moment of consternation as he sat up. It took him a moment to focus.

"Jesus *Christ*, Alv. What kind of freak show is this?"

SURVIVAL IS WHAT LIFE IS ABOUT 171

"This is your home from home."

"My hovercraft is full of eels."

Alvis laughed once. They'd both been Monty Python fanatics and that was an unforgettable line. He pedaled madly for a moment and flailed his arms, almost losing it. "I'm so out of practice. What's that doorstop you're reading?"

Talbot's eyes flicked down to the big paperback. "Gramsci."

"Huh?"

Talbot smiled. "Antonio Gramsci. A four-foot-nine-inch Italian hunchback who was one of the great political philosophers of the twentieth century. Mussolini locked him up in 1926 and threw away the key. Mr. G. was exactly as tall as Linda Hunt."

"That's a distinction." He did a 360-degree swivel in place.

"You're good, Alv. You should be in a circus."

"Four-foot-nine, huh?"

"You've got to love a feisty little person."

He teetered and finally hopped down from the unicycle with a thud. "It's good to have you here, bro. I don't get to *really* talk much."

"Talk all you want."

Alvis picked up an expired beer bottle and drank the dregs. "So how did you get involved in this horrible feud?"

* * * * *

S HE studied the home alley carefully, squatting in a shadow. A stumbling shape a block away was just a drunk, of no worry. Cautious people were the ones that made you worry.

I know you, friend alley, she thought. Sometimes the cracked pavement replied in a tired way, but not tonight. Her shoes talked, too, though it was mostly fire hydrants who kept her in the picture. They were the most reliable. They told her their names, too—Thai Top, Flathead, Domey, Ribby.

Buddha-cap at the corner always wished her well, talking very slowly. It was people who spoke too fast, gibbering so you couldn't understand. Her one human friend—Blkn—did his best to keep it slow,

172   *BOYSTOWN*

and sometimes she could keep up. He was a special human, willing to touch only her hair, without the rat-a-tat. He brought her food and never once tried to put his hand under her shirt.

Why couldn't people say one word at a time? Even with Blkn, she wasn't sure he wanted her to stay away from her place, the only reliable safety she'd known for years.

She waited and watched the fences waving all along the alley. Not speaking to her but reassuring her with their calm. What was it about that black rock? He said something. A big green trash container told her to hurry up and get inside.

She hurdled the fence effortlessly, apologizing to the grass as she landed hard. All was quiet, only city noise off somewhere, a comfort.

She ran for the small basement screen beneath Blkn's room, tugged it free and wriggled head-first through the opening before snatching it closed behind her. She listened for anything from the outside. You're okay now, the big green trash thing whispered across the yard. You can sleep.

*   *   *   *   *

M AINTAINING vigilance and stillness was one of the hardest tasks life offered.

Anything going on here, Marine?

No, sir. *Yes*, sir!

He tensed. Was he actually watching human fingers rise above the gate? Three thin pegs rose slowly and felt for the latch. A pianist's supple fingers. They curled over the wood, felt out the latch slowly and carefully, studied it by touch but made no effort to raise it. The fingers found the mock trip wire without disturbing it and withdrew.

Beck readied his Mosburg. Would the man leap the gate *right now* or find another approach? I should hit him with a Claymore.

There was a thump in the neighboring yard. Too late now. The man was trying to outflank him. New plan. *Semper Flex*. Where was he most vulnerable? That was easy; the wooden fence passed out of sight between the buildings. The man could slide along and jump the fence

SURVIVAL IS WHAT LIFE IS ABOUT 173

out of his sight. He could appear suddenly from the corner of the building, and the shallow trench would be less protection.

Beck squirreled around, reversing quietly in the trench, and swiveled the TAC-24 flashlight to face the corner of the building, still off. Slapped on, it would give out the near equivalent of sunlight. He repositioned himself belly down, keeping his aim on the corner of the building. Bring it on, dog. Come to me now.

A thud emanated faintly from the gap between the houses. Jumping that fence. Okay, Russky, if you are a Russky. Hi-yo, Silver. Come and get me.

Beck gently moved one of the grenades into reach of his left hand, his right controlling the shotgun.

A disk of sod out in the murk in mid yard shot straight up in the air like a magic trick. Oh, shit! He slapped the light on as he went down flat in his trench. Beck heard an explosion and the sizzle of shrapnel passing over his head.

A second and a third explosion filled his yard with enraged screaming scraps of metal looking for his flesh to tear into. The guy must have got here first and planted pop-up mines, like V-69 Bouncing Betties. Beck knew for sure that he wasn't facing some sloppy goofball.

He was still on top. Without raising his head, Beck fired the shotgun blindly toward the corner of the house, pumped and fired again.

"Incoming!" he shouted, as he reached out and set off the Claymore aimed nearest where the Russian had to be. It wrecked a lot of fence but probably nothing more. He hadn't aimed one of the Claymores directly up the side yard. Deep in his imagination, he felt he had, it was just too obvious, and his alter-ego tried to fire that one.

Time to get wise, Charlie. How long would it be before the cops came? For once he welcomed it.

After a terrible, pregnant silence, Beck heard a foreign voice in the yard, "I salute you, sergeant." It was a vowel-twisted accent followed by a deep soft laugh of confidence. "Nil-nil, I would say, our little match so far."

174   BOYSTOWN

Beck was reluctant to speak aloud, but something compelled him. "How many ICBMs you still got?" Beck said. "And who the hell are you?"

"My name is Sergei. And you're Charlie."

He's done more homework than me. "Staff Sergeant Charles Beck. Recon Marine."

"Third of the Fourth," Beck added on. "The Thundering Third. The Darkside. First into Baghdad. And five straight deployments."

Sergei's voice out of the night said something in another language. "*What?*"

"We were known as Thunder, too."

"Good for you."

"I'm Alpha Group. Special forces. They slipped into Kabul and took down the government in one night, but I was away on a different mission."

"So we're both great warriors beaten by fucking peasants." Beck had a hand on a grenade and was ready to rock-n-roll.

"Somebody has to cry," the Russian said.

"You got buy-in on that, Sayr-guy. Tell me, is this big furball about the butterfly man?"

He seemed to sigh. "Yes, friend, it is."

"I'm not your friend, Russky." Beck risked a glance over the timbers and saw him, a large middle-aged man kneeling calmly and vulnerably in the bright light. Dangling from one hand was the canvas harness that had recently held its nightvision mono-goggle to his eye. His other hand held something small, maybe just a cellphone. He didn't show any weapons. Beck's finger played with the trigger of the shotgun, but he wasn't certain of anything. There might be another Russky behind. Maybe several.

"How many troopies you got with you, dog?"

"Would a warrior tell that to a not-friend?" The big man hung his head a little. "I'm all target, Charles. Come out and discuss. I know you have the combat shotgun. I'm at your mercy."

SURVIVAL IS WHAT LIFE IS ABOUT 175

Beck didn't move. "You've already killed the white trash who hurt your friend, if you know what that means. I'd never choose him up for my team, but it's too late now. Just sayin'."

"Maybe it's not too late. Sergeant Not-friend, you're lying directly on top of a TC-6 land mine and one tap on this cellphone will send you into low earth orbit." He held up a cellphone, as if Beck needed a show-and-tell. "You couldn't kill me fast enough to stop it. Let's talk a little, sergeant. I'm curious about you."

Beck's belly prickled and tensed up, and all of a sudden he was quite certain it wasn't a bluff. Of course one would mine the earth behind the railroad tie barrier. "My bad, Sayr-guy. I underestimated you twice."

"Maybe more, who knows? Mustn't try to start your purple car or your motorcycle without a word to me first."

"I'll choose you for my team next time." Beck finally gave up any illusory advantage and climbed out of the trench. He sat on the timber, the shotgun across his lap.

"You may be a lot luckier than you know, Sergeant."

"So maybe we're friends now?" Beck asked.

"You did a lot of bad to my *droogs* before you killed them."

"What's *droogs*?"

"Friends."

"I needed intelligence—you understand it wasn't personal."

"Did they beg on their knees? Whine and shit themselves?"

"Jesus, no. They were soldiers."

The man smiled, harshly lit but not complaining about it. "I wasn't serious about the begging. If a warrior can't turn death into a joke, there's no way to grieve."

"What say we both take a deep breath now, Mr. Sair-guy?"

Beck had noticed how woozy he was with tension. If this Sayr-guy had it in for him, the mine below still had his name on it. There was a distant wail of sirens out in the world,

"It certainly takes a while in your country to respond to a small war," Sergei said.

"They had to finish their doughnuts. This is a civilized country. I think you better start hoofing, dog."

"I'm good."

"Is there something else we need to discuss? You called this truce." The big man seemed to be studying him.

"It never really gets better, Sergeant."

"You don't know what you're talking about. This is America."

"Is Talbot Denny going to come after me or my friends?"

"He's a pussy. Forget him."

"Arkady Belkin?"

"A petty shoplifter. You know that."

"And you—the worthy samurai? Are you going to come after me?"

Beck wondered what he should say and he waited a long time. "Probably, yeah."

"Even if I promise to kill everyone you ever met?"

The sirens were getting closer.

Sergei went on imperturbably. "Let me explain. In Lebanon, four Russian diplomats were taken hostage by terrorists. My Alpha group identified the hostage-takers in secret, and we delivered the severed heads of their close relatives, one by one, until they let the diplomats go. Just sayin'—isn't that the American phrase?"

The Old World was a hell of a lot meaner than the new one, Beck thought. "Man, you can keep those heads coming in. But it's you and me face-to-face in front of the saloon first."

"It doesn't work like that," Sergei said. "Death is not a count-down, it is unexpected." The swelling sound of the sirens finally registered with the Russian. He gave a crisp salute before starting away. "Peace out, dude," he said, holding up his cellphone like a warning. "Until we meet at the saloon."

Beck decided to get as far from there as fast as he could, expecting hell to erupt under every running step.

FOURTEEN

I Heard the Bugles Call

G o ahead and admit it, Roski thought, life scares the living crap out of you. He ruffled the bristle on his head, his old-man buzz-cut, and climbed into bed in utter darkness. He'd run out of vodka early in the night, his calm-down drug of choice these days, and his dreams had been restless, violent, world-destroying. His life-resilience was probably running on fumes. He sometimes wondered if he was an alcoholic, but he didn't want to go into it.

What would Jack Liffey have said? Hah! He admired the manic resolve that his friend Jack had on teetotaling, but he didn't seem to have access to that himself.

He was still half awake at four A.M. when the phone rang. "Walt, jump up and salute."

"Who the hell is this?"

"Be cool, fuckwad. Your lovely arson scene in West Hol has been desecrated once again. The yard next door this time. And I lost a dep-uty in the mess. He's dead as your dick."

"Aw, shit, no." Len Mars, West Hollywood Sheriff. At least Mars would give him the straight dope and not the chickenshit bureaucratic runaround arson usually got.

178   *BOYSTOWN*

"Come visit right now, fireman. I do not have the cast of mind for any more of this private war shit. You come give me some fucking clue of an idea."

"Romanie Street?"

"How many big arson scenes you got working, Sparkie?" The phone line went dead. A prickly character, but straight as a ruler.

On a whim Roski called Jack Liffey and left a message about where he was going to be. He'd grown to trust the guy's take on things, and almost everybody else could drive him batshit, including Len Mars.

*   *   *   *   *

B ECK had checked and checked the egregious purple Mercury he'd left next door, but finally opened the door with a what-the-hell tug and there was no explosion. Later, he'd parked it in the Hollywood Hills as out of sight as he could, but who was likely to see it in a winding road? He hadn't established a password with Belkin but the man was so clueless that hearing his own name through the poolhouse door, he'd opened with a bleary word.

Charlie Beck sent him back to bed and collapsed on the sofa in the living room. In the morning he'd call his wife and get her to depart Oakland forthwith and drive someplace even he didn't know. Turn off her GPS-linked cellphone, live on cash and wait a week before calling him from a pay phone. In some moods, he wouldn't have minded finding her head in a box on his porch, but no, not really, and not little Annie. It was time to stop underestimating the big Russian. Did they have a truce? Beck was still wondering why he'd lived through the encounter.

The sun was coming up when he finally got to sleep, hearing Belkin going at it in some kind of thumping masochist workout.

*   *   *   *   *

A LINA Abramovna got up very early without disturbing Petro, the city glow and false dawn just insinuating itself through their curtains. She threw on a robe and retreated to her sewing room to address

I HEARD THE BUGLES CALL

envelopes for the surprise party. Petro was so unpredictable and nosy in his wanderings—flitting around the house in his butterfly zig-zag—that it was hard to hide anything from him. He could turn up anywhere. *Allochka, what's this in the pantry?*

* * * * *

JACK Liffey had slept restlessly, exiled to Maeve's old twin bed downstairs because of his indiscretion with the girl. He'd jumped up at the second ring of the phone but found the cordless handset just too late. He went to the answering machine in the pre-dawn and then drove to the address Roski had left, an alley clotted by sheriff cars, crime-scene vans and TV news trucks. He knew the place well, he'd talked to a number of residents at the arson scene next door. He barely made it past a cordon of annoyed restless officialdom using Roski's name.

"Just in time," Roski said. "Jack, I want you to meet Sergeant Len Mars. You're both high-octane assholes."

"Who the hell is this?" The plump dark-suited cop seemed to be considering wringing Jack Liffey's neck. "You're not a damn PI, are you?"

"I look for missing children, sir. I won't get in the way."

"You're in the way right now."

"I don't touch homicides."

"You and me, *later*." The man gave Jack Liffey a furious squid-eye and then dismissed him from his universe.

"He's working with me," Roski insisted.

"That's your funeral, Smokey. Everybody stay back of the tape when we go there."

He led them through a cedar gate into a back yard swarming with investigators wearing white plastic balloon pants. Jack Liffey had never seen a crime scene marked out like this. Yellow tape was pegged at ankle-height around several manhole-size divots in the lawn. There was a much bigger crater at what had apparently been a raised vegetable garden bordered by railroad ties that were tossed aside now like losing trifecta tickets. A big section of fence had been blown down, too.

The angry cop pointed. "We don't know about those round holes yet. But that big one ... I was right over there—*Shit*—when my officer flew off supersonic and landed in three different airports. Deputy Timothy LaMott had been to the big Eye-raq with his Guard unit and he knew it all. 'Hey, sarge, look!' he says to me. 'Swear to god, that's an Italian T-6 mine. I know how to deal with that bad boy,'"

Len Mars seemed to reconsider his tone of voice. "Okay, I liked the kid's attitude. Not a lot of guys came stateside so upbeat. But most of them know they ain't trained on mine clearance and know not to show off. Just because you been in a fucking garage, you ain't a car.

"Even I know most of these things got a second thingy under or inside for any jerkoff that messes with it. The first two ambulances got most of the bigger pieces of Timmy on stretchers. For the rest, watch your step. We're gonna have to Hoover the yard and then bury the Hoover." He glared at Jack Liffey. "I didn't say any of that."

"Feds coming?" Roski asked.

The cop nodded. "ATF and Homeland Security. Like we never heard of explosives out here in the sticks. But tell the truth, we could use the help. Something is going on here and I don't know what it is, Mr. Jones. Looks like a blood feud from the Middle East. You don't buy big booms like that at the swap meet. Got any ideas, Mr. Jones?" He seemed to direct the question at Jack Liffey.

"Are there any anti-Russian vigilante groups in town?"

The policeman gave him his icy glare. "Nobody here mentioned *Russians.*"

"You arrested a Ukrainian hunchback in that alley. And two dead men from Eastern Europe were found in the carport. The Marine Charlie Beck, who lives in the building next door, worked at a machine shop owned by a Russian."

Roski was making a face to get him to stop.

"Is that enough?"

"You got your nose right up the world's asshole, don't you, PI? Give me a reason not to fuck with you."

I HEARD THE BUGLES CALL

181

Jack Liffey decided being helpful might keep him from losing his temper. "That sad-looking garage right there is not a garage," Jack Liffey said. "Beck rented it and converted it to his den and rumpus room. I think people've started calling it a man-cave."

"You think a lot of things, shitbag. How do you know all this?"

"I talked a little to his wife." What you should have done days ago, birdbrain, Jack Liffey thought in silence. Roski was still signaling him to shut up. "Sir, I'm telling you everything I know in good faith. I'm just an old man who had a heart attack and a bypass and a stroke on top and I already heard the bugles call, so I just don't care that much what can happen. If I were you, I'd get a search warrant for the garage before you waste the rest of the morning pushing me around."

"Search warrant," Mars said in mocking voice.

The policeman walked across the yard to the back door of the garage building and with one hard flat-footed kick smashed open the door. In twenty minutes, he and his deputies had found a cache of illegal military arms that were unusual outside the drug trade or white supremacist militias.

Len Mars came back out the garage door and pointed straight at Jack Liffey. "Consider yourself a material witness, shitbag. You're detained for the Grand Jury."

"He's not a flight risk, Len," Roski said.

"Sure, he is. Riley, come hook this guy up!"

* * * * *

B ELKIN was taking advantage of the safe house swimming pool even in the low morning sun and beering up in comfort on a lounger with some of its straps dangling limp under him. He wore only a towel and when Charlie Beck roused himself from finishing his night on the sofa and wandered outside, he got another eyeful of toe-to-chin prison tattoos. Beck frowned at the horrible cup of instant coffee which was all he could find.

"I hope my Mercury's better'n you look."

"Your purple thing's just hunkey-dorey, and it's all yours again after you drop me. We're square."

"This is your game, man."

He spit the coffee over the pool in disgust. "Not. I was getting to like you a little, so I got to warn you to watch your ass. The butterfly man's got some pissed-off friends." Beck thought better of saying any more, but it was only right to clue him in. "Do you know what Alpha is?"

"The *Soviet* Alpha?" Belkin had gone alert.

"Uh-huh."

"Shit, yes. It's like your Navy SEALs fucked the Devil's wife. They're famous for no holdback." He sat up and lost the towel. Beck couldn't help seeing that his large uncircumcised penis was the trunk of a crude blue elephant. Very witty.

"What makes you say they're Alpha?"

"He says his name is, like, Sayr-guy. That's Russian, right? He said Alpha, like it was something next to god. He didn't blow a cap on me when he could have, and should have, so I don't know shit about him. He did talk some nonsense about the honor of warriors."

Somebody from the main house came fast down the driveway nearby in a red Ferrari, shrieking at about a million rpm. They waited until it was out the gate and gone.

"I thought I was on top of this. I got those other two guys easy, but this one had my balls in his fist from the git-go. I'm going to collect my family and disappear into the north slope of Alaska for a century or two, and I suggest you go save any family you got."

"My family—may they rot in the dirt." Belkin went quiet thinking about something. "Can I keep the pistol?"

"You can keep the shotgun in the trunk, too. I can't deal with it now. And there's two blocks of C-4. They look like sticks of butter in brown wax paper. They won't explode without a fuse and I ain't got time to teach you, but they'll burn like a motherfucker so be careful. Better to toss 'em in a dumpster."

Charlie Beck wondered if he could risk starting the Ducati down there. This Sergei hadn't rigged the car unless it was on a very long

I HEARD THE BUGLES CALL

183

delay. Old car engines were pretty simple and he hadn't seen anything suspicious. The bike was behind a loading dock not far from the workshop. He'd take off to Payson, Arizona, where he knew a guy and hang out for his wife's call. He'd give her a week and if she didn't call, fuck it, he'd light out for the territory. This kind of fear was new to him.

"Get dressed, man," Beck said to Belkin. *Tickle-Me-Elmo*, he thought. He couldn't remember who started it, but it was what they'd said to one another heading out of the Ramadi Inn in full rattle for a night prowl.

He remembered what his brainy prick captain said when he re-upped. He'd told the captain that he'd done it to protect his guys until the end of the war, which was true enough. The college twerp had snickered and said, "Some old Greek said this a long time ago, sergeant. Only the dead see the end of the war."

* * * * *

I N the morning Talbot went out to the moped he'd left leaning against his brother's garage. It only had a pathetic cable lock, but it was still there. The little motorized French bicycles were becoming more common back East, but were almost unknown in California. It was the cheapest thing he could find on Craigslist to get him from A to B. It was basically an ordinary push-bike with a small gas engine rubbing the front tire to buzz you up to maybe fifteen mph. It got him astonishing mileage and a lot of stares around town.

Just before Talbot reached the bike, he stopped in his tracks. Something about the mopie was wrong. The whole business of the deer hunt had dialed his alert system up to eleven. Then he saw what it was. Not much, really—just a little metal box under the left pedal that shouldn't have been there. Why on earth did I even notice it? he thought. Possibly because outsiders like himself learned to watch hard for nuances, off-key intonations, unexpected speedbumps. Good old reverse gaydar.

He went back into the house to find the ball of twine he'd seen in a kitchen drawer. Back out in the endless busy white noise of West

184   *BOYSTOWN*

Hollywood he tied the twine to the moped's seat post and backed away unrolling, then around the corner of the house. It was ridiculous, but he played at it in his head. I'm in a movie and I'm the clever one. He knew he'd end up laughing at himself in a minute.

"Fire in the hole," he called, remembered from the movies. Then he pulled on the twine. The bicycle leaned and then fell over hard on the grass with a spokey *twang* of anti-climax. He was just starting to feel really foolish when the motor bicycle shot sideways spontaneously, right at him, and crashed into the corner of the house. It was accompanied by a deafening hammer blow on the great Chinese gong of the universe.

Talbot lay on his side in a fetal position, holding his hands to his ears to try to stop the steam-whistle going off inside.

* * * * *

H E should put a lawyer on retainer, Jack Liffey thought. But who was he kidding? He could barely afford to feed his dog. I'm tired of experiences that are interesting and instructive, he thought, but end with me up shit creek.

He decided the jail was probably the one true melting pot in the city. His first afternoon in the holding tank at the copshop in West Hollywood had been shared with freeway speeders, clueless young men who couldn't pay their child support, and blank-eyed possible psychopaths—*he seemed like such a quiet boy*—all awaiting bail hearings. They had the sense not to ask one another why they were there but one scarred guy yakked on about how unfair everything was.

It'd been too late in the day for bail and after booking the next day he sat on a metal bench in the lunchroom at Twin Towers central jail downtown where he'd been transported in a sticky-seat bus. He stared at his half-pint carton of milk and peanut-butter-and-jelly sandwich. How bad could PBJ be? he wondered, but he wasn't destined to find out, A furious Latino kid with a lot of Olde English lettering was on foot eyeballing his tray.

"Can I help you?"

I HEARD THE BUGLES CALL

185

The kid came quick and grabbed Jack Liffey's sandwich and retreated to his pals across the room, who erupted in applause. A really large Eight-Trey Crip named GDog, whom Jack Liffey was trying to befriend swiveled around on the bench. Probably ill-advisedly, Jack Liffey had chosen to sit with the blacks instead of the Anglos who all seemed to wear swastikas or look murderous.

"Give him the sandwich!" GDog roared. "It's his. We in this together, *esse*."

The jocularity at the kid's table died off.

"You heard me."

GDog lifted one leg, pro linebacker size, over the bench, and Jack Liffey rose with him and placed a hand on his shoulder. "Thank you, friend," Jack Liffey said softly. "Let's not do this. I'm in enough trouble."

"*Si me picas*," one of the Latinos called out, standing and grabbing his crotch. "*Te québras los dientes con mis huesos*." He tried to remember it to ask Gloria. All other sound hushed.

"*Voy sin comer, amigo*," Jack Liffey said mildly. I'll go without eating, friend.

All at once people all over the room came to their feet shouting. Then a siren wheezed to life and somewhere steel doors were clanging shut. Guards began to clatter down the metal stairs into the lunchroom.

"Hit the deck or pay!" a guard bawled.

"Lockdown!" warbled out of loudspeakers.

"I won't forget you, GDog," Jack Liffey told his defender as they all groveled on the hard tiles. Lying beside the table, he was pleased in a peculiar way that it was his stolen sandwich that had nearly set off a riot. But even more pleased that the guards were on the ball and headed it off.

* * * * *

"COULD I see the butterflies? I heard from Vlada Petrovna that they're lovely." This was all in Ukrainian, since her neighbor Masha had hardly learned a word of English beyond "Go away" and "I am fine, thank you," in ten years. She probably knew more Spanish

186   BOYSTOWN

in order to talk to her maid. It showed how insular you could become if you had no job and you burrowed into an exile community.

Alina considered. "My husband doesn't like me to show them off when he's not home. All right, it can't hurt. Be discreet."

"*Baba s vozu—kobyle legche.*" It's easier for the horse when the woman gets off the cart.

They both laughed as Alina led her up the stairs, and she opened the door at the top to Petro's sanctum. Masha oohed and aahed at the dusty glass cases, but not with any real feeling.

"This one is very nice." Alina pointed out her husband's favorite, the big divided butterfly. "This is the valuable one. Something went wrong and it's half female and half male."

"What a tragedy," Masha said. "You wouldn't know whether to beat your wife or shove a rag up your own cunt."

Alina chuckled. "Don't be vulgar, dear. The Americans are very decorous about things like that."

"I know. It's a strange country, isn't it? Freedom seems to mean endless conformity. And endless picking on people. I hate dramas. If I go farther than a *verst*, I hear only two things: Go home, foreigner! Or, Go home, Yid!"

Alina led her neighbor back downstairs. "I didn't know you'd acquired enough English to understand what they're whispering at you."

"I hear what I hear, Allochka."

The samovar on the sideboard was steaming away and the teapot on the *konforka* shelf was ready. That morning Alina had come to see how much help she needed for a party and so she invited Masha over. The dining room table had been set out with envelopes that needed to be stuffed with party invitations and then stuck with stamps. Masha could do that but Alina would write the address herself. She couldn't trust Masha with Roman letters.

"I sense that butterflies are not your special love, Masha."

"I was curious to see them, but they're just bugs. How boring it must be for you."

I HEARD THE BUGLES CALL

187

Alina wanted to agree but if she did, she would loose a long over-due laughing of derision and relief. Loyalty to Petro held her back. Husband, why don't you grow up?

"Let me get you some tea, Mash. Then we can work on the invitations."

"The Communists were right about one thing, Allochka—working together is more efficient."

"More enjoyable, too." She showed her friend one of the invitations she'd had engraved. "Petro is so vain that I didn't dare say he was turning sixty." She translated the text for her. "Join us for a very special birthday, marking a special decade for our beloved Petro Ivanchuk. We love our new land where butterflies fly free—even Jewish butterflies. After many lemons, we all appreciate sweet nectar."

Masha sat back, waiting for the tea. "I wonder if it's our nature to be haunted. I think it's much harder to leave a big country than a small one."

"Maybe. The past is so important, when you uproot yourself, it goes far far away. How can Americans know about *Cheburashka* or the Buttermilk Village? And how can we ever understand this Lone Ranger thing they have?"

"What on earth is *that*?"

* * * * *

G LORIA peered briefly out her bedroom window. Back on the days she'd been scheduled to go on shift just after dawn, she made a minor science of observing the light over East LA and what it meant for her day. Gloom meant she'd be called to wife-beatings and suicides, more than normal anyway, even family annihilators. Intermittent brightness meant liquor stores were going down. Steady sun meant you could put it all away and begin to function like an ordinary cop—responding to whatever came up.

It was sunny this morning and she was off work but she couldn't stay home and enjoy it. The phone machine had a message from Roski, dramatic even for him. He said Jack was being held in Twin Towers as a material witness. She'd only heard of a handful of those in fifteen years on the job, and all of them had been Mexicans set to run hell-bent for the border. She wondered if Jack had pissed off a cop again. He had a mouth on him, and Maeve did, too. Must run in the family. She'd never met Maeve's mother who was down in whitebread surfer land in Redondo Beach. Jack was always a punch-upward sort. I only insult what can hurt me, he'd once told her.

She badged into Twin Towers and walked past the cop-lockers because she wasn't carrying. All LAPD off-duties were required to remain armed, but medical leave wasn't the same as off-duty. She shouted down the just-out-of-training deputy who was telling her the jail was in lockdown and closed up. The jail was run by the county sheriff and there was no love lost with LAPD.

"I'm detective sergeant Gloria Ramirez, internal affairs, badge 2116. Get me Jack Liffey or apply to work in North Dakota."

The young deputy thought about it but took her to the phones at the glass visiting windows that were usually swarming with humanity but were empty now.

"Oh, no," Gloria told him. "Douchebag, get me an interview room." He grumbled a bit but she was not to be denied and eventually she got to the usual featureless room with steel table and chairs.

"You want to record it?"

"Get out of here."

After a suitable delay to punish her, another deputy brought Jack Liffey, who shuffled in sheepishly in blue jail scrubs and laceless shoes. The deputy uncuffed him and enquired with gestures if she would be okay with him.

"I know this guy. If he needs his ass kicked I can do it."

He left and made a noisy show of locking the door.

"I bet you want out of here," she said.

"Does a bear wipe his ass with a rabbit?"

She smiled in sudden relief to hear his voice, despite herself. "Jack, you never change. You make me laugh at the worst of times. In the end, that's all a woman could want."

I HEARD THE BUGLES CALL

189

"I've been told there's a lot more to it than that."

"Perspectives change as we grow desperate."

They talked of Maeve briefly.

"Do your cop colleagues ever sit around their lunchroom griping how coddled the jailbirds are?"

"A few assholes—sure. Three squares a day, no rain on your head, a blanket, TV."

"Tell them this. Breakfast was a hardened brown puddle of mush with a few lumps of gristle tucked in so it looked like the corpse of a hairless mole. It tasted even worse."

She smiled. "Good old mystery mush. You want dinner tonight in Boyle Heights?"

"Oh, yes. I'll lick it off your body if I can."

She ignored the suggestion. "There's some sort of minor lockdown going on, but I can call in favors. Jack. *Material witness.* Did you flip off a police commander?"

"Maybe something like that."

She settled back in the chair. "So other than the mole for breakfast, how do you like it in here?"

"It's a bucket of armpits, Glor. What do you think? But the company here is better than a G-8 summit."

"I don't know what that is, and I don't want to know. Be careful what you say right now, Jack. They probably got a tape going."

Somebody pounded on the door.

"Fuck off!" Gloria yelled.

"Hand me the shotgun," Jack Liffey said loud.

"Great, wiseguy. I'm doing the smalltalk thing because we got to go on yakking for a while. We can't be seen to be short-timers. That has a special meaning in here—unless you actually want a rubber glove up your asshole for drugs."

That calmed him down and he went on for a while telling her about lockdown. For now he was in a group cell for Anglos. There were group cells for blacks and two different ones for Latinos to keep the *sureños* from killing the *norteños.* Much of the time hotheads were shouting insults and challenges but he came to see it was just like dogs on ropes who knew they couldn't actually get at each other. There was a TV set on a high ledge that blared on and on. A deputy announced it was provided as a courtesy by Robert Downey, Jr. after one of his dope busts. He'd bought TVs for every group cell in the jail and paid to have them installed.

"It'll take me an hour or two to spring you."

"Understood. Honestly, I didn't mouth anybody off more than he deserved."

She smiled. "You ever gonna see somebody about that death-wish?"

Jack Liffey's eyes narrowed and she realized that he had probably been pushed near his limit.

"It's a real strain in here," he said in a flat tone. "Sadistic, impersonal, glorying in hate. It's dehumanizing. Guards and us both."

He studied his hands as if he couldn't quite control them. "I want to marry you, Glor. You always say no no no, but I could marry you twice a day forever. I want you to know that—even if I make stupid mistakes. Forget about the girl. It was dumb, it's over. I'd like to marry you before my heart gives out for good so you can inherit all my worldly wealth—that '91 Toyota pickup. Oh, minus what I still owe on the dog's surgery. Think about it, please."

It shook her a bit. She could tell he was serious, but luckily he didn't seem to be needing an immediate reply.

"I actually tried to help that Mars cop, hon. But I wouldn't kiss his angry ass. Have you heard from Maeve?"

"She left a message that there was something she had to follow up."

"Oh, *shit*. This mess is way out of control. People are blowing each other up now. It's like a cartel war in Mexico. I don't want to find a bag of heads by the roadside and have to wonder if hers is in it. No word on the kid she's looking for?"

"No, Jack. You know, you can't save the whole damn world."

"This is my daughter. I have to live with myself forever about this young woman."

I HEARD THE BUGLES CALL 191

* * * * *

R OSKI had called Maeve and warned her again that anything to do with Benjy or Russians or Ukrainians was too dangerous right now. He insisted she'd best go somewhere anonymous for a few days, and she finally took him seriously.

In turn, Maeve called Talbot. If it was dangerous for her, it was a lot worse for him. "Pack up," Maeve said. "Your death is very much the agenda."

"I kind of found that out. Pack for how long?"

"Just take a sweater and underwear you can wash. And a couple of big books."

"Where should I go?"

"I'll pick you up. I can protect you. Don't say anything more on the phone, okay. Don't even say my name. Forget your cellphone. I don't trust GPS."

"Got it," he said. "How do you feel about all this?"

"I think I'm in the middle of a long decline of my little girl assurance of being under daddy's protection." She couldn't help thinking how living in her dad's slipstream had in fact exposed her to danger many times.

"God, I used to feel lucky," he said. "Everything sort of worked out for me. Now I'm not sure if luck is in my character at all."

"Luck is just a bad idea," she said. "We can talk about metaphysics later. I promise to get you out of this alive, pal."

"Maybe I am still lucky."

FIFTEEN

Homesick for Innocence

JACK Liffey was released to Gloria's custody an hour later, with the lockdown still in force. She still had her *chutzpah* magic. Leave it to me, he thought, to parachute into town, start a war over a sandwich, and flee out the back door. It was *Yojimbo*—or the spaghetti remake *A Fistful of Dollars*. Or even *Red Harvest* before them all.

"Are you keeping count of the number of times you've rescued me?" he asked, as she drove her RAV-4 east toward the Fourth Street Bridge. It was about time one of them bought a car built in the twenty-first century, he thought. She'd been relying on the hopped-up Ford Explorers from the LAPD motor pool.

"That's not important right now."

"Saving my ass matters."

"Your ass is important, Jackie. So what are you going to do to thank me?"

He hoped he was right about the tremor in her voice. "Name it. Absolutely anything."

"Let me think about it. That's too good an offer to waste."

Almost halfway across the long bridge ahead of them, a man climbed on the concrete railing wearing a rubber lizard suit with a long green tail. Oh, not now. The lizard started waving his arms in circles, trying to keep from falling to his death on the rail yard or the concrete

194   BOYSTOWN

bed of the LA River. Gloria crammed on the brakes, the car slewed sideways, and she leapt out and ran toward the man.

"Hold on!" she hollered. "I'm here."

Jack Liffey was out of the car and running, but he was no match for cop instincts. The lizard twisted around nonchalantly to salute Gloria with two fingers like a Cub Scout and started to fall backwards before she got there.

Jack Liffey felt a spasm of horror as the man dropped out of sight. Gloria was looking over the rail as he got there to see a small square parachute deploy. The lizard woo-hoo-hooed, and the ornate Gothic bridge had its first lizard BASE jump. A half dozen people below were filming.

He took a risk and kissed Gloria's neck. She came around unexpectedly and kissed back for a moment, and that simple act made him instantly tumescent.

"If I were on the job now, I'd bust those smart-asses for stealing some heartbeats I'll never get back."

"They don't want your heartbeats, but I do." He brushed the front of the one breast that had nothing to with silicone.

"Not now, Jackie. I'm trying to live right and this crazy stuff exhausts me."

"You want me to drive home?"

"I guess I do live right," she said as she handed him the keys.

* * * * *

TALBOT set a small overnight bag at his feet in Maeve's car.

"I hope you can live out of that for a while," she said.

"We're not going to be leaving civilization, are we?"

"Let's leave metaphysics aside," she said. "Right now we're going to an all-girl unofficial UCLA dorm in the Topanga hills to pick up my stuff. Then somewhere safe."

"A lesbian house?"

"Mostly no. We just decided we'd keep the toilet seats down. My lover Bunny is probably in-between, to be honest."

HOMESICK FOR INNOCENCE

195

On the greenbelt that ran down the middle of San Vicente they passed three midgets in running trunks pissing against a coral tree. They seemed entirely un-self-conscious about it. It was the kind of thing she and her dad used to joke about in their spot-the-oddity contests, but that was long ago in a safer world. Talbot didn't seem to notice so maybe it was just a random hallucination. If only she could find a life-partner as gratifying as her dad.

"I have a question about lesbian lit, if you don't mind. You brought it up once and I looked them up. Why is it in lesbian classics that one of the lovers either dies or goes straight? It's the only genre that's trying to erase itself."

The question startled her into slowing the car so much that a Mercedes behind honked. "I guess back in the day punishment for violating the natural order was come back inside or die."

"The male gay classics can be sad but not that."

She sighed. "I guess women carry an extra burden. We're supposed to be maintaining the social order, you know."

"What you're doing is rescuing me. Thanks for true." He told her about the hunting trip and what he knew of the aftermath. "A moment of craziness and they tried to cover it up and made it all worse like Abbott and Costello. You know, I'd like to find that butterfly hunter and apologize to him on my knees, but I wouldn't know how to find him." He was quiet a moment. "Your dad's a detective."

"Let's drop it for now."

"This summer I screwed up somewhere along the line. I did my best to befriend my fellow workers. Was that so wrong?"

"Hold that thought." Maeve followed the twisty route down through Santa Monica Canyon to PCH. She'd better get this guy and herself far away before she leapt on any new "case."

They drove west on the coast highway alongside the low rollers of the Pacific.

Out of the blue he said, "The great defining moment of my nation wasn't a declaration of independence. It was a bar brawl against the police in Greenwich Village. You know, we don't have fireworks to celebrate Stonewall—we just march under a long papier maché penis."

"You're being mean."

"I guess," he said pensively.

A flight of pelicans was gliding alongside over the water, keeping pace.

"Think of the great gays," she said. "Da Vinci and Michelangelo. And how about Proust? Whitman. Virginia Woolf and Auden. Don't be dismissive."

He made a humming sound as if he required it to get his brain in gear. "I've got philosophers, too. Plato, Foucault and Wittgenstein. I guess being oppressed breeds creativity. That's what they say anyway."

"Who's 'they?'"

"People who aren't oppressed, I bet. I mean it about trying to apologize to the butterfly guy, Maeve. I think it's the right thing to do."

"I never try to keep anybody from the right thing."

Talbot went pensive as they turned up the steep green canyon toward Topanga.

* * * * *

"How tall are you?" Roski asked.

"One hundred forty-five centimeters," Gorbenko told him.

"What's that in America?"

"Figure it out yourself, asshole. The rest of the world uses real measures."

"You're not *in* the rest of the world, little man. I won't call you hunchback if we can try to get along."

"Fuck your mother, copper."

The interview room was about as plain as a room could be, though some joker had taped up an old poster of bearded men kissing by the street artist who called himself Homo Riot.

Roski had had trouble getting into Twin Towers. His arson badge didn't go very far there, and the jail seemed to be on lockdown after some race-tinged punch-up. Gorbenko was in protective custody—an

HOMESICK FOR INNOCENCE

isolation area near booking where they held transvestites, pedophiles, snitches and gangbangers who said they wanted out of their *klikas*. Presumably, a hunchback was seen to be at risk, too.

"Can I ask you a question?"

"Can you get me out of here?"

"Not really, but a good word from me wouldn't hurt."

"At least get them to turn off the shitty 24/7 hip-hop."

"Victor—may I call you Victor?"

"May I call you pussyface?"

"You've had your share of hard knocks in life, Mr. Gorbenko. I'm not without sympathy. I'm not a cop. Actually I'm an arson investigator with the fire department. If all were known, we might be on the same side."

"Then you may kiss my hump."

Roski had studied the reports on deep interrogation. Long ago, while the CIA was busy beating and waterboarding Arabs, the FBI discovered that the technique that worked was befriending them and suggesting you knew a lot more than you did. Roski did know quite a bit.

"It's too bad about your neighbor Ruslan. Shot to death and put on your bed. I hear you were good friends."

"You hear wrong, worm. He was annoying as crotchrot and he was shit at *preferans*."

"Something has come up. It's about the man that this is all about— you know who I mean. And the danger he's in. I'd like to prevent him and anybody else getting hurt." Roski offered a smile. "We need to share."

"Fuck you, doodledum, and the country you rode in on. I left one collapsing chickenshit empire. You can keep this one."

This was one angry little man, Roski thought.

"I been the guy you can hate all my life," he snapped. "I long for the day all you assholes have to wake up and look death straight in the eye, the way I do. The big D says: 'Open your eyes and beg. Maybe I'll let you live one more day. Another day being old and crippled and useless. Better just snuff yourself.'"

"About that man I mentioned, I want to help *him*, too."

Victor Gorbenko stared hard at him. "You don't know shit about this or me or him."

"I've never faced what you have," Roski said. "How could I? But we can laugh at death together. Who cares about us? Three or four people care when you're gone, then you're just gone. Poof. Maybe I could get us some sleepytime pills and we could both end our boredom."

"Good idea, crapolahead."

"But first, let's help your big pal. He needs it." Just give me a name, Roski thought. A profession, a hint. An entry point to peel back the laminations. He couldn't waterboard, but he was about to throttle the little prick.

Another half hour of humoring his obstinacy, and the little man finally seemed to accept Roski as a Swiss envoy from a hostile world.

"Pretty sophisticated stuff, the way you burned up that car. The pinetar was smart."

Gorbenko raised one bushy eyebrow. "Guerilla training. I was a tiny six-year-old Jewish cripple, doomed six ways. Shitsticks. I hung out with the Young Pioneers just to learn how to kill Germans."

"Mr. Gorbenko, there's so many people out there shooting and blowing things up I don't know what's going to happen to your friend unless I find him."

"Can you guess what we used to say in Odessa about the big storm?"

"Of course I can't."

"'When it comes, the seabirds can't make it back to the sea.' Is Petro in real danger?"

Petro. *Bingo.* "I won't lie to you, but I know he'll be a lot safer if I know who he is."

The hunchback stared at Roski. "I know you're playing me, man. Give me a good reason to trust you."

"I'm Jewish, too, Victor. *Hava Nagilah.* In our hostile world. My wife Judith left me for parts unknown and took the kids. I could never get the job I really wanted. I'm being treated for depression. I need a friend, too, more than you know."

HOMESICK FOR INNOCENCE 199

"I gave up the name Petro, didn't I?"

"Yes. But I'll trade you what I do know." He told the diminutive man that the SUV he'd burned to the ground was owned by a highly trained soldier who knew exactly why it was burned and would find Petro eventually.

They talked a while longer, and eventually he got it all: the name was Petro Ivanchuk Pogorelets, butterfly collector and community college professor at LA City College. He lived in the east end of WeHo with the other Ukrainian Jews.

"Thank you, Victor," Roski said. "I'll do everything I can for Petro and you, too."

The small man winced and wriggled. The straight aluminum chair was obviously hurting his back. "Wait, Mr. Deadass. All my life, I thought I was required to suffer. Is that nuts? Come see me again. I want to hear about Petro."

Roski shook his hand. It was about all he could really do for him.

When he got back to his office, he looked up 145 centimeters and found it was four-foot-nine. He found he was 190 centimeters himself. It didn't sound so impressive that way.

* * * * *

"YOUR affection had a good shelf life," Gloria said earnestly. She opened the fridge and took out a bottle of red wine—a departure from her usual beer. He should have told her not to refrigerate it but he hadn't. She handed him a can of ginger ale. She told him she'd been brooding about the months of rage and inner turmoil, and about how she might be driving him away.

"The affection is forever," Jack Liffey said. "The tenderness could do with a little help."

"Hush. I need to talk now. I had a real bad time with those bad cops doing their choir practice up in Bakersfield. Choir practice is cop lingo—that means drinks and wild stuff after shift. I never told you all of it, but you probably figured a lot of it out. They beat me and ... did about everything you can imagine when they had me tied up and my clothes off. It left me, like, hollowed out. I didn't know if I'd ever come back and be a woman again. This fat old lady was already self-conscious."

"You're not—"

"I said hush. I know I never been Miss Nice Guy. You know I'm a Paiute kid from a single-wide on a rez so small they call it a *rancheria*. A whore for a mother and an unknown cowboy for a father. Then a lot of rotten fostering by LA Mexicans just because I had a Mexican name. I wept inside after Bako, Jackie, seeing you so good to me over and over. And I kept pushing you away until I wanted to die out of shame and let you go free for some good woman. Saying this is really hard, you know?"

He nodded once. Hush.

"I can't pretend that all my MO is recent and just because of those assholes. People talk a lot now about this bipolar thing. You're sad as shit on one side of the line and then you're laughing and doing jumping jacks on the other side. Maybe, but I don't get the happy side much. Since I was a girl, all I mostly got was a rathole of shame and being damn tired. Why is that? Don't answer."

She was well into the second tall glass of red wine and he wished her on. He knew some of it but she'd never opened up like this. Gloria set the wine tumbler down, made a fierce face and then drew an imaginary pistol from her skirt-waist and banged it all around the kitchen. *Jesus.* But never straight at him. She gave a single quick spasm-cough of humor. "I only dreamed of shooting up the shiftroom when my blue brothers was riding me. *Squaw. Wu-wu-wu. Weepy woman. You on the rag, doll?*" A tear threaded down her cheek and she quickly brushed it away.

He fiddled with his ginger ale can as a big fart built up and he leaned and wriggled to soften it but it blatted out. *Christ*, not now. Luckily she was too inner-focused to notice.

"Jackie, what is today, Friday? Okay. I'm feeling it's good to talk like this to lift a lot of weight off. Something pulled a plug on my anger

HOMESICK FOR INNOCENCE

201

a little. Can we make Friday evening a regular talk-time? I did it with your daughter a couple days ago and it helped."

"Yes, of course. Every Friday. You're on."

She stared at him, her fierce expression hard to read. Just then Loco started baying at something in the back yard but stopped. "Jackie, I think we're both brave and strong in our ways. But—maybe I need professional help. Can you get me a shrink, but really on the QT?"

"For sure. And I'll kill them if they ever tell." He hadn't been this happy in a long time; it was what he'd pushed for years.

Her whole body seemed to slump a little, and she reached for the wine bottle. "Okay, I got an idea for a favor. Remember?"

"Oh, yes. For my indiscretion."

"I ain't looking for any off-the-wall stuff. Can you make love to me slow and careful like we're both kids and just finding out how to do it. I never seen nothing good come out of the other stuff."

"Can't hurt. I think we're both homesick for innocence."

* * * * *

M AEVE fought into a parking space on the far side of the narrow mountain road between two of her roommates' cars.

"Bravo," Talbot said. "You park a lot better than me."

"Thanks. Some of it's the cussedness you get growing up in the suburbs. We hate to ever pay for parking."

They grabbed the Thai take-aways from Cholada down on PCH, and she led him along the outside path to her garage-studio rather than running the gauntlet of the girls' whistling and hooting. What would Bunny make of it? Bunny's old Lexus wasn't there yet but Maeve would have to explain later. And what did she make of the idea of *Man on the Floor*? Nothing—she was just doing her duty, helping out like a Liffey does, but, God, was he pretty.

She couldn't stop Talbot from drifting across the big studio room to inspect her paintings. Luckily the vagina series was under a tarp. She busied herself gathering clothes and having a bit of troubled reflection. Was she playing at something bringing Talbot here? He was gay, so was she. End of story. She would finish packing and drive them to separate rooms at a motel up the coast where he'd be safe. But it was late and she was getting tired.

"You've got a lovely eye for the physical body, really. That hand is so authentic."

"Thanks, but I've hit a wall that I can't seem to get past. It keeps telling me I'm just an amateur, decorative but nothing revolutionary, no soul. And if I were serious I'd move to Paris or New York right away."

"Jeez, Maeve, give yourself a break."

"Let's eat. My spicy noodles won't be any good later."

Over dinner she told him that she was planning to get them up the coast for a while. Oxnard wasn't far and they had cheap motels. He kept saying he still wanted to find the butterfly hunter to apologize. Over dinner her spine tingled at the unmistakable scrape of Bunny's key hunting for the lock.

"Oh, god."

"Your girlfriend?"

"No, Dracula."

"Shall I hide under the bed?" Talbot suggested.

The door came open, the room mercifully lit only by city light from Santa Monica and LA coming in through the big window. "I'm sorry, babe. I'm a bit drunk." It was Bunny's softest, most trusting voice.

"Bunny, hold up, I'm being a bodyguard tonight—protecting a guy who's under threat of death. We're eating dinner here."

"Hello, Bunny," he said. "She was just telling me about you."

"Nothing happened," Maeve put in quickly. "He's gay, hon."

"Well, isn't this a TV sitcom."

"Please come in and sit with us. Meet Talbot, you'll like him. I need you to help protect him."

"Oh, piss up a rope, Maeve. You're such a little tin saint."

"Bunny, don't—"

The door slammed.

"Go to her," Talbot said.

"God, what do I say?"

HOMESICK FOR INNOCENCE

"Run and say you love her. In the end, you only regret the things you *don't* do."

"I don't know. She says I'm so terrific and then a few words take you so down."

"She was upset," Talbot said. "I don't even know what a tin saint is."

"Self-righteous, I bet. I better try to talk to her."

* * * * *

A FEW qualms had slipped in quietly to Alina Abramovna about the birthday party. Everybody deserved a festive sixtieth, but Petro was being slighted by some of his acquaintances, mostly American ones, and he wouldn't talk about it. He had found out about the surprise party, of course, and had given her a supplemental list of names.

Alina studied the list and saw it right away. One of the names—Olga Nikolayevna—had never once come up between them. She had long assumed he had a mistress. It was not the end of the world, but it might be uncomfortable. Her own lover Dr. Trachtenberg would be there, too, and she could play with that in her mind. Such a complicated Russian novel we make wherever we go, she thought. She'd come a long way in life from the Ukrainian village of Berezyne that was almost to the border of Moldova, and it was true that some of the roads along the way hadn't been paved. Her schoolteachers had told her she would have a terrible fate if she didn't learn to be more diligent, but she'd found being pretty and agreeable much more useful. The pleasures of the moment had always kept her from books.

When she had met the shy scholar Petro Ivanchuk at her aunt's house one lovely strawberry summer, she'd responded immediately to his dry and worldly humor, and the fact that his presence made her feel observed and grounded, as somebody put it to her. He could still do that. Though they'd both wandered sideways in their affections from time to time, they were deeply committed.

What had her aunt said? *However much you feed the tamed wolf, he's going to glance toward the woods from time to time.*

Da. She had found it hard to make new friends in this land, a perfect set-up for Dr. Trachtenberg who would ask her friendship as barter for their healthcare. The Ukrainian soul was always generous with those in need, as long as there might be a little recompense.

SIXTEEN
Night Watch

U NDER a little duress, Petro Pogorelets had agreed to meet Roski in the afternoon at *Traktir,* a sidewalk café in West Hollywood—after Roski swore to keep the matter from the police. Roski had his own reasons. Len Mars was out of control and he didn't want the poor man dragged off in handcuffs, or himself. He was early to the café and took a seat behind a low wall with flowerboxes. A heavyset middle-aged man with curly graying hair was approaching on foot, favoring one leg. Something was quite European about him—a business suit in the LA afternoon, a shiny-fabric dress shirt.

The other occupied tables held couples, and Petro came straight and joined him with a tentative greeting. He waved to an open bar inside where an eye-smartingly gorgeous blonde was wiping out glasses, one by one. Roski had been trying not to stare.

"If it's not too early." The man had a slight accent, but it was charming.

"It's five o'clock somewhere," Roski said. "I like single-malt Scotch."

"I know the idiom. I declare the sun over the yard'arm"

The woman arrived, and a contretemps ensued in their language, probably Ukrainian. Petro said something that circled around the word 'Scotch' and she shook her head. He responded with a gesture toward the bar where many Scotches were in evidence and said something about *vee-skee*. Her eyes lit up, her very large breasts jiggled in the low-cut dress, and she hurried away.

"You were limping quite a bit as you approached," Roski said. "Are you okay?"

"I'm sixty years old day after tomorrow. This is what I'm like now."

"I know you're a distinguished philosopher, sir, and a renowned lepidopterist, and, sadly, after changing countries, you've been forced to teach temporarily in a community college."

"My decline of expectations may be temporary."

"That's good. I had to trade knowing signs and representation for learning signs of a fire-accelerant."

Petro shrugged. "You can push all your furniture against the door, and the bad luck will get in the window."

"What was your specialty in philosophy, if you had specialties in Ukraine?"

"My landmarks were Nietzsche, Epstein, and some Eastern Europeans you've never heard of."

"I bet I have, but we're not here for that. We're here because of several dead men scattered round West Hollywood. Don't worry, I'm not the police. I'm just a fireman investigating an arson, but I know you're in danger."

The waitress arrived with their drinks. Petro had a vodka, of course. Roski gave up not looking and side-eyed the spilling breasts for a moment. Jesus.

"Nothing more unless we call," Roski said, and Petro seemed to translate for her.

He didn't know if Ukrainian waitresses butted in like Americans with incessant "Is your drink okay? What more would you like?"

"About your leg," Roski said when she was gone. "Three men—no, *four* including a sheriff's deputy—are now dead because of your leg. If you don't tell me what you know, sir, you'll have to tell someone a whole lot nastier."

"Is that a threat?"

"It's much more a belief."

NIGHT WATCH

"Things have a tendency to go on happening despite beliefs, wouldn't you say? The British dictionary-maker Samuel Johnson kicked a rock to prove the rock exists. Primitive but functional, so very British. Today, a man walks on the moon. Tomorrow, we all go on picking our noses."

Roski took a pleasurable first sip and decided he rather liked the big garrulous guy.

"I'll match you and raise. Lacan said, 'We're all just defects in the perfection of non-being.'"

"A trashy aphorism, sir. The French are possessed by rhetoric, they have no deep soul. Mr. Roski, you can't argue me into telling you what I don't know, no matter how post-modern you make it."

"You're very much in danger, sir. Tell me what you don't know."

He made a face and sipped his vodka. "I tripped hiking in the Sierra mountains when I was chasing a fairly rare sulphur or *colias*. It looks a lot like a leaf of cabbage. Falling broke a killing bottle I had with me and it stabbed my thigh. My skin tone has degraded with age and the jagged glass left a deep wound. Do you need to see it? I can show you the wound, as our savior offered the great Christian skeptic, St. Doubting Thomas."

Far too much detail, Roski thought. "Please don't take your pants off for me. I'm not a worthy skeptic. I do wonder if you might know a Victor Antonenkovich Gorbenko. He's a hunchback, I don't really have a more polite word. He seems to know you well."

He held a pretty good poker face, then gulped down the vodka. "No, sir. Nor do I know Dr. Frankenstein's hunchback assistant Igor."

The man was getting ready to stand up and depart.

"When things get dangerous, call me," Roski said and handed across his card.

Petro smiled briefly. "My grandmother always said, *Bog ne vydast, svin'ya ne s'yest.* 'God willing, everything will be all right, and the pigs won't eat you. I have nothing more to say.'" He left a ten on the table.

"Look," Roski said quickly. "A sign." A small white butterfly had settled on a geranium in the nearest flower box.

"A hairstreak." Petro couldn't resist identifying it. "*Ministrymon.* Common in the Hollywood Hills chaparral, but not so common down here."

Roski watched the man closely. "That butterfly is quite the vision of freedom, flitting around, but to the caterpillar it came from, it represents extinction, the end of its universe."

"Good afternoon, Mr. Roski. I don't think I like you."

Things can always get lousier, Roski thought.

* * * * *

S ERGEI had found out that his bicycle bomb had missed killing Talbot. The young man was irrelevant but would have to go. In a contingent world, every loose end raised the odds of failure.

He lifted his weekly pot of *shchi*—cabbage soup—off the stovetop in his anonymous furnished rental and carried it to the window to stare out. He made a large pot every week and ate little else except brown bread. The *shchi* kept easily without refrigeration. *Rodnoi otets nadoyest, a shchi—nikogda,* he thought. One may tire of one's own father, but never of *shchi.* He never used the oven, being unclear how the indicated Fahrenheit temperatures related to the gasmarks 1-7 he had grown up with.

He had had no missions against anyone worthy in quite some time, though the American Marine was a question mark. He hadn't backed down an inch when Sergei offered a truce, a lie of course. His cellphone fuse simply failed to work. Inexcusable. We are two *ronin* wandering lost in the world and one of them is getting sloppy.

He emptied a small plastic tub of Russian sour cream into the soup and used his worn wooden spoon to eat it cold. He kept the spoon with him always. It had been his grandmother's, the color on the delicately carved flowers of the handle worn off but for ghosts of paint-stain in the wood. It was the only tangible item he had left of his unpleasant youth and it had been used to rap his knuckles hard.

Sergei had a feeling that Charlie Beck would not be his problem in the end. That would be the street waif who'd seen him make the first mistake at Belkin's window. He knew she panhandled and scrounged

NIGHT WATCH

on the strange night-centric Hollywood Boulevard. Easy prey. In darkness he knew how to hide and watch ten hours or more in plain sight.

The *shchi* was not tasting right. Garlic, onion, pepper, cabbage and a bag of chopped up cooked chicken he'd bought on the way home. His spoon dabbled with it, favoring the *smetana* sour cream. He was beginning to wonder about all his self-control in a world that no longer wanted it or him.

* * * * *

B ELKIN played *pasyanz*—what Americans called solitaire—with a deck of repulsive sado-porn cards he'd found in the safe house. Beck had not returned as promised. No one had come down from the main house to shout at him and apparently they didn't care. He tried not to look closely at the photos of women being sexually assaulted by multiple men. Plopping the cards face up he could ignore them. The pictures sent his mind into overdrive, worrying about poor defenseless Cat. The rich were so damn sick. He worried that Cat might have come home to peek over the back fence for the rock that was their signal. Or had moved it herself to try to signal him.

Belkin opened his last beer and sat back daydreaming about him and Cat—if only he could take her to a safe place liked this up in the mountains somewhere. He couldn't stop himself imagining a chaste kiss and he worried about life crushing him like an insect for daydreaming about happiness. He held the deck behind his back as he took the next card.

Red three goes on the four of spades. Why do men find sex cruelty appealing? he wondered. Do we hate women so very much? How could guys not think of their own mothers? And all those childhood tormenters—the bullies, the brutal teachers, the commissars. Maybe men had to be cruel to pretend they weren't vulnerable. Even when I came to like breaking rules, I only stole cars and robbed money, running free at night with the other guys. I never hurt nobody if I could help it. But so many people are all twisted and bent. He wondered if there would be an afterlife in a better world.

210   *BOYSTOWN*

* * * * *

"*STOP!*" Talbot yelled.

Maeve knew he felt the car going off a cliff, made worse by the evening light.

"It's okay," she said.

Her Echo slapped a bit on its springs as it plopped down into the steep descent.

His palms were crossed on his chest to hold his heart inside.

"You just took a year off my life."

"A warning wouldn't have helped. It's in the gut. It happened to me the first time."

"I'll do better later in life." He said.

"You'll like this guy. He might be able to out-philosophize you."

She hadn't called ahead but only decided to come as they left Topanga. If Roski wasn't home, she'd head for the freeway and the nearest exit.

Lights were on inside though, and she hurried toward the door ahead of Talbot, suddenly spooked by the thought of murderers out in the twilight.

"*Maeve*. What's up?" Roski opened the door wearing a long red plaid bathrobe.

"Hi, Mr. Roski. By all rights we should be on our way out of town at a hundred miles an hour, but I felt we could help each other. This is Talbot Denny. I think he's at the root of everything."

"Come in, come in."

"They're trying to kill him now."

"Should I arm myself?" Roski said, kidding.

"I'd feel safer," Talbot said.

"Ah."

There was very little seating in the front room—mostly exercise equipment—and he took them to a scruffy breakfast room off the kitchen.

"Can I offer adult beverages? Coffee? Six-guns? You tell me."

"It's serious," Maeve said. "Beer would be super."

NIGHT WATCH

They settled onto the wraparound wooden bench with Coronas, and Talbot told him the tale of the hunting party and the ridiculous shooting and then the bitter arguments and trying to hunt the victim down. Also the small explosive attached to his bike pedal. He offered a lot more detail than Roski needed to hear, Maeve thought, but he was compulsive about explaining the "grounding" of events. Okay, sure.

"I feel I owe the poor man an apology," Talbot said. "It all feels so stupid and I should have found a way to stop it."

"You couldn't have at the time. Do you know that four men are dead now? At least one from your hunting party. That guy of the butterfly net has friends and some of them have a lot of weaponry and military training. I've been warning your dad off. There's a war going on out there, and yes, you should have come forward sooner, son."

Talbot's face fell. "Aww. Who's dead?"

"Do you really care? One body is probably the idiot who shot first, your workmate Zeke something. One is an unlucky cop. The others are nameless foreigners who may as well have dropped in by parachute. No one will ever find out their names. There's another one of those on the loose. It's the cop's death should worry you most in the long run. A madly punitive DA could hit you through very slitted eyes with a charge of felony murder. You know, the poor guy who was just waiting in the car when the bank robbers killed the guard. You've seen it in cop shows."

"Really?"

"Oh, yes, I know of a woman who spent half her life in prison just for carrying a few guns to Mississippi so the SNCC guys could defend themselves against the Klan."

"Aw, *shit*," Talbot banged his forehead on the table.

"Do it again, son. If your brains leak out, it'll save everybody a lot of trouble. Maeve, there's such a thing as accessory *after* the fact, too. I should be calling the police right now. So you listen hard."

"Can I hit my head, too?"

"Just listen: I'm not a lawyer and I'm not sworn law enforcement, so I'm not considered what's called an officer of the court. It would be a real stretch to prosecute me but even defense lawyers, believe me, always say, if you did it, don't tell me."

There was a gunshot outside, in mid distance, and all three of them stared hard at the outer wall of the kitchen as if something would come crashing through at them.

"Car backfire?" Talbot said.

Roski shook his head. "This is the edge of gangland, but isn't everywhere. A police helicopter will be circling in a minute. What a country. We pour dumptrucks full of guns in the poor neighborhoods and then lock everybody up for touching them."

"Can we talk about this 'accessory' business?" Maeve said.

Roski stared hard at them in turn as he pursed his lips. "Will you two agree to follow my advice?"

"Oh, *yes*."

"Yes, sir."

"You're out of your depth—are we agreed?"

Distressed head bobs.

"First, let's have no panicky runaway. Maeve, I'll take your car keys."

She hated to relinquish the key ring with the keys to her studio, Gloria's house and her mom's, but she didn't hesitate.

"You're probably not going to be sent to the hoosgow, but everybody gets to pay for bad judgment in some way. You two will stay right here tonight. You'll be safe. There's a back bedroom down the hall with one big bed. Make your own arrangements. I'll put your car in my garage and put mine on the street."

"What about getting in touch with my dad?" Maeve said.

"Not tonight."

* * * * *

A FTER dark Sergei got to the post where he would keep watch for the waif. He had just walked over a bronze star for Charles Boyer, whoever that was. A recessed shop entry for Tabu Tattoos would be for him, not far from Hollywood and Vine, names that resonated in the recesses of his memory but he didn't know why. A metal shutter

NIGHT WATCH

had been rolled down to guard the window. Skinny letters on the over-hang offered Expert Tattoos, Piercings, Souvenirs, Smoke Paraphernalia, and weirdly, Googly Eyes. It seemed unlikely that rich movie stars had ever hung out here. A fleapit cinema next door was running "Film Orgy: Dead Flesh Feast." Across the street was an empty shop that said "Retail for Lease," then Chuey's Pupusas, and Passion Nails, all dark for the night.

He heel-squatted in the deep alcove and his narrow slice of the world out there was occasionally crossed by strollers, mostly alone. A girl in thigh-high leather boots, a non-obvious gender with long green hair, a bare male chest with nipple rings. Some of the passers-by were in a hurry and some were not. A few had companions. In a lifetime of strange, Sergei had never been in a place where people tried so hard to look peculiar.

He knew he could hold his place for the rest of the night. If you don't move, no one notices you. But even if they paused and stared, he was sure they would get alarmed and hurry away.

After midnight the pedestrians thinned out and even the cars passed more infrequently. He could see their wash of headlights approach in the angled windows on either side of him, glare briefly then vanish. The trick of a night watch was not to see except what you needed to see. You stilled your senses to the basics. Long ago his trainer had told him—though Sergei had never been sure how serious he'd been—that he had learned the rule in Angola by watching herds of impala. *Comrade, there are only two states of consciousness: grazing and flight. In our case as soldiers, it's waiting and attack.* The trick, he'd said with a little grin, as with the impala, was to be able to switch in an instant.

A rattling sound approached, with breaks of changing tempo. Atop a skateboard, a young woman in an old-fashioned party dress and red high-top tennis shoes rattled past him. Nothing, just grazing. Stay light in your attention, his instructor had said. But *heavy* light, so your mind doesn't drift like a balloon. You could always be killed in an instant, too.

After midnight, a dog somewhere switched from its dot-dash barking to an ugly snarl. A throaty old American *strassenkreuzer* passed slowly and suddenly accelerated. A police car switched on its siren and flashed across his narrow world. Eventually most noises died away. It was odd, but a far more peaceful night than the scorched darkness near his firebase in Chechnya. A damp wind blew from the west where he knew the Pacific Ocean waited fifteen kilometers away.

At one o'clock, a couple of angry kids stomped into sight and halted abruptly in full view to carry on an argument about total freedom and their right to music downloads. The boys moved on without a glance into his shadows. Later, a barefoot young boy in torn T-shirt and jeans stumbled into view and waited, shuffling his feet and coughed softly into a rag. The boy glanced at the rag and then dropped it like poison. Sergei could see blood on the rag.

Enough, Sergei's heart cried out. Where was his soul hiding in this world? Why didn't he just rush out to this boy and get him to a doctor. Feed him, adopt him as a son. Caution interrupted and told him there was pain clinging to every life, and sympathy was promiscuous. It was better to keep your steel shutters down. The dog barked for a long time and then stopped. The cessation of a sound was rarely a good sign. An eerie A.M. quiet held sway for a while, with only distant urban whisperings.

Was steel shutters on his soul the real problem? he thought—the waking to loneliness and despair. It could take him five long minutes now to gather the willpower to sit and greet the new day. Another day of being the stone he needed to be. How delicious it would be to sleep on and on or wake and join a laughing friendly football match.

Sergei wondered if he really was in the line that carried down from Chapayev, Spartacus, Shaka Zulu, Caesar, Alexander. He was a better warrior than the American Marine for sure, but he wasn't certain any more of his belonging to the very top.

Scrape-scrape. An old man with wild hair came into view dragging along a ladder like a dray horse with stuffed plastic bags tied on. The man hacked and spit directly into the alcove before plodding on. Wind whistled and keened sending two cold fingers to stroke his neck. It reminded him of standing in the mudroom of his uncle's house out

NIGHT WATCH

on the steppe and opening the door. By morning the snow would be a meter deep.

Then only the *shush-shush* of faraway traffic, the city snoring in sleep.

He finally put his monkey-mind to rest, banishing unprofessional thoughts that swung from tree to tree. He was on soldier watch, soldier intensity.

Sergei, anything to report?

No, sir. Neither threats nor targets. I'm in focus now. I needed this night to rebuild my efficiency.

Are you sure you have done so?

Oh, yes. I'm efficient in every fucking particular. Test me.

Test yourself, soldier.

Zam!

The young woman appeared in his limited view like a lightning-strike. She stared straight at him from the sidewalk, slit-focused on him with a cat's night vision. Barefoot, ragged, but intense. He could see she recognized him from their confrontation at the bedroom window. Then she vanished without seeming to move at all—as she came.

Dammit, Sergei. You're still grazing while your prey is in flight. Chase.

SEVENTEEN

Love Is a Dreadful Loss

ROSKI felt heavy when he woke, as if he was holding up the world. The sad hunchback, and Maeve, and friend. The deaths, the feud-war of some sort. What was it all? He might be the only nexus of enough information to put it to rest. He could see how UN mediators felt facing intractable wars. Why on earth had identical-looking Serbs and Croats and Albanians fought each other so cruelly after centuries of intermarrying? They spoke the same damn language and no one else could tell them apart. And everyone swearing they were the real victims, the only victims! What craziness.

His breath was sour as he heaped in extra coffee. Maeve stumbled in wearing only a T-shirt and undies. "Put something on, please. You're a little too fetching. There's a robe on the bathroom door."

"Sure, Unca Walt. Fetching, am I?"

She came back wearing his man's cotton kimono. "This is cool. Like the ones with storks and cherry trees the Japanese women wear. Where did you get it?"

"It's too early to blather."

"Okay, make me some coffee."

He nodded to the coffeemaker, which was starting to gargle.

"You must be a morning person," Roski said. "How about the boy?"

"I'm the same cheerful pain-in-the-butt all day. I don't know about him. We're not an item, you know. I'm just trying to save his life."

"Keep him here today while I do reconnaissance out in the cruel world. Guns and bombs. If people don't have those, they get machetes and clubs. They'd end up killing each other with staplers if they had to."

"I don't think people are nasty unless somebody makes them that way," Maeve said.

"Sure. Eggs? Bacon?"

"I'm vegetarian but not Vegan. I can fix the eggs for all of us if you'll take scrambled."

"Chop up some onion."

"I'm there." She crossed the kitchen and hugged him a little too intimately, and he stiffened. "Help me, Jesus."

* * * * *

J ACK Liffey was making Gloria's favorite breakfast, *machaca*, stirring shredded beef, chopped peppers and onion and then scrambling eggs into it. At the end he added a small can of the hot *Herdez* to one side. Last night, they'd gently toyed with a little sex after six months of abeyance and he was a lot happier for it.

She came down in street clothes for the first time in a long time, microwaved a half mug of milk and filled the rest with coffee. "Thanks for going slow last night, Jackie. I been a hard nut, I know."

"You've been what you had to be."

"Why do you think I'm so angry all the time?" It sounded like a real question.

"You a had a tough life and you built yourself protections. The armor had to grow a few cracks sooner or later. That's how the truth gets out. I admire you, Gloria."

She set down her coffee mug and came over to hug him from behind at the stove, resting her head against his shoulder, exactly as *he* had for a long time without response.

"How long we been together?" she whispered.

"Six years? I'm not sure."

LOVE IS A DREADFUL LOSS 219

"The first few were pretty good, weren't they?"

"They've all been good. Neither of us runs for cover when it rains."

He felt her shudder for a few moments as if crying and then it stopped. When he turned around, she backed off and offered a fist to be popped. He did.

"You moved heaven and earth to get me out of the can," he said.

"You and me are always back to back in fights."

"Why does loving always feel like some kind of dreadful loss hanging up there?"

He wasn't sure where "up there" was. They kissed briefly and he could feel the mood had turned. He'd find her a discreet therapist of some kind.

"*Comamos,*" He tried out. "*Algún machaca picante.*"

She smiled. "Don't even try. You sound like you're reading it through a coffee filter."

As they ate, a skattling announced Loco's claws coming along the linoleum. He didn't come out of his hidey-hole much anymore, sleeping about 18 hours a day and going deaf. It was sad. The half-coyote had once been a fierce handful. Age and cancer and chemo had just about crushed his spirit. He flopped on Jack Liffey's feet and went back to sleep.

"Oh, Jackie, I better tell you. I called Maeve's place, and one of her roommates said she'd driven off with a guy last night and said she'd be away for a few days. Does that ring any bells?"

He alerted as if stung. "Why didn't you tell me sooner?"

"I knew you'd go ballistic and I want my breakfast. Calm down, we're back-to-back, remember. I've got a lot more resources than you."

* * * * *

L ATE in the night, Belkin had realized he had to check on Cat or go crazy, so he'd started walking. He didn't know the roads up here but downhill was pretty easy. One downhill fork was a dead end and he had to retrace. When the sun came up it helped. East was east and his apartment was to the south and a little over that way. On the flat he knew the streets.

He kept to the shadow side of the long alley as he made his way to the back gate. The cold air had risk in it, making him very alert. Like that moment right before breaking a window to hot-wire a big Zil. Then he hadn't really cared what the authorities did to him—the worse it was, the more prestige.

This was new, a desperate need to protect, and it made him fearful. A kind of pain, really. He wasn't sure he liked the feeling at all, but he couldn't push it away. He wondered if it meant he was in love with Cat. He had no way to know. He'd done the old in-and-out plenty but that wasn't love.

He stood on tiptoes to peek over the gate. His heart rose when he saw that the stone had moved. Cat was back! She might even be waiting for him! He went in cautiously, wincing at a creak the gate made, and walked stealthily to the house. The owner had put cardboard over the shot-up window.

He unlocked his outside entry and turned the knob warily, then pushed in. His heart fell into his shoes.

"Bleen!"

The room had been searched crudely, without any concern for concealment. His goldfish had been de-bowled and lay at rest among the decorative rocks.

After inspecting all possible hiding places, he was sure he was alone, and it made him annoyed. The room knew things and was refusing to let on. Cat, are you out in the sub-basement?

He retrieved his flashlight and found it worked at half power. Danger hid nearby somewhere, and it was new that it worried him instead of invigorating him. He went outside quietly to the basement vent and yanked out the screen. The weak flashlight beam poked around under the house.

"Cat! This is me. You moved the stone. Good girl."

He listened, but heard nothing. Did an immobile, terrified person give off the same silence as no person at all? There were suggestive

LOVE IS A DREADFUL LOSS 221

shadows, lumps and house piers, backlit by light from the other vents—
the usual. Okay, you got to go in, Belkin.

* * * * *

A LINA Abramovna had bought a big plastic bag of green garden
stakes at a nursery and she had hidden them for days in the laundry hamper. Now she was pressing them into the water-softened back
lawn according to an elaborate plan she had drawn up. She consulted
her drawing over and over to help her position the pegs. All this with a
sense of mischief that she hadn't known since Berezyne, liberating her
father's sweetcorn. He had been an early booster of American sweetcorn, filling his private plot with it after Khrushchev's decree. Up in the
colder steppe, it had failed disastrously but her father grew lovely crops
year after year. It was primarily to feed the cows and pigs, of course,
but she fondly remembered sneaking some inside, boiling it and slathering it with sour cream. The kernels had been much tougher than the
sweetcorn she bought now in American supermarkets.

She heard his car crunching in the driveway, quickly tossed the
remaining stakes behind a bush and hurried inside.

* * * * *

"R OSKI didn't say where your Butterfly man lives, but I'm sure
he knows," Maeve whispered. "'You kiddies just twiddle your
thumbs and stay here.' He's such an old maid."

A bleary Talbot had finally drifted into the kitchen. They could
hear Roski working out hard with his barbells clanging in the living
room and Beethoven was playing away.

"He'll be leaving soon, and I bet he's going straight to the butterfly
man," Maeve whispered. "Get dressed quick and we'll follow him."

"Didn't we make him a solemn promise to stay here?"

"And violating that is wrong *why*?"

"Well, let's start with Kant. He said lying was a violation of the duty
to be true to yourself. He insisted you have to tell the truth—he said that
even if a murderer comes looking for his victim and asks, you can't lie.

The definitive answer to that is, of course, 'Oh come *on!*' Nietzsche said the problem with lying was it corrupts a relationship. Sartre said lying is a perfect example of bad faith because the inner self knows what's true. Foucault wrote a whole book about lying—"

"Stop! You'll still be yakking when Roski is halfway across town. Put on your shoes."

* * * * *

ALINA Abromovna had discovered the crunching noise was just the mailman so she hurried upstairs to get an overview of the stakes. She didn't normally go into Petro's study, but this visit was for him. A good third of the yard was hidden by the lower roof but she'd allowed for that. She could see her design and it was working.

She was startled by the sudden chime of the doorbell that Petro had set to the first bars of "Katyusha." Petro wouldn't ring the bell. As she hurried down she sang along in her head to the tune from the Great Patriotic War, "Apple and pear trees were blooming." She wondered if Petro had meant it as ironic.

She expected one of the friends she'd asked to help with the party. Petro would be out for the rest of Saturday in Plummer Park with his cronies.

"Are you Mrs. Pogorelets?" It was a nice-looking muscular American man holding out a leather wallet that held a badge and card that said he was some kind of investigator. The word *arson* she didn't know, but she certainly knew investigator.

"What is it that you want, sir?"

"I need to speak to your husband. Is he here?"

"He's with his friends today."

"Do you know where they are?"

Of course I do, you dumbwit. What sort of fool do you think I am? "No, I don't." Automatic denial was ingrained in every citizen of the former Soviet Union, may it rot in hell. Even the non Jews. Every language should have a super emphatic *no* for *apparatchiks* like this—some-

LOVE IS A DREADFUL LOSS 223

thing on the order of, That I would speak to such as you, *where* would such a thing happen?

"Do you know when he'll be home, ma'am?"

"Right after his car arrives," she said.

He smiled. "I'm not his enemy, ma'am. I've spoken to him once already and I believe he's in grave danger. I want to protect him."

And I may be the daughter of a flying green cannibal. "I'm sorry, sir, I can't help you."

"All right. Please ask him to call me."

She took the card. May you shit on the sidewalk as you walk away and fall into it.

"Pardon?"

My G-d, she thought, did I speak aloud?

* * * * *

M AEVE and Talbot hunkered down quickly as Roski came out the door and drove away. It was a large old Hollywood house with a smaller second story off-center on a large roof.

"Mr. Butterfly's probably not home," Maeve suggested.

"In movies the detective goes out and sits smoking away in the car and waits," Talbot said. "The scene dissolves to a big pile of butts in the street and we know it's a lot later."

"Believe it or not, I've done surveillance."

"I thought you were a painter."

"Nobody is just one thing. Are you just a gay guy? I'm messing with you, sorry. I've been helping my dad for donkey's years. Maybe I'll give up art and study Detecting 101."

"Don't."

"When Dad's down in the dumps, he says finding missing kids is more honorable than delivering pizzas." She puffed her cheeks once. "LA is the world capital of runaways. I love to imagine my mom's horror at the idea."

Talbot seemed to relax. "I guess I've never had an ambition that's so situated in the real world. I'm going to end up explaining semiotics to bored freshmen at North Dakota State U."

"You carrying any bud? Talking about smoking got me interested."

"I might have a wrinkly number in my pocket."

* * * * *

"I'LL make some calls around the Department, Jack. That'll do a lot more good than driving randomly around LA county."

"I'm a worry-wort," Jack Liffey said.

"I'll come up with something."

It was only on TV that an apoplectic police sergeant could bellow into a microphone, "Put out an APB on a small white foreign sedan!" Uh-huh. Six million cars in the county and eighty of them new to the hotsheet every day. Even if it had a bumper sticker saying "Powered by Tofu," it wasn't the way to go.

On the phone she said, "Paula, I've got a big favor to ask—"

* * * * *

BELKIN wriggled into the cobwebby crawl-space. A spider web grazed his ear and he brushed it away with horror. A little bump would help right now, he thought, but he didn't have any crank. Cat tended to nest over on the left, directly under his room, where he saw a low mound. He hoped it wasn't human shit.

He touched the mound gingerly. Rags. He found a broken-spined picture book, *Green Eggs and Ham* and it made him wonder if Cat could read. Dozens of empty cardboard food boxes, pizza boxes, french fry scoops, Chinese fold-ups.

He shined the flashlight around the center of her nest and found a scatter of thread spools, a small glass pig full of pennies, a scissors. There was a chaise pad that was her bed, with a tattered old comforter beside it. In a basket were four plastic dolls with rags tied over them to conceal their nakedness. Cat's only family?

LOVE IS A DREADFUL LOSS

Straight ahead was the only possible concealment, a Roman numeral III of sewer pipes from the house above. Someone had stuck cardboard against the pipes to create a blind. He crept cautiously toward the blind. *"Ya idu tebya iskat'! Kto ne spryatalsya, ya ne vinovat!"* I'm coming to find you! Whoever isn't hidden yet, it's not my fault!

At the left side of the blind he saw a long low shadow. Some prowler lying in wait? He touched Beck's tiny pistol in his shirt pocket for comfort.

"Who is it? I have an *oruzhie!* A gun!" The shadow didn't budge. He crawled nearer and prodded the shape.

When he grasped what it was, he sat up so fast that he bashed his head and fell on his face, stupefied. Some time later he came conscious again with a feeling of utter desolation. The Cossacks had ridden through and torched the village. It was such awfulness that he bashed his head a second time. This time the blow only dazed him.

Her skin was too cold to be alive. It was funny how you could know something truly, instantly, but your mind not accept it. There was a small hole in the center of her forehead. Eventually, feeling dull and faraway, he grasped her lifeless wrists and dragged her body out of the crawl-space. He lay her in a dignified way on the grass. He wanted to pray over her, but he didn't know any prayers and didn't believe in them, anyway. My Cat—you were so precious and innocent. I got to teach myself how to mourn.

For a long time he did his best to honor the girl. He hoped suffering would grant her soul a special right into any special happy place there was. But inside, he knew that was nonsense. The girl was dead. This was meat, bone. Wise up, Belkin. Cat, please forgive me for failing you. That set him weeping. Never to be able to offer food again.

Eventually it was evening and he opened his eyes to see a large square man sitting on the grass on the far side of Cat's body. Belkin wasn't frightened because nothing mattered now. He knew immediately that this man was a warrior—a man destined to kill him.

"Bog dal, bog i vzyal," the man said gently. God gave, God took back.

"God didn't take her back, *you* did," he replied in Ukrainian.

"She was too damaged for this world. You know that."

"Fuck you," Belkin said in English.

"Do you know who I am?"

"Maybe. You're the famous Sergei. It's not a real name."

"To friends I used to be Vyacheslav Milanchuk. But I've been Sergei for a long time."

"Why did you kill her?"

"She recognized me. She would know me again. She was just an incompletion, son, like you. That can't be allowed." Sergei crossed his arms, which seemed to mean he was invulnerable, invincible.

"I brought her food," Belkin said. "I talked to her every day. What makes you think I won't try to kill you?"

"Because there's no way you can, son. And I'm afraid the opposite is fated."

"Would you at least tell me what this is about?"

"Don't be naive, countryman. You were on the hunting party when your fool of a friend shot my friend in the leg. For absolutely no reason. The madness of it almost makes me forgive him. Almost. I hate reasons and people who go on and on about their *reasons*. But a friend is a friend."

"Can you vouch for the actions of every friend of yours at every moment?"

"It doesn't matter. It's simply not manly to rest without making somebody pay. Life is payback."

"I heard once the best revenge was the laughter of your children," Belkin said.

"I got no children. I bet you neither. You want a cigarette? *Belomorkanals*. Strong and cheap, oh-so soviet times."

"Sure." Sergei shook one up for him and lit it with an American Zippo that had a US Marine Corps insignia on it.

A helicopter began to circle overhead, but it wasn't interested in them.

"The cops are so polite here," Sergei said, glancing up. "They almost seem like Christians."

LOVE IS A DREADFUL LOSS

"Fuck you!" Belkin said. He scrabbled out his tiny .25-caliber pistol. Sergei glanced at it but didn't react.

"Oh, ha! Son, that's the Yugo of pistols. It'll jam or misfire. Probably the trigger won't even pull. Let's make a bet—"

Belkin pulled the trigger, and felt the pistol react in his hand, putting one shot into the startled man's chest. The sound of the shot was quite mild, a pop like an air-rifle.

Sergei slapped a palm to his chest and then yanked it away to stare at it, startled to see real blood on his hand, his own blood. "*Chyort poberi!*" The devil take it!

Belkin fired five more times into the big man's chest until the Yugo of pistols was empty.

The big man toppled to a knee and then fell forward.

EIGHTEEN

Quake

I T felt like somebody big and clumsy had blundered into him and was still shaking him. Victor Antonenkovich Gorbenko opened one eye to darkness.

He heard a nightstick rapping along the bars in the hall.

"Wake up!" the public address blasted away the last of his sleep. "Drop, cover and hold on. This is a little earthquake."

A siren started to wail mercilessly and he scrambled under the steel shelf, then reached back up and dragged the blankets to the floor with him. A jailer had finally taken pity and given him extra blankets to roll up for his back. He'd heard about LA earthquakes, but in the dark it was much scarier than he'd imagined.

* * * * *

M AEVE sat up abruptly in bed, knowing precisely what was happening. The world slammed left, then right. She'd been far too young to remember Whittier Narrows, but she and her mom had ridden out the awful Northridge at Richter 6.9.

"Under the bed, man," she snapped.

She and Talbot wedged themselves beneath as Roski's creaking bungalow went on rocking. "A side-roller," she said. She wondered why they always seemed to come in the darkness.

230 BOYSTOWN

"Tell it to knock it off."

"They used to say to stand in a doorframe, but now it's sturdy furniture. Gives you a nice private coffin."

"*Please!*"

She realized he was terrified. "Sorry. This is just a little one." It might not turn out to be, but yesterday they'd dispensed philosophically with lies.

"Is it over?"

"Enjoy. Be thankful we're not a hundred feet up a steep hill in a stilt house."

Two years ago, she and her father had taken refuge in a bathtub against a gigantic rumbling mudslide that had killed others in the house. They'd been trapped in the tub for hours. It hadn't affected her too bad, but her father was pathological about claustrophobia and it might have contributed to his heart trouble. Poor dad—his bank account was always full of the wrong currency.

* * * * *

J ACK Liffey opened one eye and said, "Earthquake."

"Yes, dear. I know."

"That last shake was something. Have you been awake?"

"I'm having trouble sleeping." They were hurled into each other by the wobbly resilience of the upper floor of her century-old wood frame house.

"What's police wisdom?"

"Drop under a table and stay away from breakables. Don't run into the street."

"The coffee table downstairs is about as sturdy as furniture gets," Jack Liffey said. "Good luck getting there." He dared not let himself imagine being buried in the rubble.

"Let's just lie here and pretend it's a roller coaster," Gloria said. "I had fun in the Sylmar quake because it fit my destructive urges at the time. I wanted my fosters' house to collapse."

"*Jack!*"

QUAKE   231

A big slam had thrown them sideways.

* * * * *

A LINA woke first. "Petya!"
"What is it? Oh, it's one of their famous earthquakes. I've been
wanting to experience one."

"You're a madman."

They turned in bed to stare at one another in a longing way they
hadn't felt for a long time.

"*Ne boysya sobaki, shto layet, a bosya toy, shto molchit, da khvostom vilyayet,*"
he said softly. Dearest, don't be afraid of the dog who barks, be afraid
of the one who is silent and wags its tail. "I'm sorry to wait so long to
say this to you, but I seem to have acquired some nasty enemies." After
the earthquake died away, he told her ruefully about the hunters, the
Russian warrior and the fire inspector.

"The fireman came again, Petya. I told him to fuck off."

He smiled. "Good."

"Oh, Petya. Happy birthday to you."

She reached into his pajamas. The house creaked and groaned,
but they didn't notice.

* * * * *

B ELKIN woke in fighting temper at the jolt, jumping out of bed in
his undies to pose like a Bruce Lee. He'd been dreaming hideous
dreams about Cat, and he remembered now that she was gone. She
was in fact directly under his room again, along with Sergei. It had
been a struggle to get the big man through the vent, like pushing tooth-
paste into the tube. With a heavy feeling, he wondered what to do with
this terrible collection he was growing, but he didn't care really. There
was only one thing he wanted to do.

* * * * *

W HEN the rolling came, Paula Green had been clearing rubbish
out of the Police Interceptor she'd just bought at the LAPD

auction—standard patrol car back in the day, rebadged from a Crown Victoria with a bigger engine and harsher suspension. She was imperturbable and the sway only triggered a moment of recognition.

Now she was driving her battleship deep into south LA with Gloria beside her and Jack Liffey in the back. They passed a few toppled chimneys but there wasn't much to see south of Jefferson.

"You didn't get enough of this big hooptie on the job?" Gloria asked.

"I like the horsepower. It's a big comfy motherfucker. You push down on some guy's head, you can get him into the seat easy. Reluctant dates, you know."

"You still gotta arrest them to get any?"

"Hey, how about you?" Paula asked.

"Jack has been a saint and a half for a long time. The shaking got me excited." She laughed. "He's a sinner again."

"You ought to make him get hitched up," Paula said.

"That's a thought."

Am I here or not? Jack Liffey thought, hearing about himself in the third person. He was too worried about Maeve to let it matter. Gloria reached back toward him and he took her hand for a moment, roughened and cool.

They'd turned off the Harbor at Slauson and were driving down Vermont now, staying in the center to avoid a few pools of broken window glass. Some people were out on the street looking around. In a vacant lot a few Latino families had set up a tent city. Probably re-enacting the Zona Rosa quake in Mexico City.

Paula turned off on sixty-second. "There," she said. She was referring to a beat-up white Toyota Echo, windows all smashed and trunk yawning. "Jack."

The car didn't look right, but he got out and approached it cautiously. Radio gone, even a seat. A tiny pine tree dangled from the mirror—not a Maeve item. On the far side the front fender had been replaced some time ago with a deep green one. No evidence of bumper stickers.

The big throbbing Ford awaited. "Not," he said, climbing back in.

QUAKE   233

"I just took a shot," Paula said. "Guy said there was no plate. Tell me what Maeve is up to, and I'll do better. But you've got to promise to do the beast on this girl here."

Gloria gasped and swatted her.

* * * * *

PETRO Pogorelets had been ordered out of the house so he could enact his surprise later, and he took his walking cane, as much psychological as physical, on the long stroll. Not much damage to see along Santa Monica Boulevard. A tree limb had snapped off and lay in the street. Some bricks from a false parapet had toppled onto the sidewalk and he had to cane carefully through them.

There was something gratifying about an earthquake. His life had been upended by exile, so why shouldn't everybody experience a little disruption? It equalizes things.

With the arrival of the special forces protector things had gone topsy-turvey again. No matter how many times he set up a new normal, it fled toward the forest.

A few of his friends were at their usual card tables.

"*Dobryy ranok.*"

"Good morning to you, sir."

"*Chy khtos' postrazhdav pid chas zemletrusu?*" Anybody hurt in the earthquake?

"Not me. The TV was frantic about a little broken glass and a few soup cans on the floor. If these people knew real war—"

"We have a little war," Vadim said. "Right here in our Little Ukraine." Vadim was a tall skinny elderly man who had once been a commercial airline pilot until a very hard landing at Pulkovo had put cracks in the tail assembly of his Tupolev-154. "All these police coming around acting bigshot and waving their sausages at us."

"And all the shooting and burning."

"I don't know what you mean," Petro said.

"Don't tell me you haven't heard a thing?"

He shrugged. "Americans are all cowboys. Let them shoot each other."

Vadim let it drop. "Anybody seen Victor the runt? He owes me money."

"How about giving us a rest from the *tsuris*, Vadim?" one of the players said.

"Petro, sit and join the game. Take the weight off the bad leg."

Some of the feud was beginning to surface. *Menishe vy znayete—tym mitnishe spyte*, he thought. The less you know, the more soundly you sleep.

* * * * *

W HEN she wasn't looking, Roski had slipped a card that looked interesting off a tiny table by the door. The woman had made it quite clear she hated his guts and would not cooperate. Everybody who'd had the misfortune to live under the Soviets seemed to have learned to fear, detest and thwart authority whenever possible, going mute, or piling lie upon lie. He had extraordinary affection for people who could occasionally paralyze a powerful tyranny by so simple a method.

The card was an invitation to a surprise sixtieth birthday party. And now he knew for sure how to reach Petro at two that afternoon.

* * * * *

"F RIEND, have you seen the butterfly man this morning?"

"What are you talking about?"

Belkin stopped an old woman with a cart. "Do you know a Ukrainian man who hunts butterflies?"

Proshu zalyshty. Please leave.

In a mini-mart:

"I'm looking for a big man who loves butterflies."

Hey do bisa! Get the fuck out!

QUAKE 235

Belkin knew he looked scary and he was used to rudeness. He tried to keep his voice light and casual. In another shop, a whole family was putting quake-toppled cans back on the shelves.

"Do you people know a man who loves butterflies?"

The man shrugged and the kids looked at their mother. "Absolutely not," she said.

Belkin would not take rejection as a sign of rejection. Who cares any more if I have feelings? he thought. He headed toward Plummer Park. It was a well-known hangout for old-country men, and he bet somebody there would react to "the butterfly man."

* * * * *

"CAN I have a phone," Jack Liffey asked. He hated cellphones and did not have one.

"Glove compartment," Paula said.

Gloria extracted a small flip-phone, stared at it for a moment like something from another planet and handed it to Jack.

"I took it off a drug dealer," Paula said. "If the other end has caller ID, it'll say you're Dr. Feelgood. Have fun but don't promise anything."

He checked the tiny address book he carried and called Roski's home.

After a few rings it was answered by a ridiculously false girl's voice, holding her nose.

Oh, *no!* he thought.

"Mr. Roski is away right now. May I take a message for him?"

"*Maeve!*" Jack Liffey shouted.

"Oh, dad! Who's this Dr. Feelgood?"

"We're worried to death about you. What's going on?"

He felt Paula steer over to the side of the road and stop, and both women turned to stare at him.

"Why are you at Roski's?"

"I'm not. I'm in Fresno."

"You're on Roski's home phone."

236   *BOYSTOWN*

Maeve laughed. "Got me. I'm perfectly safe, dad. Uncle Walt's guarding us."

"*Us?* Put Walt on."

"He can't come to the phone right now. He'll be right back."

"Stay where you are."

"If you insist."

"Don't you hang up—"

She hung up, and he howled at the roof of the car.

"Calm down, Jack. Give me the address."

He did and the big car growled up to speed.

*   *   *   *   *

B ELKIN had found his car near where Beck usually stored his motorcycle. It was hard to miss the purple glow. Luckily the old owner had kept a spare key in a little magnetic box.

In the park he saw a number of heavyset men playing basketball. He didn't think this flat-footed back-and-forth clomp was quite the way the game was meant to be played, but so what? A woman and three kids sat on the grass watching them dutifully with a picnic spread of sausage and *blinchiki*—cottage cheese and honey crepes. His mouth watered and he realized how hungry he was.

"Ma'am, have you seen the butterfly man this morning?"

"He's with his pals."

The woman pointed toward the crowded picnic benches swarming with old men.

He drifted closer to the tables, maybe thirty old men and *kibitzers*. *Patyenz*—he despised it, like all games. It was time lost forever that had nothing to do with survival?

Slowly and inconspicuously he floated past the tables. One group was much too young. Then all at once—*bozhe miy!*—there was the butterfly man in the flesh, a black cane resting on the edge of the table. Seeing him, Belkin relived that moment of Zeke's mad potshot, and this man collapsing on the mountain path. A moment that had killed Cat as

QUAKE 237

surely as Sergei's shots did later. A chain of fate or whatever someone smarter than me would call it. This man did it. He had sent the killer.

Koly drova rubyat—trisky letyat. When wood is chopped, wood-chips will fly.

* * * * *

"*WALTER, what the hell is my daughter doing at your house?*"
"Calm down, Jack. I can almost hear you without my cell."
"What the fuck is my daughter doing at your house?"
"She's helping out a nice-enough guy who's on the run from all the hostilities. He puts the key in the lock, Jack. He was there when this started and knows what it's all about."
"Walt, one last time, why is Maeve at your house?"
"They're safe. I made them stay in my spare room and she promised to keep him there, too."
"You don't know her. She has to be at the center of things. Where is *that*?" Jack Liffey made a shush gesture to the women.
"Why are you Dr. Feelgood, Jack?
"Just shut up and tell me where to go." A sort of doom swam in the air around him, and he didn't like it at all.

NINETEEN

Things Worth Finding Out

THEY saw Roski parked a half block from the arts-and-crafts house he'd led them to the day before and she parked discreetly behind a big SUV. "How you feeling?"

"I still want to apologize," Talbot said. "But you know, you go and make an appointment for a root canal and it seemed like an okay idea at the time, but when the time rolls around, you sure wish you hadn't."

She chuckled. "If he gets hella nasty, Mr. Roski is there to save us."

A little boy in cowboy chaps was pedaling a bright plastic big-wheels up the narrow street and stopped to aim a squirt gun at them. Talbot made a fierce face and the kid rolled on without firing.

"You wear rosy glasses, you know," Talbot said. "In my experience, the thing you worry about giggles at you from behind the door and then does something unexpected that's a whole lot worse."

"Maybe I've had a charmed life. I think I live a lot in my dad's world. It seems more real than ours. You know, Pogo and Woodstock and Vietnam and Malcolm X. I carry a lot of my dad's stuff around."

"It was a rich time for sure but it was a lot harder to come out of the closet," he said.

"I forgot that."

"I think I'd like to meet this dad of yours."

"Why don't we go up to the house and see if Mr. Butterfly lets us in before the Great Roski goes ballistic."

* * * * *

A T the samovar, a few people and early arrivals were milling around. Alina called Petro and told him he could come home. She said to hurry before the Bolsheviks come back.

The night before, after the quake and the surprise of making love they had wept a little and talked deeply. They had made the birthday milestone into a *sumo-krytyk* session, acknowledging that their silences had grown longer, their arguments more frequent. He said he knew how hard it had been for her. Whereas in Kiev she'd been a day's train journey from her close and loving family in the village. Here she was impossibly far away, while he had his teaching, his butterflies, and friends. If she had ever used her good sense, she would have flown home.

She was touched he'd noticed her unhappiness. She was indeed frightened of ending up alone in an unfeeling place where even God would forget about her, and after the worms began eating her, no person would ever speak her name. She told him he was a fine man and she knew he'd had his own challenges with low status in a country that had little interest in him or his learning or even his butterflies.

She choked up even now thinking of his last words.

"What a man dies of," he'd said and sighed a big Ukrainian sigh from somewhere deep in the soul and stalled there for a while. "A man's spirit dies of trying, despite all, to stay strong. It's such vanity."

* * * * *

B ELKIN sat on a low decorative wall at the park's west entrance, behind spiky aloes. He was maybe 50 meters from the table where he watched the man take a phone call and then excuse himself and pick up his cane.

A lovely red-haired woman with a small boy in tow approached Belkin, the boy's eyes fixed fiercely on him. "Papa," he called possessively, English with Ukrainian vowels.

THINGS WORTH FINDING OUT

241

Belkin smiled. "Sorry, not me."

"It happens with every thin man he sees, I apologize," the young woman said. "Yuri wouldn't even recognize the *suchyy sin*." The son of a bitch.

He couldn't help considering what it would be like to be this gutsy boychild's father. He'd need someone broken, like Cat, to be mother, not a normal attractive woman. Normal women intimidated him.

There was a parting jeer of "*Vislyuk!*" Donkey-fucker. A kid with spirit. Belkin stayed put for a few moments so he wouldn't be obvious.

* * * * *

"LOOK!" Gloria cried, and Paula brought the huge street-cruiser to a stop. The little white Toyota was parked on the street ahead of them. Maeve was visible slumped down at the wheel with a young man beside her.

"Block it," Jack Liffey snapped.

Paula managed to spurt the big Ford to a foot from the Echo, locking it against a Chrysler van.

"Don't even touch the controls," Jack Liffey snapped, about a foot from his daughter's face when shed cranked the window down.

"Dad! Gloria! Don't shoot!"

"This isn't a joke."

"I'll try to proceed from there," Maeve said, fighting a grin.

It was so hard to knock her off her high horse. "What do you think you're *doing* here?"

"Shutup, Jack." Gloria was beside him. "You're too invested. Maeve, I have a feeling that the young man who's trying to make himself invisible would love to explain things. But right *now*."

After some wriggling, he got out.

"I'm so sorry."

By this time Roski had seen the commotion a half block away and joined the party with quick double-takes and grudged greetings all around. There was enough weekend street life that they weren't attracting much attention yet. The young man managed to get out what he knew about the hunting trip where a jerky workmate named Zeke had semi-accidentally wounded the butterfly hunter and then his co-workers at Gusev had freaked out. He gathered that bad things connected to the shooting had been happening and he wanted to try to apologize to the Butterfly Man.

Roski pushed in and nodded wearily to Talbot. "Hello, son. So many Liffeys around, so much trouble. Here's the deal, all of you. I was here first, and I have dibs on Petro Pogorelets for a few minutes to clear up my issues."

"Is that the Butterfly Man?" Talbot asked.

"Shutup. A certain amount of discretion is called for right now. In about fifteen minutes there's going to be a surprise party for the man's birthday. I'll let them surprise him for a few minutes then I'm going to crash the party. Give me fifteen minutes after I go in to get a couple things straight. Throw up an armed perimeter if you like. Nobody is going to get away. Do this out of the kindness of your hearts."

"You're looking ill," Jack Liffey said.

"I had a bad night. Thanks for asking."

Gloria nudged Jack aside and looked Roski over as if she were a hungry predator eying a tasty nugget. "One way or another I'm responsible for every stinking person here. Forget Jack. Forget your bad night. I'm the boss. Talk to me."

He gave in and they walked out of the earshot of the others and argued with animation.

* * * * *

"**D**AD, are you mad at me?" Maeve asked him.

Part of him was beyond furious, but he couldn't lose it now.

"You're supposed to be tucked away safely in college. When do you give up playing Nancy Drew?"

"I'm never tucked away. It was Bunny's vulnerable brother, Dad. One thing led to another. You weren't born a detective, you know. You just started helping people when you were a lush."

THINGS WORTH FINDING OUT 243

"After I quit." Jack Liffey glared at a new dent in the little Echo that he and her mother had bought her ages ago, then back at her maturing face. She's not a child, Jack. The young man looked away quickly, scared to death. Finally his eye caught on Paula.

"Yeah, I'm on leave. Tell you some time."

Gloria and Roski were still arguing away, and he had to say something to Maeve. "I never deny I was a lush, hon. I hope you never have to visit bottom. The redeeming thing about detectives is they still believe there's things in the world worth finding out."

An out-of-place Rolls honked lightly as it drove past them, but Rollses always looked out of place. He could see the Gloria-Roski conclave was about to break up.

"I love you, Dad," came out of the firmament.

* * * * *

I N the back yard, an officious woman was lining up thirty or so older people including Olga Kuchin along some stupid stakes poked in the grass. It was likely, and banal as shit, that from the upstairs windows they'd be arranged as the digits six-zero. Oh, so clever. She deeply resented being relegated to one of the common herd who knew Petro only peripherally. The honored guests would not be asked to be dancing bears. They were inside starting on their *mlyntsi* and caviar with vodka. She deserved better and she would get it. He truly belongs to me. *Boh berezhe tykh, khto berezhe sebe.* God keeps safe those who keep themselves safe.

"Relax for a few minutes," the woman announced. "I'll alert you when they go upstairs."

Everyone else seemed to be enjoying the prospect of the shadow-play and they applauded softly, happy to be a lesser part of the celebration. She knew so few of them she began to wonder if she should have come at all. But she would make a disturbance to plant a flag in front of his known world.

Give me Alina, she thought. Let us wrestle and slap and bite and scratch. Winner take Petya.

*　*　*　*　*

THEY'D all gone back to their cars and Paula had reparked her beast. Earlier Roski had seen the man waiting alone in the park and assumed his wife would summon him when things were set. He had no idea what sort of commotion his own arrival might set off, but he didn't give a damn. A stocky woman on the house-wide verandah appeared to be keeping lookout. Next to the front door a card table held a tub with a sign on it. Party favors? He couldn't read it. A middle-aged couple arrived and the stocky woman barred them as she talked. The man deposited something in the barrel. Probably a Ukrainian birthday custom.

The winter light was pale and sinister. Gypsy-like music started up from the house, and a long block away he saw Petro Pogorelets approaching, banging slowly along with a cane. The stocky woman saw him approaching, too, opened the door, shouted inside and the soundtrack cut off.

His concentration was interrupted momentarily by an old show-off purple Mercury that paused to block his view. The driver stared for a while and then went on. His face had been a rictus of determination. That's one unhappy man, Roski thought. Go with charity. Roski checked his watch as Petro Pogorelets mounted the front steps. Two on the dot.

TWENTY

Homesick for a Place He'd Never Been

J ACK Liffey watched a purple bathtub-shaped Mercury—1950 he thought—come around for a second time. Probably casing the neighborhood for a burglary. The sinewy-looking driver didn't appear Latino but the menacing flame job screamed it. Good luck, he thought, with all the cops here.

"Folkses," Paula said. "I should be calling for backup. I'm the only one on the job here, even if I'm off duty. In my world the arson man doesn't count. I'm personally gonna piss on the guy's corpse if things break to the dogs."

"Stand in line," Gloria said.

* * * * *

A LINA led Petya upstairs past all the butterflies imprisoned under glass to the back window of his big study.

"Be surprised," she said evenly.

He helped her budge the sticky sash up and peered out through the bars that enclosed the entire house like Lubyanka. So American, this land of freedom, guns and burglar tools.

"Ooooh," he said with mock surprise. "They're telling me I'm sixty." He made a lot of noise approximating surprise and thanks and called that he wasn't sixty yet, he'd been going backwards since forty-nine. They applauded and he applauded back.

"Oh, love, it really was wonderful of you," Petro said and he embraced her flamboyantly in front of the window to another roar of applause that became rhythmic and grew faster and faster until he broke off the kiss and the ovation tore itself into cheers and laughter. People were noisily clomping up the staircase.

In front was David Gurevich, a younger colleague at city college, who burst into the room with a shout, drank down a shot glass and hurled it into the far corner of the room, where it only bounced on the wood. The party was on. Petro hoped it would tone down, but he knew Ukrainians could be pathologically high-spirited in parties.

* * * * *

B ELKIN brooded, thinking about Cat until he walked back to the trunk and examined what he had available in this new deranged existence. Cat, I'm so sorry and confused.

He unzipped the long khaki bag that Charlie Beck had left him. There were two assault rifles, and he left them where they were. Guns only caused trouble—look at Zeke.

There were several flat bricks of C-4 explosive wrapped in wax paper. He felt dizzy. Belkin, stay in *this* world for a while. There was also his red metal tool box, that contained a drill, a saw, many kinds of glues, a hammer and sack of big nails. In the back seat were a dozen cut-off short ends he'd collected at a building site.

* * * * *

G LORIA reached over the seat and pressed her hand to his temple like a nurse. "You okay, Jack?"

"No."

"There goes Roski," Paula said, as the man stepped out of his car and headed for the bungalow. "How long do we give him?"

HOMESICK FOR A PLACE HE'D NEVER BEEN

Nobody answered. They watched Roski knock and go in but he was immediately thrust back out by a fierce-looking woman who made him deposit something in the tub.

"His badge wallet?" Gloria wondered.

"Couldn't see."

"Be easy, girl."

"How?"

* * * * *

ALINA and Petro came back down to the tables placed end to end diagonally from the sitting room into the dining room, set out with giant *kurniks*—pies full of chicken and delicacies. There were bowls of beef and cabbage soup, two geese stuffed with kasha, towers of bread loaves, boiled *vareniki* and the piece-de-resistance, a meter long grilled sturgeon she'd had flown in from Riga.

Petro and Alina called out the back door to invite everybody in.

"Please refortify yourselves for my wonderful husband."

Crowds immediately formed at the drink table and many of the guests had to make do quickly by dipping Dixie cups into the punch-bowls of kvass—fermented ryebread.

A tall wildly bearded man who looked uncannily like Rasputin raised a paper cup and shouted, "*Ukrayna! Podali vid ichey-blizhche do sert-sya!*" Ukraine! Away from the eye—closer to the heart.

Most emptied their Dixie cups compulsively and then crumpled them to make an enthusiastic white hail.

Alina knew there were some who did not speak Ukrainian so she toasted in English. She would not use Russian. "To all of us who have done our best to adapt to exile, we know that life does not always go according to plan." Her eyes passed over Petro's mistress Olga, who had been lurking nearby trying to make eye-contact with him. "Dearest, Petya may you advance to a job in America that is worthy of your scholarship and your value on earth. And may you capture the butterfly of your dreams! Happy Birthday, Petya!"

248   *BOYSTOWN*

There was a big hoot, another neck-snap of drinking and another hail of Dixie cups.

"Please hold your other toasts for the dinner table," Alina called out quickly to fend off Olga who had stepped forward aggressively.

Rasputin raised a ham-size hand into the air and waved it about. "Let's go eat our fill, *panove!* Stuffing ourselves is the national pastime."

Kitchen helpers bringing more food were kicking aside the noisy snowdrift of crushed paper cups. A short man with a dyed black forelock pasted to his forehead like Napoleon in a cognac ad grabbed Petro and gave him a bearhug and a double cheek kiss. "Sixty, my friend. What is to be can't be avoided. I myself am approaching seventy and the life ahead is provisional. Maybe I'll get younger, too, and become the first Ukrainian astronaut!"

This Napoleon was someone Petro knew, though not intimately. His memory for names was beginning to fail with an early drink and the sensory overload.

"May you rocket into space, *dyadko*," Petro said. Uncle was a safe form of address.

Alina saw Olga striding toward them and thought fast. "Before we eat, my wonderful husband wants to lead a small tour of the highlights of his magnificent butterfly collection!" She backed in front of Olga and waved her arms to gather a crowd.

Petro seemed bemused but happy enough to lead a contingent away from the noise and clamor. He plucked a tiny powder blue-and-yellow Ukrainian flag off an aspic and held it up overhead with two fingers like an Asian tour guide. "On to the *metelyky*, follow me."

Alina watched Olga push clumsily into the crowd moving up the staircase. Whatever happened up there would not be her problem because she would not have witnessed it. That cheap-looking whore from Odessa would only become a problem if people saw Alina notice.

There was a small commotion in the entry and her battleaxe door guardian—a true valkyrie from a pig farm in the Carpathians—was holding back a man Alina couldn't see clearly. And then she could; it was that pushy fire inspector. She sighed. Why now?

HOMESICK FOR A PLACE HE'D NEVER BEEN

"Madame Pogorelets!" the man called out as she came over. "Rescue me. I think I'm going to be crushed."

"We have plenty of mincemeat already. Let him go, Ninochka."

The big woman released him and he tried to reach across to offer his hand to Alina. She recoiled. "Don't you know not to shake hands across a threshold. What do you want now, Mr. Roski?"

The large woman stepped back but watched with a vigilant gaze.

"I need to speak to your husband," he said. "Right away."

"Can't you see that this is a special day? Perhaps Americans don't honor birthdays."

"Ma'am, I'm sorry. What I've learned can save his life. Don't you know he's in the middle of a small violent war?"

Alina closed her eyes. "No and yes. Is he in immediate danger?"

"Yes. Five or six men are dead, I can't keep count, and I'm sure whoever it is knows he's home right now just like me."

She sighed. "I'll bring him aside. He is what I love the most dearly in this perilous world."

"Please."

* * * * *

PAULA led their rambling approach to the bungalow and because she had the badge, Gloria and Jack Liffey straggled a pace behind.

"What if I call SWAT," Paula said darkly.

"Easy, girl," Gloria said. "Roski's in there. Don't start shooting them."

Coming up the path toward the wide verandah, they could hear music and hilarity within. A siren approached and then receded. Paula had a fine ear for sirens. "Ambulance," she said.

The sign on the tub at the door said:

A day of respect, please
All cell phones in here

The message was repeated in Cyrillic script. A real battle-ax of a woman came out, hands on hips, as enforcer. Paula badged her,

250   *BOYSTOWN*

but she insisted on seeing their phones go into the tub that was nearly brimming.

Jack Liffey glanced behind at a footscrape and was irritated to see Maeve and Talbot coattailing.

"We have police business here," Paula insisted. "Don't make us shut the party down."

Maeve and Talbot caught up, and in the end they all deposited their cells in the barrel in order to avoid a scene. She didn't believe Jack Liffey didn't have one and he had to endure an airport pat-down. Perhaps Ukrainian women were less inhibited than TSA. His left ball shrieked at him after the tweak she'd given it. And she'd winked at him.

* * * * *

O N foot Belkin had been up and down the block and around the house. The neighborhood was parked up for blocks around, a few cars even hanging over into driveways. He'd been lucky to get a spot earlier. He heard party music from the house, Nina Bannova, some singer, wailing away. The place was packed and bodies drifted across all the barred windows like a jailhouse party. So much the better, he thought. There weren't enough souls in the universe to pay him back for the loss. He couldn't think of anybody besides Cat who had ever really listened to him. How many of those partying in there realized that the things they'd been waiting and waiting for all their lives might be snatched away. Well, aunties and uncles, it's all tough shit.

He got out and foraged in the trunk, packing items into a small shoulder bag. The reloaded .25-caliber purse-pistol, the Yugo of guns, that had ended Sergei's smugness. Two waxpaper-wrapped soapbars of C-4 plastic explosive. And from his tool kit: a big tube of superglue, a roofing hammer, and big handfuls of ninepenny galvanized nails. He slung the bag over his shoulder and grabbed an armload of the meter-long bords.

Long ago Belkin learned that he had been born in Lithuania. Nowhere he'd ever been taken or lived had ever suited him. Now he was homesick for someplace he'd never been.

HOMESICK FOR A PLACE HE'D NEVER BEEN

251

* * * * *

"T HE women in America are ugly and aggressive!" the Rasputin bellowed. "The vodka is foul! The children sulk or go wild!" He thumped his chest. "Nobody here has a soul!"

People with drinks and hors d'oeuvres did their best to ignore him.

"Don't shout, Valenteyn. You must stop reading books with big words in them." An aging blonde stood on tiptoe to kiss the big man's cheek.

"*Zamovkny!*" someone called. "Petro is descending."

The butterfly tour was clattering back down the staircase, greeted by cheers and toasts. Petro was immediately kidnapped by his wife.

"We'll be with you all in no time," she announced. "Eat, enjoy!" Alina turned to block out the approaching mistress and led her husband urgently toward the sewing room. Petro's dark glance finally turned his mistress back.

The American party crashers were waiting in a loose formation, like a peace delegation from an invading army. Roski took command. "How is your wounded leg, sir?"

"Why are you here? I don't have time for good manners."

"I understand." Roski explained that he'd learned all he needed about the hunting accident and the small war after it, and someone was certainly on the way to kill him. "You need to suspend the party for another time for everyone's safety and come away with us. Bring your wife. We can protect you."

"That is out of the question. You saw the room."

Talbot pushed forward. "Sir, I was with those foolish hunters and I know the man who shot you. He's dead now, and I did nothing. I want to apologize with all my heart—"

"I don't want to hear any more. All of you, leave my house right now or I'll call the police."

Paula held up her badge. "Sir."

He leaned forward to look at it. "All right, remain as my guests, but stay in this room, I'll have some food brought."

"That isn't necessary."

At that moment there were excited shouts from the party, not good-natured at all, and a thunderous hammering.

Gloria and Paula glanced at one another. "I think we're going into the party."

Just as they spilled out of the room, an unmistakable gunshot sent people screaming and scattering away from the entry.

TWENTY-ONE

The Captain Goes Last

JUST after the gunshot, Jack Liffey heard and felt a visceral whoomp. Whatever it was, this was not the place to be. On instinct he grabbed Maeve and Talbot and pulled them toward a double sash window at the back of the sewing room. Just outside the glass were wrought iron burglar bars. In a fit of obstinacy he threw up the sash and hurled his shoulder at the bars. That was futile.

"Sir!" Talbot had picked up a bench and together they backed off and ran the bench at the window. They staggered back at the impact, the bars only ringing dully.

"One of them will have an emergency release," Jack Liffey called.

"Dad!" At a smaller window Maeve held out a handle like a stirrup attached to a chain that ran into a metal ring in the wall. She tugged hard but nothing happened, then she yielded to her father who put his whole leg strength into a heave that also did nothing.

The hubbub from the house was becoming panicky. A wild-haired man popped in the door and shouted: "Fire in the house!"

Talbot grasped Jack Liffey's arm and shoulder

"Together. Three—two—*pull!*"

A terrible snap and their joint dive to the Persian carpet said the chain had broken.

254   BOYSTOWN

Jack Liffey glared at the empty hole in the wall. The chain must have rusted away.

"There have to be more exits."

* * * * *

ROSKI slipstreamed behind Paula and Gloria working through the crowd that was starting to go berserk. A terrible hammering was still going on outside somewhere. The crowd was driven sideways suddenly by a crash and a shower of flying glass. The policewomen were buffeted back and forth ahead of him. They made it to the front door and Paula yanked her 9mm out of the holster at the back of her skirt, which sent partiers into shrieks and dives away from them.

In the skinny full-height sidelights beside the door they could see that boards had been nailed haphazardly across the doorframe, and flames boiled up fiercely from two places just outside. Roski could think of few accelerants as rapid and compact as what he was seeing— not even a pail of acetone or a meth lab. It had to be something exotic. Trapped under the verandah roof those flames would quickly eat into the roof and the house itself.

"Don't get trapped near the door," Roski called. Paula led back toward the dining room where a grinning drunk was grabbing up handfuls of the flesh of a long decorated fish amidst the general wailing and panic. A big man with unruly black hair was bellowing incomprehensibly with a woman clinging to his back.

Roski took note of the burglar bars all around. "Find the windows with emergency pulls!" he shouted. "It's code."

The women pushed toward the front room which held worse mayhem. By jumping in the air, Roski could see above the surging crowd that French doors had been nailed shut, too, and a fire was kindling out back. A mass murder arson. He'd never run into such a thing but he thought something like it had happened to the architect Frank Lloyd Wright.

"Upstairs!" Roski shouted. "There'll be an escape." The hammering was still going on, beyond a kitchen archway where the caterers were

THE CAPTAIN GOES LAST   255

huddled. Whoever it was scurrying around nailing them in wouldn't get to the upper floor. Roski's party fought their way to the staircase. A dozen people had already taken refuge up there with mounted butterflies all around and were frantically opening sash windows for air to reveal more bars. Wrong tactic. It created a chimney draft that Roski knew would suck the smoke and fire upward, but he'd never get panicky people to close the windows.

He saw the release-pull immediately, the handle nearly hidden beside a filing cabinet. He ran across, shoved the file aside and pulled. Like a cruel joke, the handle came free in his hand with no resistance at all, carrying a foot of chain. Had it been sabotaged?

He turned to see the owner coming up with his wife. "Tools!" Roski shouted at him. "Do you have any tools here?"

Petro heard, shook his head and shouted no. More people were spilling upward behind them.

The best option Roski could see now was to tear out a section of the lath and plaster wall and kick out the outer clapboards. There probably wasn't insulation in this old house and sixteen inches between studs should give enough room to escape, though the stout would have to be pushed. Getting the infirm off the roof was a problem for later if the fire gave them time. The captain of the ship goes last, he thought dismally.

* * * * *

S TANDING in the doorway of the sewing room, Jack Liffey saw red-yellow flames billow and boil all across the front verandah. How long before a neighbor saw it and called 911? He tried to think clearly. Some way out. Next to him Talbot and Maeve were clinging to one another talking earnestly. Toward the main rooms, the initial panic seemed to be subsiding into babbling and to-and-fro consternation.

"Did anyone sneak in a cellphone?" he shouted to a chorus of negatives all around. Shielding his head against the searing heat, he reached to a small alcove that held an old-fashioned black telephone which offered his ear no sound at all. He ran a few steps to glance toward the kitchen. The doorway was jammed tight with people. Obviously no exit there. He heard Roski's voice upstairs, just as two more gunshots sent people diving and tumbling away from windows.

"Jack, get up here, I need you!" Roski called.

He grabbed Maeve and Talbot and took them up the staircase with a tailwind of heat and smoke to where Roski was preparing to smash a butterfly display.

"Jack, we need to cut through the plaster. Broken glass might saw it."

Clinging to the wood frame Roski tried to smash it diagonally but it shattered into a million pieces.

There was a howling across the room. "Those are priceless!"

Jack Liffey had to throw a bodyblock to keep the man off Roski. He spoke calmly into the man's face, "Human life is what's priceless, sir."

The man clenched his eyes shut, his face a rictus of horror. "I must be mad. Smash them all." He took a dull paper opener out of a drawer and handed it to Roski who started stabbing at the plaster. It reminded Jack Liffey of his pocket knife and he got on his knees and the two of them flailed at the century-old lath and plaster.

Modern drywall would have been a lot easier to break through, Jack Liffey thought. Their attack located one of the studs behind the brittle laths, and Jack Liffey refocused his Boy Scout knife to where the next stud would be, stabbing, tearing, punching. Others in the room saw what they were up to and initiated their own assaults on the inner wall with scissors, a paperweight and a curtain rod. Over the din of deconstruction, Jack Liffey could just hear a siren far off. At last.

People were still spilling into the study from below. The brawny doorkeeper woman rushed up beside them and ripped back lath and plaster chunks with her bare hands. The crowd was backing away from the stairs where smoke and heat were issuing.

The smoke was collecting against the ceiling. Jack Liffey was wearying beyond endurance at the frantic hacking. That damn feeling of being old and weak.

"How you coming, Walt?" he asked.

Roski was only a foot away. "Life really clears up in a crisis, doesn't it?"

"Not mine."

THE CAPTAIN GOES LAST 257

An oversize man with wild hair grabbed Jack Liffey's shoulder to get his attention and gently took the knife from him. "My turn, uncle."

He looked very strong and stabbed and sawed with abandon. He ripped away laths and small plaster polygons. There was no insulation at all and soon they'd revealed enough outer wall to get at the clapboards. He hoped they were rotten, but the boards resisted even the big man's kicks as stubbornly as the burglar bars. Half-risen Jack Liffey could see out the window to where flames were beginning to lick up over the eaves in front.

"Back away!" Paula shouted.

She pushed forward with her pistol extended and fired again and again along an imaginary dotted line. Seventeen times, he counted. She ejected the empty magazine and reloaded.

"Warning! I'm shooting again!"

She emptied another magazine and the board was fraying badly. The big man drew a leg back and kicked two boards that crackled as they broke outward. The sirens were closer, but not close enough. An elderly woman in a wheelchair was gallantly being hoiked up the stairs, two or three steps at a time, her head wagging at each lift. Maeve and Talbot waited by the desk with many others while the other work group was fighting another section of wall with less progress.

"Is everybody up?" Jack Liffey asked Gloria, who was resting a hand on his shoulder as he gasped for breath.

"If anybody's in the kitchen, they're ashes, all fall down. My Jack, being around you is such damn bad luck."

He had nothing to say.

The giant had cleared away enough clapboards to start pushing women out through the opening.

"Some strong men get out there!" Roski shouted over the fire roaring from down below like a wounded beast. He indicated the woman in the wheelchair. "You need to help the others out and down!"

Jack caught the huge man's eye and pointed at Roski. He pushed Roski toward the man who got the idea and bearhugged him, then virtually hurled him out the gap. "Take charge where you're needed!" Jack Liffey yelled. "Don't be an asshole and try to get back!"

At the front of the house something pounded up through the shake roof and a filament of flame spurted out its new escape. From below, the fire's crunching, grinding noise grew louder, and waves of super-heat flowed out the stairwell. The smoke was accumulating deeper. The terrified and overdressed birthday guests had crowded into the corners of the big study away from the stairs. All the sash windows were sucking flat rivers of smoke down from the ceiling and outside. A queue of women had gathered or been forced to gather behind the big man to be thrust out one after another between the studs. He saw the wheelchair sitting empty and presumably she'd made it out. The evacuation wasn't fast enough, Jack Liffey thought.

He hurried to the section of wall beside where Roski had been working and began tearing at it. "Help me here!" Talbot came imme-diately and a young man in a ridiculous tuxedo, and they all ripped at the laths until the tuxedo kid tore his hand on an exposed nail and screamed and another man took his place. The fire siren cut off abrupt-ly nearby with a terrible sound of crunching metal.

Jack Liffey grew overtired again, and an olive-skinned man with a bushy Stalin moustache pushed him aside and took over stabbing at the laths. He stood up wearily and looked out to see Roski assembling a line of the fittest to help the women and older men down the sloped roof. At the edge two strong men were making them sit, put their legs over, and then, dangled them by the arms and let them drop, maybe to somebody below.

Fire licking up through the roof was eating its way along the shingles toward the bucket line of men helping the women and old men along. They all seemed amazingly calm, as if Ukrainians were professionals at crisis. Jack Liffey remembered the volunteers who had swum directly under the runaway core of Chernobyl on what were suicide missions to prevent a far worse tragedy. How was someone that selfless?

A pulsing upside-down lake of smoke was growing downward from the ceiling, and an ominous spot on the floor beside the door

THE CAPTAIN GOES LAST 259

was bulging up and beginning to steam. He felt a mesmerizing drowse and wondered about his heart and all that. Where were the damn fire trucks? The floor bulge was actually glowing. The women had all got out and a last handful of old men were stooping into the hole in the wall. I'm old, he thought, nearing a panicky state—his lifelong claustrophobia. The floor blister burst open to a small bright window into hell and blowtorch heat knocked him to the floor.

Somebody grabbed his arms. "Uncle, *come!*"

The rumpling gray blanket of smoke was descending toward his face. A foot away an obese man was being pushed through the opening. Smoke rippled just above him and those remaining were flattening themselves on the floor. A pity to miss escape by a few seconds, he thought.

"We'll make it, uncle," a man said. It was the last thing Jack Liffey heard as acrid smoke engulfed his face and triggered a ripping sensation in his chest.

TWENTY-TWO

There's No Gradual Bad News

ROSKI looked back from the eave-edge to see the giant bearded man tug and twist Jack Liffey out feet-first between the studs. The big man carried him as gently as a mother to the edge of the roof. A flame burst from where they had exited, and the house gave a doomed bellow, like a huge dying animal.

"Down below!" Roski yelled. The shingles around him were venting smoke. Where the hell were the firefighters? "Catch this man! He's precious!"

The captain could now abandon ship. He lay half off the scorching roof to help the big man lower his unconscious friend to several men below.

"What's your name?" Walt asked the big man.

"Valenteyn."

"I'm Walter. God bless you, Valenteyn."

"Same to you, Small Walt."

"Clear the area, we're jumping!" Roski called.

He and Valenteyn were the last two, not counting those left inside who were surely dead, and they dangled from the eaves and dropped to the grass. Roski yelped at a twinge in his ankle. The giant offered Roski a hand to get to his feet but his ankle wouldn't hold him. He lay there and heard the unmistakable blast of a flameover as all the combustion gasses trapped against the ceilings igniting in one go. It was just too much, too much. It was his punishment for a life spent in investigation, devoting himself to arson and the behavior of fire, and not contemplation. He began to weep as the man pulled him up.

"I believe in things, Small Walt," Valenteyn said. "And I act on what I believe. That is what makes life valuable."

He lifted Roski as easily as he had Jack Liffey and hurried him away from the building. Behind them was only hellfire.

* * * * *

M AEVE kept far from the house as she ran across the lawn to her father's inert body. He was making tiny thwarted gasps. She knelt quickly and palpated his neck. The throbbing seemed to flutter, but it was strong. She opened his mouth, swept his throat with her fingers and began rescue breathing.

Paula and Gloria knelt beside them and Gloria loosened his shirt tenderly. "Smoke inhalation," Paula said confidently. "I've seen it."

"And none of them died, ever?" Maeve whickered.

"Don't get all up in this. I'm in the house." She pressed Maeve aside and took over.

Before long Talbot rested a hand on her shoulder to get her attention. "If you can bear to leave your dad for a moment, there's something you really need to see."

She sat, considering the whole unsatisfactory universe for a time. At least her fragile father had good care. Behind her the upstairs windows spouted flames like the burner turned high on a stove. It gave out a frightening roar. Why were no fire hoses pouring water onto the flames? There were sirens in the far distance. Her whole life at UCLA, Bunny, her own painting seemed so unimportant.

"Please," he said. "Really."

Eventually she followed Talbot through a low hedge to the next yard where a large group of the partiers were gawking at something in the street. Talbot took her to a vantage point where she could see a thin

THERE'S NO GRADUAL BAD NEWS 263

man pinned face down in the middle of the street by three firemen in full fire uniform. The man didn't seem to be resisting.

Beyond that—and it took her a moment to make out just what she was seeing—a purple car just like the lo-riders in Gloria's barrio had rammed hard into the side of a long ladder truck. The collision had been hella strong because the fire truck had smashed into a row of parked cars and was now jackknifed and tilted, blocking the road. Behind it, other fire trucks one behind another were trying to back away but it was a complicated maneuver on the narrow parked-up street.

"Look up front," Talbot said.

The first car hit had been her loyal little Echo that was about two-thirds its original length.

Her favorite vagina painting was in the trunk. So what. She had to get back to her dad.

* * * * *

"CONSIDER this an official call, fuckhead," Len Mars' sour voice bleated out of the answering machine as Roski was monitoring. "This Mr. Russian Tattoos that we're holding, the guy that insists on doing pushups all day long—he's going to be your torcher for sure but it's out of my hands. He says his name is Belkin, first or last, who knows? The LAPD's Russian mafia unit doesn't know him, and the State Department is mum as usual. By the way, tell your fire boys it was super work putting out that fire so quick."

Roski considered, but decided to pick up before Mars could hang up. He'd had two long bearable days to recover from his long dark night of the soul. "I'm here, Len. Thanks for your update. Didn't you know we always let structures burn to the ground if we can? What's up with all this?"

"Oh, hi there, Sparks. Not so much up from me. Major Cases downtown grabbed it. Lots of TV and chances to show stony heroic faces. Just the facts, Ma'am. They're on it like ants on Jell-O. Okay, there's more I'll give you for free. After having their fun tearing up the inside of this Belkin guy's apartment, somebody had a brainstorm and

264 BOYSTOWN

found three bodies in the crawl under the house. One's just street trash, runaway girl—spare change for a blowjob. She was double-tapped twice from close on. One body is a big buff guy from some ginzo country far away, soldier-of-fortune maybe. He's got a bunch of old bullet wounds. Plus some brand new little tiny ones. The third body was a young man that was probably beat to death, maybe just fists, and he's starting to smell bad. The Belkin guy gets all emotional when the girl comes up, but shrugs on the others. I hope the old boys downtown get the TV they want. Fat and slow, most of them."

"Like you and me," Roski said. "Does anybody have a name on the dead boy?"

"No."

"Okay, have I got a gift for you. If you want some points, check your missing-persons files for a Benjy—Benjamin—Walker. Not that you'd want to score any points on Downtown."

"Hey, *thanks*, Walter. That just might make my week."

Roski thought over the news. Jack Liffey had been in the hospital for three days now with a collapsed lung—apparently the smoke had retriggered a trauma from years ago. But Jack was reportedly conscious now. He'd have to go tell him the Walker boy was probably dead. And tell Maeve, too. There was nothing in any of that to look forward to.

Life was what it was, he thought, and everybody lived in some relation to unpleasant duties.

* * * * *

J ACK Liffey woke with the steady puffing of oxygen from a nasal cannula tickling his nose but he couldn't roll because of a large stiff tube rising out of his chest. It was attached to a gurgling machine. He knew he was sedated enough so he could lie back and fatuously welcome anything at all right up to nuclear war. Men have died from time to time and worms have eaten them, he thought, but not without first paying their hospital bills.

THERE'S NO GRADUAL BAD NEWS 265

What did happen was a knock at the door and the arrival of the two women he loved who were bearing magazines, a paperback book and a candy bar. No annoying flowers.

"Oh, wonderful women!"

"You're awake!" Maeve rushed toward him but stopped seeing the sputtering tube from his chest. She took his hand.

"Hi, hon. How are you?"

"I'm fine, dad. I'm staying on the east side with Gloria for a while."

"Why is that?" He was instantly suspicious.

"Her car got totaled, Jackie," Gloria put in. She went around and held his other hand and it was going to drive him nuts, rolling his head back and forth.

"I've always wanted a nice three-series Beemer," she went on. "As soon as I pick it out I'm going to give her the RAV-4."

"Can we afford a BMW?"

"Who's *we*, kemo sabe? Old pukeface reinstated me. I'm back at Harbor Division next month. Full pay."

"That's all the changes I can handle right now," he said. "Sorry, the world is a bit with me."

"Jack, how about looking into a different profession—like accounting? You end up in County so often they're going to build a Jack Liffey wing."

"Back in the day, I sat in a nice calm cubicle and typed and ..." He got confused and let it tail off. "Tell me about the fire. I think I missed the end of it."

"You were kind of a hero. Your pal Roski, too. Eight people are dead, nobody we know. The guy who started it is in custody. It all seems to have been some kind of feud. Male madness."

"Must be my fault then. Have you heard anything about Bunny's brother?"

Maeve squeezed his hand and made a sour face. "Roski called and told me he had some bad news and he'd see me soon. That's so dumbhead. I knew immediately it had to be about Benjy. I'm sure he thought he was breaking it gradually, but there's no such thing. Call up

266   *BOYSTOWN*

a fiancé and say you've been rethinking the relationship, right? Just isn't any gradual bad news."

Jack Liffey squeezed her hand. "You're so right, hon. You're always a smart fortune cookie. What do you see in my future?"

"I think I see two people getting hitched," Maeve said, looking across the bed toward Gloria.

Uh-oh, he thought and rolled his head.

Gloria was outside the curtain that was faintly stirring. Maybe gradual bad news.